HEROES OF TIME LEGENDS
A prequel of the Heroes of Time series

THE HEALER

By Wayne D. Kramer

Copyright © 2024 by Wayne D. Kramer
First Edition

Heroes of Time® is a registered trademark of Heroes of Time Productions LLC

Published by Heroes of Time Productions

All rights reserved.
This book, or parts thereof, may not be reproduced in any form without permission.

Library of Congress Control Number: 2024905944

Illustrations by Jade Zivanovic and Steam Power Studios
(copyright retained by Heroes of Time Productions)

Interior Formatting by Melissa Williams Design

This book is a work of fiction. Characters, names, places, and events portrayed in this novel are either products of the author's imagination or are used fictitiously.

Publisher's Cataloging-in-Publication Data:

Names:	Kramer, Wayne D., author.
Title:	Heroes of time legends : the healer / by Wayne Kramer.
Other titles:	Healer.
Description:	[Louisville, Kentucky] Heroes of Time Productions LLC, [2024] | Series: Heroes of time series. | Audience: young adult.
Identifiers:	ISBN: 9781955997188 (hardcover) | 9781955997171 (paperback) | 9781955997164 (ebook)
Subjects:	LCSH: Healers--Fiction. | Rogues and vagabonds--Fiction. | Thieves--Fiction. | Magic--Fiction. | Magnetism--Fiction. | Talismans--Fiction. | Danger--Fiction. | Loss (Psychology)--Fiction. | Magicians--Fiction. | Medicine, Magic, mystic, and spagiric--Fiction. | Spirits--Fiction. | Adventure stories. | LCGFT: Fantasy fiction. | Action and adventure fiction. | Science fiction.

Classification: LCC: PS3611.R3636 H43 2024 | DDC: 813/.6--dc23

For Kaly, the most amazing wife that an author with a bonkers schedule like mine could ever hope to have.

PREFACE & ACKNOWLEDGEMENTS

This book was originally going to be a little bit different.
    When I set out to write *The Healer*—a prequel volume for the "Heroes of Time" series—I intended for it to be a novella, maybe something in the vicinity of 40,000 words in length. As I continued writing, soon enough it became evident that this adventurous tale needed more room to be properly told. So, I ran with it, and now we have something nearly twice the originally intended length.
    Fulgar Geth is the star of this story, set about 25 years before the events of *Murdoch's Choice*. If you haven't yet read the Murdoch books, Fulgar is the healer and spiritual guide introduced in *Murdoch's Choice* that soon became a fan-favorite character. In this book, we go back in time to Fulgar's origins, answering many of the questions existing readers might have about the framework of this unique character. I truly hope you will enjoy the experience.
    This book can be enjoyed whether or not you have already read any other books in the series. The publication order is *Murdoch's Choice*, *Murdoch's Shadow*, and *The Healer*... and you can totally enjoy them in that order. You can also start with *The Healer*, as it was written to be a primer into the series.
    In fact, this book has been crafted to be a primer into *either* the Murdoch tie-in series or the *main* series. To quickly explain

that, *The Healer* and the Murdoch novels are all part of the *Legends* portion of the "Heroes of Time" series. *The Healer* is the first of the Fulgar story arc, and *Murdoch's Choice* is the first of the Murdoch story arc. (This isn't to say that there will or will not be a direct sequel to *The Healer*, even though we have designated its volume number as "F1" on the spine.)

Think of the Marvel Cinematic Universe. You've got the massive *Avengers* storyline that plays out with a certain set of primary characters. Meanwhile, you've got smaller stories that focus on one or a few of the major characters—like *Iron Man* and *Captain America*.

Everything under the *Legends* books is considered a tie-in series. These are more focused stories. They're not necessarily small individually, but they are meant to tie into the larger, more *Avengers*-like storyline that will be the main "Heroes of Time" series.

That "main" series will begin with *Heroes of Time: The First Ethereal*. As of writing this preface, that novel has gone through drafting, initial editing, beta reading, and review and critique by various professionals, including superstar fantasy author Patrick Rothfuss. We can all look forward to its future release, as well as the release of the third Murdoch installment.

Interestingly, writing these novels does not necessarily get easier as more of them come out. I think part of the reason is because there are so many more details to obsess about. In writing *The Healer*, I consistently had to check and recheck small details that had already been written, including in the previous books. It's so important to me that we have continuity across the series, even if it takes more time. Of course, the business side of being an author also gets more and more complex the more books I publish.

I'd like to start the acknowledgements off with a heartfelt thanks to my business team—Jacob Kuntzman, Michelle Fields, and James Reed—who provide critical support for my work and help make sure what we do in Heroes of Time Productions is the best it can be. An extra-special thanks to Jacob for his extensive work as my alpha

PREFACE

reader, ads manager, media specialist, and a variety of other tasks.

We had a particularly lively bunch of beta readers this time, who all provided extremely valuable feedback that helped shape the final novel. A very big thanks to all of you (in no particular order): Ryan Harger, Alex McHaddad, Dawn Montoya, Kaylein Sheppard, Jade Zivanovic, Janelle Reinhardt, Heather Schultz, and Diana Noel.

Much appreciation to all the professionals involved with helping to make this novel shine its brightest. Thanks to Linda Branam, Josiah Davis, and Pauline Harris for their insightful editing services. Thanks to Michelle Argyle for her quick and adept formatting skills. Thanks to my audiobook narrator, Ed Romanoff, for his partnership in creating some really fantastic productions. Thanks to David Sherrer for insightful marketing advice and to Ben Wolf for being a great events resource and neighbor.

Huge thanks to Jade Zivanovic, who continues to do such excellent work on the cover art, maps, and character illustrations. Jade also illustrates my children's picture book series, "Penny Pangolin." It's a completely different style of art and looks absolutely beautiful. Please check out those books if you've got kids around the 3-8 years age range.

Thanks to Artificial Intelligence (AI) for playing absolutely NO part in the creation of this book or any future book of mine. That also goes for any illustrations and audiobooks associated with my work.

Thank you to Patrick Rothfuss for providing the opportunity years ago that allowed me to gain his review and critique of *The First Ethereal*, and for spending over four and a half hours on a video call with me to discuss it and publishing in general. Similarly, thanks to Robin Sullivan (wife of Michael J. Sullivan) for many insights into the business and valuable resources.

I wholeheartedly appreciate all the author friends who have supported and befriended me on this journey, in ways both big and small: Lydia Sherrer ("Loves, Lies and Hocus Pocus" series), E.R.

Paskey ("The Guardians" and "Finder" series), Chris A. Jackson ("Blood Sea Tales" series), Jonathon Mast ("Madelyn of the Sky" series), JMD Reid ("The Storm Below" and "Jewels of Illumination" series), Shannon Everhart (*Moments at McBride*), Clayton Wood ("The Magic of Havenwood" and "Runic" series), and so many more who have become great friends and colleagues.

I'd get absolutely nowhere without the support of my family. To my mother-in-law, Lona Person, thanks for your thoughtfulness and for being an awesome "Mamaw Gangy" to the kids. Thanks to my parents, Greg and Joy Kramer, who helped teach me the virtues of hard work and being detail-oriented. Thanks to my brother, Brandon, for being there to lend a helping hand at so many times when we've needed it.

And, of course, thanks into infinity to my wife, Kaly and our daughters, Dawn, Brooke, Holly, Ivy, and Jade. It's so gratifying to see my kids picking up their own love for reading and writing. At times when work and responsibilities have felt overwhelming, their love, patience, and encouragement have helped to pull me through. Whenever Kaly wears her "I Love My Writer" shirt, it's a subtle yet powerful reminder that she's on my team.

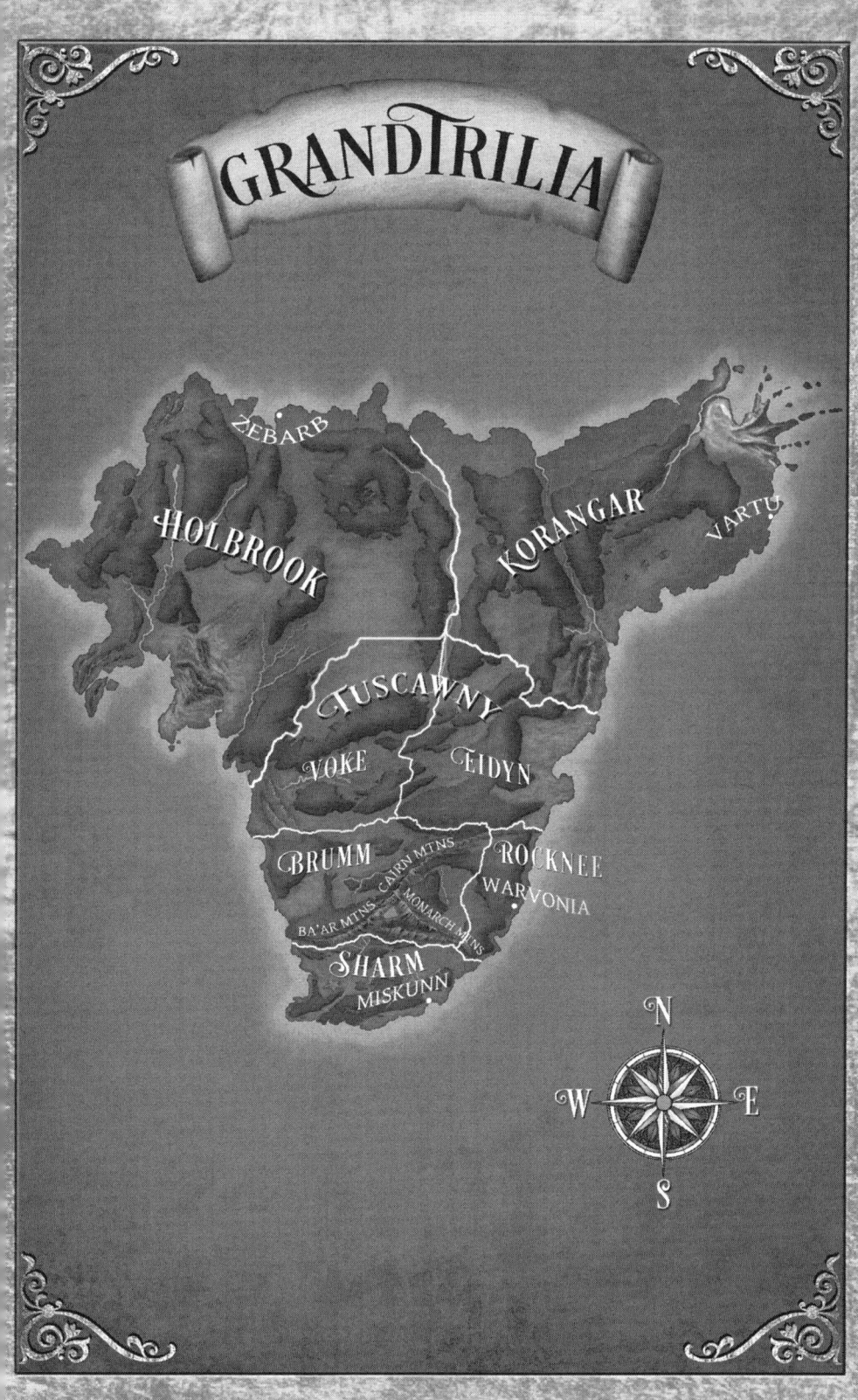

Map

- Ekron
- Whiteland
- Kelau
- Grandtrilia
  - Holbrook
  - Korangar
  - Tuscawny
- Coral Ash Islands

THE GREAT CRESCENT

Gukhan

Ska'ard

Zuar

Akkadia

The Border Crescent

Aviania

Kingdom of
PROVINCES OF ROCKNEE A

Patrol Route

R. Helltoth

Prickly Trout Inn

Tree Blossom Inn

Belltown

Warvoid

FREEMANTLE
METSADA PALACE
ALPHA MAKUTU
RUCA
MILLTOWN

MAIN ROAD — — —
MINOR ROAD • • • • •

prologue

A PLAN FOR WEIRD THINGS

3/6/3161 P.A.

F ulgar Geth could heal with his fingertips.
At least, that's what he believed as he knelt in the meadow amid trampled wildflowers. That's what seemed to happen when he lifted the head of a vibrant, orange lily and pinched its broken stem—when the tiny burst of whiteness appeared between his fingers and the stem stood up straight, once again holding the blossom's weight.

He released the restored lily and smiled as it pointed toward the evening sun, whose brightness contrasted with the planetary rings crossing the sky in the south. The unfortunate flower had been one of many victims of his friends as they stampeded about the field of wildflowers and feathery, purple heather.

Fulgar jumped up and took off after the three boys, hoping to intercept and tag one of them. At eight years old, he was the youngest of the bunch, which only made him more determined. His thick hair of black with hints of white and blue was tousled by the crisp ocean breeze blowing in from the south. Across the field, maybe a hundred paces away, tall flamethyst torches were lit around an open-air shelter beside a playground, where some of the boys' parents conversed and watched their younger children. Fulgar's parents weren't among them—he lived close enough to walk home—and certainly not his best friend Binny's, for different reasons.

Three colors of hair, his friends declared, should make Fulgar a superhero. One or two colors were common. Binny's dark-brown hair was streaked with two stripes of blond, from his bangs to the back of his neck. Rare as it was to have three, those colors were currently of no help to Fulgar. His friends were still outrunning him.

He stopped, huffing. This was going to take more than his legs alone. Binny was especially lanky and tall and hard to catch.

Unseen by his fleeing friends, Fulgar dropped to the ground, disappearing under a canopy of heather.

A laugh drifted back to him. "Little Fully's the squirtiest squirt that ever was!" jeered one of the boys.

"Hey," said Binny, "where'd he go?" Fulgar imagined Binny turning vainly in circles, and he cracked a smile.

"Maybe he ran home to his momma," said another one of the boys.

"Nah, he was right behind us." Their steps came a little nearer. "C'mon, we gotta find him. If I leave him behind again, his parents'll kill me."

They came closer. Fulgar remained within the weeds, still as a rock. At least three little bugs were itching trails along his skin, but he remained vigilant, waiting for just the right moment.

A gentle buzz ran through his arms—a warm, tingly sensation he often felt when near metal—a light internal tickle, like a parade of tiny ants running through his veins.

One of the boys had a metal belt buckle, a second boy some-

Prologue

thing smaller. Buttons, maybe? Fulgar concentrated on his senses. The buckle he could work with; the buttons probably not.

Two pairs of legs stopped within inches of him, one in front and one behind. He reached toward the buckle, felt for the shiver of magnetism, and tugged back his arm. Simultaneously, he used his leg to swipe away the pair behind him. Two kids plopped to the ground at once, yelping in shock.

Fulgar sprang up. "Ha!"

Binny was right before him, flinching. Fulgar reached out to tag him, but Binny ducked away and slammed an arm into Fulgar's gut.

"*Ugh!*" gasped Fulgar, hunching over.

Binny pulled Fulgar back up, shaking his head. "Nice move. Too predictable. You gave me too much time to react."

"I still tagged two of you at once," Fulgar replied in his gently lilting but currently strained voice. The other two were back on their feet. They brushed weed chaff from their clothes and tried, with limited success, to look unfazed, their eyes fixed on Binny.

Binny gave Fulgar's shoulders a firm pat and leaned in close. "A true hero would've gotten all three."

Fulgar fixed him with a glare.

Dorin looked up from his belt buckle and shot an accusing finger at Fulgar. "He's a witch or something!"

"I'm *not* a witch!" Fulgar yelled back.

"A sorcerer, then!"

"I am not!"

The other boy, Finn, spat to the side. "Nah, he's just a weirdo."

Binny held up both hands to calm the others. "No, no. What you all mean to say is *cursed*." Fulgar dropped his jaw, feeling betrayed. "But in a good way!" Binny amended.

"I'm not *cursed*, either!" Fulgar stomped his foot, wind gusted from the spot, and the torch-fires around the shelter flared dramatically to twice their height, turning every head.

"Nothing to be ashamed of, scamp," said Binny, regaining everyone's attention. He looked at the other boys. "Don't you chumps know? He was saved by *magic* at birth!"

Fulgar slumped his shoulders with a conspicuous eyeroll. "*Binny* . . ."

"Right when he was being born," Binny continued, "some mage touched him with an ancient staff. Since then he's always been . . . different."

Dorin and Finn stared at Fulgar, their wide eyes taking him in.

Then they spluttered with laughter. Fulgar wondered if this day could possibly get any worse.

"*Fulgar!*" It was his mother, calling from the shelter. The edge to her voice, sharper than usual, caused him to whip around. "Fulgar, your father's home. Let's go. Now, please!"

Dorin and Finn had already wandered off. Binny met Fulgar's puzzled gaze. "I'll see you later, 'kay?"

Fulgar nodded and ran to meet his mother. As they started home, it took him only a moment to realize that her steps were uneven. She was limping.

"Mum," he said, "why are you walking like that?"

She sighed, her face looking tired and puffy. "It's just work. I'll be fine."

"Barrels again?"

She nodded.

Currently, the guilders of Milltown, a tiny village in the kingdom of Tuscawny's southernmost province of Sharm, had her working mercantile deliveries. The work was strenuous and often involved hauling barrels of ale for delivery to taverns. There were stronger folk in the labor force, better suited for that sort of work, but sometimes it seemed the guilders liked putting less-educated people through turmoil. Fulgar didn't understand why anyone would enjoy that.

"You should tell them to get someone else," said Fulgar.

Prologue

"That's just the way work is. Some days are harder than others, my starlight."

Fulgar glanced all around for anyone in earshot. "Mum, don't call me that—not *here*."

She stopped, looked down at him, and ran gentle fingers through his tousled hair. He saw watery little glints in her eyes for a moment, until she blinked, took his hand, and started walking again.

Despite her gimping stride, his mother moved quickly and didn't show any pain. If his father had already gotten home, Fulgar briefly wondered, why hadn't his dad come instead of his mother?

They were home in little more than fifteen minutes. Their house was at least three generations old, a faded yellowish color of stucco, with plenty of cracks and windows that sometimes felt warm or cool around the edges, depending on the weather. Many other houses in the district had plumbing. Theirs had a rickety wooden outhouse. Fulgar had mastered the skill of holding his breath while using it.

His father was seated on the couch, rubbing the bridge of his nose. On the table beside him was a half-emptied bottle of "the brown stuff"—a bottle, usually in the cupboard, that Fulgar wasn't allowed to touch.

There was a heavy, unsettling aura inside the house. It made Fulgar feel rigid and cool. Adding to the coolness, the room's one window was cracked open.

His father acknowledged Fulgar with a short nod, his face looking distant. "Hey, buddy."

Behind Fulgar, his mother placed her hands on his shoulders. "Fulgar," she said through a breath, "we have something to tell you."

"Belinda, I don't get it," said his father, interrupting. "The more I think about it, the less sense it makes. You, a mere civilian, going off with a long-distance caravan, for a merchant you only just started with . . . !"

His mother spun Fulgar around so he faced her. "Fulgar, dear, wait in your room while your father and I have a quick talk, or you can play outside if you'd like . . . but please stay close."

"Moon hasn't said anything about tenure, right?" continued his father, undeterred. Fulgar, far too riveted by the gravity in his parents' words, didn't go to his room. "There's not even a commitment!" Fulgar figured his father must be referring to Moon's Mercantile, where his mother had recently been assigned an assistant's job. His father shook his head emphatically. "No, no, no. We have to challenge this."

"We can't, Koen," she replied, her voice sounding resigned. "I've already talked to them. Going to the guild chief will only make things worse. The guilders make things hard enough. What happens when they find we've gone over their heads? I don't want them giving you and—" She glanced at Fulgar. "Giving *us* any more trouble."

Fulgar felt the rising tension in the room, felt his fists clench into tight balls.

His father shot up from the couch. "I'm talking to your labor assigner, then. First thing tomorrow. Who is it this time—Berle?"

"*Please* don't. We can't risk you going into grievance . . . or worse. We'll just get through this and be done."

Looking anxious, his father rose and paced back and forth behind the couch, fingers pressed against his forehead. "But for how long? Weeks? *Months?*"

Across the room, a decorative metal plate sitting upon a shelf seemed to bounce the tension back to Fulgar, joining with him in magnetic connection. Without a second thought, he raised his arm and sent the plate soaring across the room, where it clanged hard against the wall and fell dented upon the floor.

His parents stopped talking, their wide eyes now on him.

Fulgar had startled even himself. He wasn't sure why he'd done that. Maybe he just didn't want to hear his parents going round and

PROLOGUE

round like this.

"Mum, Dad . . . why am I a freak?"

"Oh, Fulgar," said his mother.

"Who told you that?" demanded his father.

Fulgar looked at the floor. "My friends. But it's true. I do weird things."

"Weird things," his father repeated sharply. "Your friends—*they're* the weird ones."

A teapot whistled in the kitchen.

"I'll be back in a minute," said his father.

His mother leaned in and combed her fingers through Fulgar's hair. "Don't dwell on this, Fulgar. *Weird* is just another word for *misunderstood* . . . but, perhaps, Eloh has a plan even for the weird things."

"I was cursed at birth," Fulgar added.

"You were *blessed* at birth. We all were . . . by the miracle of *you*. What you have is a gift. Pray to learn the purpose behind the talents you have."

Cupboard doors slammed in the kitchen. Something fell and broke, followed by a curse from his father.

"You're going away, aren't you?" asked Fulgar. "Somewhere far."

"Yes, my dear," she replied. "It's a merchant trip. We have to cross the mountains in the north. You'll be a big helper for your father while I'm away, won't you?"

Fulgar nodded. He felt numb, crushed by the weight of something significant that he knew he didn't fully understand.

His mother hugged him, and the strength of her embrace brought both the full weight of her love and the gravity of change.

"I love you, my starlight," she said.

"I love you, Mum," he replied.

Fulgar went back outside, feeling the need for fresh air. Hands in his pockets and head downcast, he walked quietly away from the porch and toward the gate at the edge of their yard.

Binny appeared from around the gate. "Wow, that was a real tear-jerker."

Fulgar's body tensed, his jaw clenched at the sudden intrusion. "Why are you here? Were you *listening*?"

Binny raised his hands in a calming fashion. "Sorry, man, didn't mean to. I wanted to tell you something I couldn't in front of the others—something exciting, something *big*. You okay?"

"I guess," Fulgar replied, shuffling his feet in the loose dirt.

Binny gave Fulgar's arm a light jab. "Hey, goof-brain, you know I've got your back, right?"

"Yeah. Thanks."

"You know the problem with this world?" said Binny. "There's always someone who thinks they're better—that they can control you. Not with me, though. I've got a plan to change all that."

Intrigued, Fulgar looked at him. "You mean, you could stop the guilders from treating my parents so mean?"

"Guilders, bosses, soldiers, teachers, parents—anyone trying to make you do things you don't want to do. Let me show you something. But you've got to keep it just between us, okay?"

Fulgar's eyebrows lifted, a scandalous pang swelling within at the promise of something secretive and only for him. "Okay," he replied.

Binny dug a hand into his pocket and pulled out a round object on a string, a kind of medallion with a coppery-red shimmer. From a swirling pattern in the center emanated fiery tongues, like little flames blown by a gust.

"It's a talisman," said Binny. "Got it from my uncle's place last week."

"You took it?"

"He said I could have it."

Fulgar frowned. "Is this the uncle your mum said to stay away from?"

PROLOGUE

Binny snorted a laugh. "What's it matter? Listen, thickhead, there's a legend around this. Whenever this talisman changes hands, the new owner is challenged to find the old shrine where it came from. It's hidden and ancient. It's a place of *magic*, Fulgar."

Fulgar's eyes bulged. He'd heard stories about ancient powers before, dormant energies hidden within Eliorin since the great cataclysmic ages of the distant past, just waiting to be discovered.

"Did your uncle ever find the shrine?" Fulgar asked.

Binny shrugged. "Nope. But he's something of a git. He never tried very hard."

"You think it's for real?"

"It's out there," Binny replied. "I know it. Finding the shrine grants these ancient powers to *you*. Some say it's a force even stronger than the Light of the Land."

Fulgar shook his head. "Nothing's *that* strong."

Binny shrugged. "Depends who you listen to. Even if the magic is half as strong, that's a lot."

"I dunno," Fulgar replied with a slight smirk. "I already have powers."

"Sure, man, but this is a whole other level. You can't just be born into this—you have to *earn* it."

"How do you get these powers?"

A mischievous grin stretched Binny's mouth. "All you have to do is want it."

Fulgar furrowed his brow. "Want it?"

"Yeah, like bad enough to find it, you know, and willing to accept it. Not just anyone can handle power, but *you've* already got a head start." He leaned toward Fulgar. "Listen, mate. It's my dream to find this place. I figure, maybe it could be our dream together, you and me. We can find this place, both of us, if we really put our minds to it. Can you be committed, though?"

Fulgar blinked in thought, glancing back at his house, where at this very moment his parents struggled with the demands of others.

THE HEALER

"Yeah, I can commit."

"Look, I can't stop your mum from leaving or your dad from working tomorrow. That's still gonna happen. This is a longer-term thing. It's gonna take some time to find what we need. You understand?"

Fulgar sagged a bit, but he knew that was reasonable. "Yeah."

"Imagine it, Fulgar. Power over anyone—and not to boss people around or do boring stuff like rule a land—but just so *they* can't rule over *you* and those you care about. That's what real freedom is."

Real freedom. Fulgar ran it over in his mind, trying to grasp it. Over and over, he had seen his parents ordered and pushed around by the guilders in town. Neither of them had made it into university when they'd had the chance, back when they were seventeen years old, because some so-called masters who didn't even know them decided they weren't suited for the higher studies they'd desired.

On top of that, Milltown, deep in the kingdom's rural south, was far too small for job stability. His mother might work a daycare one week and muck stables the next. Now she was a mercantile assistant, but later she might be something else. Father might tend gardens one week and dig postholes the week after. It seemed the jobs only got harder for them, more and more demanding.

But had they been allowed to pursue their desired disciplines and careers, they might now live a better life. They might have meat instead of porridge, plumbing instead of a freezing outhouse. It wasn't all bad, of course, but things could be easier, and it was only because of other people that they were stuck with hard work and minimal pay for the foreseeable future. There was no escape from the vicious cycle.

"Okay," Fulgar said. "I'm in."

Binny clapped Fulgar's shoulder. "Alright, squirt, I'll leave you be." He veered off, thrusting a fist into the air. "Freedom!"

Fulgar couldn't help but smile just a little.

He kept walking, thinking of his parents, what it would be

Prologue

like living alone with his dad, how long his mother might be forced away. Before he knew it, he was back in the field where he'd played with his friends earlier.

By now, everyone else was gone, and the torches around the shelter had been snuffed out. The sun was mostly set, the sky in twilight. He cut across the field and found the paths they'd trampled through the heather and field grass.

A little dot, lighter than everything else, caught his eye, and he stopped. There, in the path, was a white butterfly. It had only one wing, which it raised and lowered rhythmically, its tiny body shuddering.

Feeling intense guilt, he approached it. "We did this to you, didn't we?" He spoke in a gentle voice, as though soothing an injured friend. "I don't think I've ever seen such a perfectly white butterfly before. I'm so sorry about your wing."

Fulgar searched the ground among the demolished flowers. It took a few moments, but he finally found it—the butterfly's missing wing.

He stooped down and carefully plucked the wing from the ground with two fingers. Then, just as gently, he guided the butterfly into his other hand and lifted it up before his face.

Like a flood, emotion filled him. Thoughts of his mother rushed into his mind, amplified by the sadness he now felt for this helpless, innocent creature that had simply been in the wrong place at the wrong moment.

"Dear Eloh," he said softly, "just as through me you can heal this butterfly . . . please, show me purpose."

Then he put the severed wing back on the butterfly, right where it belonged. It stayed in place, and the butterfly, no longer shuddering, moved its antennae about in a curious fashion. Seconds later, it beat its wings and took to the sky in perfect flight.

Fulgar watched the butterfly for just a few moments, smiled, and turned back toward home.

chapter 1

BLARKLE HEIST

5/9/3177 P.A.

"I imagine you have quite a high opinion of yourself right now," said Fulgar, blood rushing to his head, adding color to his already-tanned skin. Hanging upside down in fishing net tended to have that effect.

Entering via the rooftop had seemed like a good idea at the time, a means of avoiding detection. The upper lofts of the cargo warehouse were sturdy and free of watchful eyes. Normally, the facilities of Miskunn's harbor were kept in tiptop shape.

But he had hit a collapsible spot in the floor, clearly a trap, and fallen right through. If that'd been the extent of it, he would at least be properly upright. Instead, he'd landed roughly upon a slippery ramp, fallen backward, and slid headfirst through the hole that brought him to this dismal, inverted state.

The room looked like a simple administrative office, with a sturdy wooden table and a hefty metal door, like the sort that might conceal a vault or prison cell. Standing there was a tall, burly man with tousled, greasy-black hair. His big head was shaped like a chunk of building stone, oblong with a rather uneven-looking face.

He guffawed at Fulgar's plight, like a poacher with a fresh catch.

Fulgar struggled against the netting, trying but failing to reach the sword sheathed at his side.

The man sauntered up and palmed Fulgar's head within a massive hand, turning him so their eyes met. The man had big eyes—ugly, gray, and bloodshot—with yellowed whites. Drool pooled in the corner of his lopsided mouth.

"Already had a pretty good opinion o' meself." The man spoke through a husky accent, reminiscent of one from the northwest fringe of Sharm province, near the mountainous border with the province of Brumm. He gestured at Fulgar's inverted position.

"O' course, this *does* improve it. Ye fell right int' me trap!" The man grinned wickedly and chuckled through the gaps in his teeth. A few of the ones he did have were gold. "Fulgar Geth, ain't it?"

Fulgar extended a hand through the netting. "And you'll be Volk Vorovka. It is such a pleasure for you to meet me."

Volk scowled at the hand as though Fulgar were offering a cut of rancid meat. "Royal Guard'll be glad t' get ahold o' you, I reckon. It be all over the harbor that yer wanted. Stealin' pocket change, no doubt, bein' too pathetic t' snatch any respectable dosh." He reached through the net and pulled the sword from beside Fulgar's waist. "Cain't be havin' this, now." He tossed it to the floor with a series of clangs and walked back toward the table.

"Oh, bad form!" Fulgar protested. "Now you're stealing my sword?"

Volk snorted. "Little street rodent like you prob'ly stole it in th' first place."

"That . . . is entirely beside the point!" Fulgar squirmed about in the net, trying to keep his eyes on Volk. "Besides, you'll find it's not worth much."

Volk whirled around, coming close again. "Prob'ly worth more than *you*! Usually, ye'd not even be worth the trouble o' turnin' ye in."

Blarkle Heist

He plucked a few of the hairs from Fulgar's head, snatching strands of black and blue but missing the white. Having an unusual three colors, his hair was long and thick, often with long strands swaying this way or that, all of it presently reaching toward the floor.

Volk chuckled darkly, the drool in his mouth threatening to spill over. "But I knows, t' the right folks, yer worth more fer different reasons." He rubbed the hairs between two fingers, right in front of Fulgar's face, then let them fall to the floor.

"If you're referring to my three colors of hair," Fulgar said, watching the hairs fall, "that's nothing new. I'm already registered, you know."

There was no consensus among commoners as to why kingdom officials cared to know about people with three hair colors. Some believed it a means of segregation, perhaps to privilege certain people or to indicate lineages of noble interest. Some saw it as just another arbitrary way to track the population. Some felt it steeped in superstition, as if to indicate special traits or abilities. Naturally, Fulgar knew nothing of privilege or lineage but saw plenty of merit in the notion of unique abilities.

Out on the streets, hair like his might earn the occasional lingering glance—mystified or curious or, sometimes, suspicious. Many people didn't even notice immediately, and even if they did, Fulgar found that most people weren't bothered by it. Most interpreted it simply as they saw it—different hair colors—and weren't convinced it meant much more than that.

Volk's awful eyes narrowed. "But I knows yer not registered, and that's part o' the value."

"Oh, please. There aren't many twenty-four-year-olds who can skirt registration requirements. I'm rather well-known to the Guard, you know, and get along quite well with a few of them."

"Yer a useless whelp, and soon you'll be wettin' yer britches in prison. After I gets a nice reward, o' course."

"Ah," Fulgar chirped, "but you only *think* I'm caught!"

He flicked his right wrist, frowned when nothing appeared from his sleeve, and flicked it again with the same result.

"Lookin' fer that?" Volk pointed to the floorboards, where rested a small dagger.

Fulgar tittered. "Well, I see how you could *think* that's what I'm looking for."

Volk grunted, subjecting Fulgar to a rancid whiff of something like pickled herring and onions. "Barmy little maggot," the man growled, walking off toward the table. "After me cargo, no doubt."

"It's not like you're the victim here," Fulgar ventured. "I have it on good authority that the cargo you're about to load is already stolen."

"*Yer* just a common thief, a little rat scrappin' fer a bit o' cheddar." He collected some papers from the table. "Me, I'm a legitimate businessman. A reseller, as it were."

"You mean to tell me all that pretty, sparkling metal you have in here is *not* stolen, then?"

Volk pointed an ominous finger. "I mean t' say, me source an' cargo be none o' yer business." He pulled open the heavy door and shouted, "Oy, mates, load it up!" He pushed the door shut again with a resounding metallic boom.

"How perfectly boring," said Fulgar. "You mean to just leave me hanging here until the soldiers show up?"

Volk gave a dreadful smirk. "I knows yer not here alone, Fulgar Geth. Binny, right? You two are partners. We had a feelin' you mangy thieves might show up. He'll be along any moment t' double me reward."

"We're like brothers," Fulgar replied, "but you'll have no such luck with him. It's not like he's just going to walk in right through the door."

With dramatic flourish, the door flew open and slammed against the wall. There stood Binny in a dark frock coat, holding something like a handheld ballista, larger than a typical crossbow.

Blarkle Heist

Wearing a sly grin beneath the hooked nose of his rectangular face, he coolly brushed a wavy lock of hair away from his forehead. The blond streaks of his otherwise dark-brown hair made him look especially wild, like an anthropod badger loaded for bear. "Ahoy, ye brainless picaroon! Lookee what I found!"

Volk stuffed his papers into a coat pocket with an agitated growl. "Binny! *Yer* the brainless one fer showin' yer face 'ere!"

Binny addressed Volk with a short bow. "Greetings, my good man! Beg pardon, but I was actually talking to *him*." He pointed at Fulgar.

Volk took the bait and turned to glare at Fulgar. Binny fired the ballistic weapon with a loud *twang*, and its bolt sheared through the net's tether above. Fulgar writhed enough to keep from landing directly on his head, but the back of his neck took a hit against the floor, hard enough to blur his vision and deaden his hearing.

When his senses returned moments later, Volk had overturned the heavy wooden table and grabbed a crossbow. Binny flung aside his bulky weapon and rolled away just as Volk shot and shattered a terracotta pot.

Fulgar struggled with the net, flailing about for the opening. Volk cursed and started loading another crossbow bolt. Binny drew a single-edged shortsword, leapt up, and dashed toward Volk from across the room.

Volk's thick hands must have made him clumsy with the crossbow. He glared up at Binny, gave up loading the crossbow, placed both huge hands upon the upturned side of the table, and shoved it with impressive force.

"Binny, look out!" Fulgar shouted.

Binny clearly hadn't expected to see a table zooming toward him with such aggressive speed. He leapt just as the table came at him, but he was a hair too late. The table slammed into his shins mid-jump and toppled him heels over head.

Volk took up his unloaded crossbow and ran out the door,

THE HEALER

slamming it behind him. Metallic clicking followed that could only mean the door had been locked.

"Great," muttered Binny through gritted teeth, rubbing at his shins. "It locks from the *outside*."

Fulgar finally managed to free himself of the net. "Are you insane? Did it not occur to you that he could catch both of us in here? Clearly this room is rigged. Why else would they have a prison door and a trap in the ceiling?"

"I got you out of the net, didn't I? You're welcome, by the way." He pointed a thumb at the door. "Can you do something about this?"

"Well, I can't trip the lock, not from this side on a door like *this*." He approached the door and placed his hands on it. "Solid metal, sure enough. It's going to be noisy . . ."

Binny rubbed his hands together in eager anticipation. "Yeah, fine. Come on! If we make straight for the holding area, we can still get out of here with some of that cosmic metal."

Fulgar shook his head. "Binny, this job is blown. These people are armed with crossbows and Eloh knows what else. Assuming we make it out of here alive, this is going to turn the officials' attention right at us! Volk already knew we were coming!"

Binny clapped a hand on Fulgar's shoulder. "Hey, everything will work out just fine. You'll see. Remember, even just a satchel-full, and—"

"We'll be set for months," Fulgar finished. "I know. But I'd rather be poor and free than rich and dead."

"Maybe even *years*, mate. We *need* this, or the officials might be the *least* of our problems."

Fulgar rolled his eyes. "You don't even know what this stuff is, do you?"

"Sure I do. It's a valuable metal, black with sparkles. Blarkle."

Fulgar's brow furrowed. "And that reminds me. You've told me next to nothing about this prospective client of yours. How do you

18

know they're good for it?"

Binny tilted his head with an exaggerated sigh. "Some secretive group, if you must know, like religious fanatics or something. But here's the thing: They might have information about the talisman, clues how to find where it belongs or even about the nature of its power. Plus, they have sway with the soldiers, the Palace, anyone they need. Which, of course, makes our success that much more important. They can help keep the officials off our backs." He slapped Fulgar's arm with vigor, a twinkle in his eye. "See? We're doing real king's work now, like good model citizens!" He gestured toward the door. "Now we just need to get to the blarkle before they load it."

Fulgar groaned, went back to the heap of net, and retrieved his tiny dagger and sword from the floor, sheathing the sword. "I hope you know what you're getting us into." He stretched his arms toward the door. "Stand back."

Fulgar felt the tingles of magnetism vibrate from inside his arms, growing in strength. His arms began to shake as the attraction intensified, and he slowly turned his forearms upward and pulled back, as if trying to move a loaded wagon tied to his arms. Creaking sounded from all around the door, and the surrounding wooden frame started to split. With a firm yank from Fulgar, the door flew open with a dramatic shower of splinters.

"Now *that's* breaking out in style!" cheered Binny. He flung himself through the doorway, sword held before him.

Fulgar shook out his shoulders, feeling the slight drain of energy leaving his body. With a sigh, he drew his own sword and followed behind.

The landing outside the door overlooked a sea of containers far below. Stairs led down to the left. Binny was already halfway to another landing, which branched off to a narrow, wooden elevated walkway. The warehouse below was a complex tangle of carts and pulley systems for moving hundreds of crates between vessels in the harbor, throughout the facility, and to any variety of drays for further transport inland. Fulgar heard men shouting from somewhere within the expanse but saw no one.

"How are we supposed to know which one has our metal?" Fulgar called out.

"Whichever one they try to keep us from!" Binny shouted back, only deepening Fulgar's anxiety about this job.

Binny stopped just before he reached the landing and held up a finger. Fulgar halted at the signal, and Binny turned his head, listening. "This way!" He hopped the last few stairs and took off to the left, darting down the elevated walkway.

Just below them on both sides were rows of tall crates, most of them sealed and ready for transport.

"Binny, wait!" Fulgar hissed. "They're going to see—"

A crossbow bolt struck the railing to Binny's right, followed by shouts from below of "There!" and "They escaped!" and "I want 'em alive so t' gets me reward!" Fulgar and Binny ducked down instinctively, but there was little cover to be had in this vulnerable position.

"If we get out of this," Fulgar said, "*I'm* leading the next job!"

"Nice sentiment," Binny replied, "but I prefer bigger fish to street crumbs." His attention snapped to the action below. "Out the way!" he shouted as he lunged into Fulgar, narrowly dodging another bolt.

The move cost Fulgar his footing. He tripped over the railing and fell atop one of the tall crates, landing hard on his back and knocking the wind from his lungs. He sucked in a breath and raised his head with a groan.

"Good idea!" Binny called from the walkway. "We'll split up and draw them out!"

Before Fulgar could protest everything about that statement, Binny leapt off the other side of the walkway. Instead of landing solidly upon a crate, he fell right through the top with a resonating crack of wood.

Blarkle Heist

Fulgar turned over, able to see the cargo beneath him from between the boards of the crate. His eyes were met with tiny, sparkling pinpoints amid a sea of black.

Despite their predicament, he took a moment to stare at the unusual material, unable to turn away. Its beauty was striking to him, irresistible. He felt drawn to it, as if the stuff beckoned him to reach out and take it.

Completely unbidden, his intrinsic power surged with sudden excitement, a rush of buzzing warmth pulsing through his veins.

"The metal!" he gasped. This was the material they were after. He was sure of it.

He heard another crack of wood and realized that Binny had just kicked his way out of the side of his crate.

From his vantage point, Fulgar saw four men, including Volk, spread throughout the area, making their way toward Binny. None of them seemed to realize that Fulgar lay atop the prized cargo.

Fulgar turned back to the sparkling metal, so close to the greatest fortune they had ever achieved, desiring more than anything to hold it. He turned back to the scene below, scanning for Binny.

He found him after a few moments.

One of Volk's men, a wiry-looking redhead, was coming right into Binny's path, a loaded crossbow held ready in his hands.

Binny was about to be shot.

Fulgar slid off the crate and ran between the carts and roller conveyors where the larger crates rested, wending his way to Binny's position. He passed beneath the elevated walkway, sword in hand, his breaths rapid and anxious.

He rounded the corner of a crate just in time to see Binny and the redhead meet up. Binny's hands were raised, and the crossbow was aimed directly at him.

"You're comin' with us," said the redhead. "No matter if you're bloodied and unable to walk." He shifted his aim toward Binny's legs, ready to squeeze the weapon's trigger lever.

An instinct, increasingly familiar with time and practice, pulsed within Fulgar and evoked a forward thrust of his free arm. An energetic jolt passed from his sword arm through to the one now outstretched, like a tiny, prickly ocean wave coursing through his limbs.

At that moment, the crossbow twanged.

Fulgar's eyes were on the bolt as it sprang from the crossbow, and with a deliberate upward jerk of his arm, the bolt's path skewed over Binny's head, leaving the projectile to puncture a crate just above him. With a following downward twitch of Fulgar's arm, the redhead's crossbow smacked to the floor.

Confusion twisted the redhead's face, and Binny wasted no time reacting. He charged into the redhead with his shoulder, slamming him into a crate. He pushed off a feeble sweep of the man's arm and punched him square in the face, decking him.

Binny turned around and found Fulgar. "I take it that bolt didn't change course due to some bizarre *indoor* gust of wind."

"No," Fulgar said, still staring at the crossbow. "No, that was me." The power pulsing through him was unusually strong, had been since landing near that dazzling metal. Attracting and moving something as large as the metal door was easy compared to this. An object in motion was very difficult to alter. He'd never done it with something as potent as a just-fired crossbow bolt.

He didn't always understand his abilities with metal and magnetism. Innate instinct told him it was all connected to other strange powers, such as the healing of small things like flowers and minor injuries, which he'd known since childhood. It was sometimes stronger in the heat of a tense moment or when his will was especially high, but he couldn't remember it ever feeling quite as strong as it did now.

"Well," said Binny, "that was *fantastic*."

"I heard 'em over this way!" someone shouted.

BLARKLE HEIST

Binny grabbed Fulgar by the biceps and guided him around the corner of a crate. "We've gotta lose these guys!" he said in an urgent whisper.

"I . . . found the sparkling metal," Fulgar said, barely gathering his thoughts, "in the crate I landed on."

Binny's face lit up like Candletide. "Ha! That's brilliant! So, we go wide in two directions, spread these guys out, and circle back to the crate."

"Move it out, *now*!" roared Volk. Rattling sounds followed, the cargo rollers turning.

"Gheol's foul flames!" Binny seethed.

"We'll never be able to get to it if they're all around it," said Fulgar, "which is probably why they're now focused on the container rather than us."

"I know, I know." Binny thought a moment, looking aside. "Okay . . . we're gonna have to get out of here."

Fulgar raised his eyebrows. "We're giving up?"

Binny's eyes snapped back to Fulgar. "Jostle your brain or something? Of course not! We need to watch where they load it, maybe get to it before the ship leaves port."

Fulgar gave him a wide-eyed look. "You mean get from here to their ship, then take the sparkling metal from their ship, and then get ourselves *off* of their ship without being apprehended?"

"Yes."

"You're mad."

"Look, *this* is our chance. Once aboard, they'll disperse to get the ship ready. After a bit, they'll think we've given up. We'll pose as dockhands—they're constantly bringing crates on and off ships—and make a quick break for it."

"We're more likely to get shoved overboard," Fulgar grumbled.

Determination shining in his eyes, Binny looked about. "There, that way!" He pointed down the length of an aisle toward a stairwell leading to the lower floor.

Fulgar glared at the stairs, then at the sunlight from bay doors somewhere to their right, then at Binny. "We should exit *that* way, toward the daylight."

Binny shook his head adamantly. "This is one of those double-decker facilities for loading the bigger ships at deck height. Ground level will be another floor down."

Voices and the rattling sounds of the rolling container drew closer. They were out of time to debate. Fulgar nodded, and they made a break for the stairs. He had no idea if anyone saw where they went. They were just lucky to be alive at this point, although he had a bad feeling their luck was running out.

It felt like the stairs went down three floors rather than one, with a landing in between that switched back the other direction. They finally emerged into an expansive holding area with more crates and rows of locked, barred doors that resembled a wooden cellblock. The soft lapidary glow of flocalcite lighting illuminated the space.

Fulgar was focused on the lighting and the lack of any active cargo doors. "Binny," he said in an accusatory tone, "where's the sunlight?"

"Hmm," Binny replied, scratching his chin. "This must be where they keep more valuable cargoes under lock and key. I've heard of places like this."

Shouts echoed from the stairs above. "Yer both trapped like rats down there now! Be down in a wee spell t' collect yer sorry hides, don'cha worry."

"I *knew* it!" Fulgar shouted. "They saw us go down here, and there're no open exits. We should've made for the bay doors upstairs!"

Binny held out his hands in a calming gesture. "This'll work out just fine." He picked a row and started forward. "Come on. Let's just . . . find another way out."

"You won't find it," said a female voice. "At least, not on your own."

BLARKLE HEIST

Fulgar and Binny halted in their tracks, looking around dumbly for the source.

"Over here, you two."

Fulgar saw her first, standing within one of the barred holding containers, a dark-complexioned woman about his height and, he guessed, about the same age. She was skinny, dressed in a dingy, tattered shirt and a torn length of skirt, her black hair flecked with tiny patches of white and curling over her shoulders. Her lean, triangular face was both sharp and soft at once, with vibrant brown eyes like spicy cinnamon bark.

Fulgar stared at her, at a loss for words. Slovenly as she appeared, he was struck by the keen, searching expression of her face and the rolling accent of her voice, like chimes ringing in perfect singsong succession. He loved the sound of chimes.

"Are you . . . cargo?" asked Binny.

"Well, kind of," she replied. "I mean, I'm in a container, aren't I?"

"But . . . why?"

She seemed to search the container's ceiling for an answer. "Wrong place, wrong time, you could say."

"Ah," replied Binny with a knowing laugh. "Stealing?"

"Something like that."

They heard steps and voices descending the stairs.

Binny gave the woman a short nod. "Well, best of luck to you." He started off. Fulgar didn't move, as though the woman herself were magnetic and wouldn't let him.

"Wait! You've got to break me out of here."

Binny turned back, an eyebrow sharply arched. "Oh, and why is that? Because, in a couple of minutes, we're going to be target practice for some crossbows."

She placed a hand over her chest in grandiose fashion. "Because *I* can help you escape without getting killed. There's only one other way out of here, and I know where it is."

Fulgar snapped his gaze to Binny. "We can't just leave her here."

"Really?" said Binny. "Because I rather think we can."

Fulgar gestured at the bars on the crate. "This same fate could be our own! She can help us."

"Oh, come on. She's a petty thief—just like us, maybe, but clearly not as good." He looked at the woman. "No offense."

She responded with a cross-armed glare. "Let's just give it a minute, then. I can wait."

"I'm helping her," said Fulgar. "You can go if you want."

"There's a good man!" she cheered as Binny threw up his hands.

"What's your name?" Fulgar asked her.

"The name's Jinx." She reached between the bars and shook his hand. It was a wonderful hand, dainty and strong.

"Jinx?" replied Binny. "Not really selling yourself as much of a good-luck charm, milady." He backhanded Fulgar's arm. "Okay, well, if you've got some grand scheme, now's the time, me bucko."

"Right," said Fulgar, looking down at the door's lock. "This is just a simple lever tumbler lock, the sort they probably have a skeleton key for. So, the levers inside just need to be pushed into the right position to open it."

"And you have a way to do that?" asked Jinx. "Without the key?"

"Yeah," said Binny, "you have a way to do that?"

"As I said," replied Fulgar, his voice calm, "it's a matter of positioning the levers inside."

Jinx gave them a sideways, inquisitive stare. "Who *are* you guys?"

Fulgar placed his hands around the lock. "Like no one you've ever met." He stooped down and placed an ear against the front of the lock.

Binny stared at him, his stance jittery. "Okay, Fulgar, you do that . . . and I'll be right back." He took off down the aisle and turned a corner out of sight.

Blarkle Heist

"Fulgar," Jinx repeated. "I like that name—has a strong, rugged sound to it."

"Thanks."

"What's your friend doing?"

Fulgar coughed a laugh. "What he does best: mischief." He closed his eyes, concentrating on the lock. "Now, please, I must listen to the levers."

This was a trick he'd practiced on many a lock ever since he'd first sensed the buzz of magnetism within his body. The trick didn't always work, but the surge of energy he felt right now gave him confidence. Sometimes the internal lock parts were made of nonferrous metals—tin, copper, brass—but that didn't really matter. He could make things magnetic that weren't before, if only for a short time.

Jinx stood very close, practically against the door on the other side, looking down at him. "I *love* your hair. Three colors, too! That's amazing. Never change it."

"Please," said Fulgar, "I really need to concen—"

He stopped at a series of clicks within the lock, and the door swung open.

"Oh!" Jinx squealed. "Fulgar, you're *brilliant*!" As soon as he stood, she ruffled his hair with both hands, yanked him forward, kissed him on the mouth, and wrapped her arms around his neck. Wide-eyed, and not knowing how else to react, he hugged her back, his arms encircling her slender waist. It was a brief moment, short and sweet and invigorating, filling him with warmth like an exquisite mulled wine that made his every sense demand more of everything he'd just felt.

"Come on out, ye whelps!" shouted Volk from the stairs.

Somewhere else in the huge room, a loud cracking sound whipped into the air, followed by something of a *whoosh*.

Fulgar chanced a glance around the corner of the crate he stood halfway in with Jinx. Volk was flanked by four of his cronies, pointing toward the source of the sudden commotion. "Over there!" He ran off with two of his men, while the other two stayed behind to guard the stairs.

"What was that?" asked Jinx.

Fulgar smiled. "That'll be Binny."

Perfectly on cue, Binny showed up, slightly out of breath. "Right—best be on our way, then. That crate of flamethyst won't distract them for long."

"Oh, I *like* you guys!" said Jinx. "Alright, then, let's get out of here."

Cricket song blended with the crackling of woodfire, and a pleasant, smoky aroma hung in the air, a scent that Fulgar had come to associate with the relaxing end of a long day. The planetary rings of Eliorin were bright across the southern sky, their perimeter washing away the light of any stars that were near them. Higher in view, a crescent moon seemed to smirk in the mostly clear sky.

Typically, this was a view he shared only with Binny. Tonight, after having escaped the cargo warehouse, they were joined by Jinx. Their wiry new companion had been true to her word and led them through a service door nestled in the farthest possible corner of the facility's lower floor.

Binny had not been totally wrong about the building's layout. The floor above was indeed for loading larger ships. It just turned out that both larger and smaller ships were loaded from there, reserving the lower level for special containment. Hence, highly volatile minerals, like flamethyst, and more concealed shipments, such as people intended as cargo, were kept in the same separated area.

The flamethyst fire had been a stroke of brilliance on Binny's part. What started from within a small container soon erupted into

Blarkle Heist

a large enough blaze to threaten the entire facility. It completely flummoxed Volk's pursuit and attracted the attention of harbor authorities, providing all the cover they needed to slip away unhindered.

Unfortunately, that which gave them cover to escape also made it impossible for them to go back and find their desired prize, whether still in the warehouse or aboard Volk's ship. If they ever got another chance at "blarkle," it would have to be another day.

Once north of the harbor, they continued west, running as fast as they could until reaching the Miskunn city limits, where just beyond sat the edge of a large, dense forest. On their way through the fish markets, they had managed to snag a few snappers from the edge of a cart, the ones most likely to be discarded anyway if left unsold much longer.

Now seated beside the campfire, Fulgar couldn't keep himself from casting frequent glances at Jinx as she sat cross-legged, roasting stick in hand, the firelight adding a certain edge to her already fine features. She was rugged yet dainty, gangly yet strong, and despite her tattered clothing, or even partly because of it, she was very attractive.

When she looked back at him, he averted his eyes on some insufferably bizarre instinct and poked his stick needlessly at the firewood, sending up sparks. He had just finished his portion of fish, the warm morsels settling pleasantly in his stomach.

"So, then, what's the story on you two?" she asked after long moments of silence, mostly the result of exhaustion.

"Story?" said Binny midway in the act of sitting on a log. "What makes you think there's a story?"

Jinx shrugged, speaking through a bite of snapper. "Roaming about a cargo basement, getting chased by a gang, picking locks with your hands—that one's *still* got me reeling—nicking fish like it's no big deal, and clearly you neither one have got a proper home. Are you vagabonds or something?"

"We're your classic sob story," Binny answered. "My parents were worked so hard in the wheat fields during the hottest summer in modern history, without any breaks or water, that they collapsed within an hour of each other." He nodded toward Fulgar. "His mum was forced into a merchant convoy that never came back, and his dad descended into a drunken stupor. All of 'em were victims of the guilders in some way or another."

"Wow," said Fulgar flatly with a turn of his stick, "it sounds so poetic to hear you tell it."

"And so no one ever taught you it isn't nice to steal?" asked Jinx with half a smirk.

"We take only from those we believe can afford to lose it," Fulgar replied. "Sometimes we share our spoils with others who struggle more than we do."

"You justify it, then." She held up her free hand. "Look, I'm not judging or anything. Me, I'm just trying to get by and survive . . . you know, till some better luck comes along." She bit off another piece of fish, talking between chews. "I don't quite get that from you guys, though—the survival thing. Whatever you want to call it, you clearly justify it."

"Everyone justifies their choices," Fulgar replied. "I'm not really happy about it, I admit, but we are justified by a system that is foundationally unjust."

"You mean the labor system?" asked Jinx. Fulgar nodded.

"We grew up watching it ruin our parents," Binny replied. "One chance—*one*—to impress a bunch of power-hungry university snobs enough to let you pursue what, at the time, you *think* might be your desired occupation. Some people do well, sure, but we got the other side of that coin. We got to watch our folks get beat down by guilders who valued them about as much as pack animals. We got to watch their hope for anything better erode with every job that only got harder and harder, more and more degrading."

"Despite all that," added Fulgar, "I actually still tried doing things their way."

Jinx wore a look of confusion. "What's *their* way?"

"You know," said Binny, "march yourself to the university at the age of seventeen to declare what you're good enough at to pursue further studies." He exhaled a laugh. "Good-boy Fulgar here gave it a shot. I didn't even bother. Told him to come find me when the masters screwed him over, too."

Fulgar sighed with a weak smile of reminiscence. "I tried to have faith that maybe it could work out better for me. It was ... faith misplaced."

"And what did you try to declare?" asked Jinx.

"Medicine, herbalist—medical practice as a physicker. It's not that I didn't know enough. It's not that I lacked ability. Standing there before the professors, I was nervous—terrified, and I choked on my answers. My confidence evaporated. I was so scared that what had happened to my parents would happen to me that I manifested that very outcome upon myself. The masters voted me down. And that was it—my one chance. I was on my own. If I ever wanted *honest* work, in the eyes of officials, it would be whatever the guilders assigned me."

Jinx's eyes were wide. "And there's no way to change that outcome? Challenge it or ask for another chance?"

"The only way is to be adopted—chosen—by an expert with enough influence to attain guilder or royal approval. I have no such person to turn to. Always, your fate is in the hands of someone else."

"We've got big goals for the future, though," said Binny. "We won't always be scrapping around like this."

"What about you, Jinx?" asked Fulgar. "How did you end up in that cargo container?"

Jinx gazed at the fire, setting her roasting stick and fish bones aside. "Simple enough, I guess. You two are citizens here, so you can come and go and do ... your justified things well enough. I washed up on the western shores, apparently from a shipwreck, barely alive and remembering nothing. My real name isn't Jinx, but it's the only name I know. Soldiers found me, kept me from dying, found no evidence of me being a citizen of Tuscawny, and designated me for 'kingdom service.'"

"And what does that mean?" asked Binny.

"You get assigned—maybe to a guild chief or a knight or a noble's household—and you work, not for money you can do what you want to with, but basically to be kept alive."

"Sounds almost like slavery."

"Yeah," she replied reflectively. "Yeah, you could call it that, even if *they* don't."

Fulgar felt a heavy weight in his stomach. "And you have no memory from before washing ashore?"

Jinx shook her head. "None. I still know how to speak, what words mean. I know I look like someone from the Coral Ash Islands, because I've heard people say that. But I don't remember my family or who I was with or what happened at sea. I've never had enough freedom to figure that out. Smarted off one time to my last master, the steward of Fort Morga—a real galoot, that guy. He didn't like that, so he went out of his way to have me traded off to some other land. I was set to be deported. So, I guess you guys aren't really the lowest of your labor force after all."

"Wait a minute," said Binny. "I thought you were caught stealing."

"And that bit was true. How many of you 'proper' citizens get caged up in a crate for stealing food scraps? I managed to escape from the steward, but I got caught."

Fulgar and Binny shared a look, both a mix of surprise and disgust. Forced servitude in the kingdom of Tuscawny was the kind of thing sometimes rumored about but almost never overtly confirmed.

"You should stick with us," said Fulgar, noting the guarded expression on Binny's face. "At least for a while, to give you some time to find a direction."

Binny slumped his shoulders and stared at the fire. "Well... yeah, I suppose a little while won't hurt. Just follow our lead. We've got important jobs to be done and can't afford too many slip-ups."

"Like this last one, eh?" she replied wryly.

Fulgar turned to Binny. "We almost died on this job, you know."

Binny half-smiled back at Fulgar. "*Almost*. Wouldn't be the first near miss."

Fulgar moved to the ground to rest his head upon the log. "So close to that enchanting metal, only to come up empty-handed."

"Well," said Binny, "not exactly." He dug a hand into his satchel and pulled out a palmful of small, sparkling diamonds. Amidst his awe, Fulgar frowned, trying to determine when Binny could have retrieved them. Then he remembered the crate that Binny had fallen into.

The diamonds weren't what they had been after, but at least they were something.

"See, Fulgar—don't I always take care of things?" He moved to rest against his own log. "Now, let's get some sleep."

chapter 2

A BORROWED SECRET

5/30/3177 P.A.

Binny sat within the Shadow Wood Taphouse, drumming his fingers upon a bar counter of black wood, made of what must have been the darkest variety of ebony ever found to exist. Situated off a dodgy little alleyway several blocks from Miskunn's Jade Artery, the entire tavern was constructed of the same wood, making for a profoundly dark interior.

As Binny gazed around, it looked to him as if the whole place could have once caught fire, every inch of the walls and ceiling now ashen like the wood of a doused campfire. Come to think of it, the place did carry something of a burnt smell. It was oddly calming.

He sat with the collar of his frock coat turned up, a mug of frothy pale ale in front of him. The long coat nicely hid the sword sheathed at his side, just a little precaution in case things got dicey.

He was here to meet someone. Someone he didn't know. The note had been handed to him in the street by a dirty little messenger boy. Before Binny could say a word, the street urchin had dashed away.

Glancing left and right, Binny pulled the folded flaxsheet from his coat pocket. He was at the right place, and this was the right time. His eyes lingered over the rest of the message: *Let's discuss your talisman.* It was signed *Afonso, of the Order.*

A note of that nature made Binny instantly wary. But it was just as irresistible. He placed the message back in his pocket.

He didn't look away from his mug as the chair beside him slid back from the counter. Someone sat down heavily beside him and scooted forward.

"Afonso," said Binny.

"Binny," Afonso replied in a gruff voice.

Binny sipped his ale. "I thought your sort were never late."

"Of course we are, if we want to be." He signaled the bartender with a gesture at Binny's drink, indicating he'd have the same. "If we went around acting like perfect little astrals, we wouldn't exactly blend in, would we?"

Binny shifted to face Afonso. Aside from a crooked nose, he had reasonably handsome features—a lean, stubbly face, black hair mussed as though by the wind, and he was perhaps a few years past middle-aged. "I'll give you that, I suppose. You look far more mediocre than I expected of an underground cult follower. I mean no offense, of course."

Afonso snorted a laugh. "*Cult.* How typical. It's an ancient order which has existed in this kingdom for generations, its purpose to protect certain people—even kings—and resources of immeasurable value, under the devotion of Eloh."

"Religious folk, then, just the sort who would love magical metal. But, the first time, we communicated through an intermediary." He pulled out the note, giving it a little wave. "What's your interest in my talisman? Why this sudden desire to meet face-to-face? I already told your associate that we failed to retrieve the metal."

Afonso sputtered out a wheezy cackle. "So, they went through with the job after all. *Ha ha!* Sending smalltime thieves after their lost treasures. How quickly they descend."

Binny thumped down his mug with a scowl. "We're a little more than *smalltime*. If you've got a point, best get to it, and you still haven't answered about my talisman."

"Yes, yes. Upon learning of your talisman, quite an ancient relic, I decided it best to meet you for myself."

Binny arched an eyebrow. "You and your fanatics have been watching me, then?"

"Not really. The Order's associate, the fellow who engaged you for the Volk job, described it to me." Afonso leaned in, speaking lower. "We're old friends, you see."

Binny leaned an elbow on the counter, eyes narrowed in suspicion. "What's your association with the Order again?"

Afonso straightened with a flash of indignation. "My devotion is . . . a former one. I do not come to you as a part of the Order."

"So, you were kicked out?"

The man's expression hardened. "We had our differences, the details of which are irrelevant to this conversation."

Binny casually traced a finger around the ring of his mug. "That depends. I believed the Order—whatever *that* is—to be the end client of our last job, a job that yet remains incomplete. In talking with you, I'd hate for there to be a conflict of interest."

"If a conflict is what you want," Afonso practically hissed, "then all you need do is wait for the Order to discover your talisman for themselves. They would seek to confiscate it. They would sooner see it locked away, just another curio in their vast collection."

"But not you, huh? Or maybe just for your own collection?"

"No. I see an opportunity, I daresay much like you do. This talisman is a key to unlocking mysteries the Order has struggled to unravel for millennia. It is a chance to understand powers of the Shadow Age in ways they never have."

Binny nodded wistfully. "It belongs to an ancient shrine, one that I mean to find. I'm not about to give it up to you or the Order or anyone else, not for all the king's lyra."

"No need to worry. I do not mean to hinder your quest but to aid it."

Binny frowned. "And why would you do that?"

"I want you to find where the talisman belongs. I want you to find it, learn of its power, and remember me when you do."

"You mean . . . pass the talisman on to you next."

"Exactly."

Binny stared at the bar counter in thought. This seemed a resource too valuable to pass up. Plus, once he and Fulgar finally achieved the power they sought, Binny had not committed the talisman to any specific person. By legend, it had to be passed on to someone.

"Okay," Binny replied. "If the help you offer is valuable enough, then I agree."

Afonso took Binny's hand in a firm shake. "Very good! I do warn you, young sir, that I have very powerful friends. Do not forget this commitment."

"Understood. What have you got?"

Grinning, Afonso pulled a small glass vial from his pocket. "What I offer are the location and clues to show you exactly the place you are looking for." He dangled the vial before Binny's eyes. "And a little something to help you retrieve it. Now, please listen carefully, and be sure to bring your talisman . . ."

Bright and early the next morning, Fulgar and Jinx were led by Binny to Glory of Saint Brinon Cathedral, one of Miskunn's oldest and most elaborate of the Soladrien Orthodox tradition. It was situated along one of the streams which ran through Miskunn, with a sluice gate that channeled a steady flow of water into and back out of the main sanctuary, effectively an indoor creek famous for fostering an environment of peace and spiritual serenity by the sounds of natural creation.

As they stepped through the massive, fortress-like cathedral doors, Fulgar decided that if *old building* had a scent, it was a pungent mixture of incense and dusty air.

"Um, is this where you *meant* to take us?" asked Jinx. They took wary steps through the empty vestibule, a tall, narrow entrance area, with a large door positioned diagonally on the right for entry into the sanctuary, and a door on the left for egress.

Last night, after spending the day capering about town, Binny had returned to their woodside campsite with renewed excitement. He had promised them something big, a real life-changer, elaborating no further. "I'll show you tomorrow" was all he said, but Fulgar knew that look in his eyes.

Binny had, or at least he believed he had, made a development toward finding the origin of his uncle's talisman.

"I never took you for the churchgoing type, Binny," said Fulgar.

Binny pressed a finger to his lips. "*Shh.* Show a little respect, will ya?" He reached behind the statue of a robed, stern-faced woman, feeling around with particular interest in the vicinity of its buttocks.

"What are you *doing*?" asked Jinx with a look of disgust.

"Looking for something," Binny replied, stepping back from the statue. "Something that'll be on or in a statue and out of sight."

Fulgar leaned closer to Binny. "This is another one of your *leads*, isn't it? Why didn't you just tell us last night that you wanted to come here?"

"I figured it would be more effective to just explain as we went."

Binny pushed through the door on the right with no small effort. It was so thick and heavy it must've taken about half a giant roastwood to make. This brought them into the main sanctuary, where the ceiling was so high it seemed possible to have formed its own ecosystem up in the rafters, like the canopy of a jungle. A thin haze hung in the vastness of the room, penetrated by colorful rays of light which shone through stained-glass windows. Even the windows seemed about as tall as the trees used to make the doors.

Fulgar's face was hardened with indignation. He and Binny had been at their quest to discover the origin of the talisman for years. Their search had been exhaustive. No museum, library, cathedral, statue, monument, plaza, business, tavern, cellar, ship, harbor, or any other sight or structure they'd investigated had yielded useful clues.

It had started to feel like the legends behind the talisman truly led nowhere, that they might forever be stuck in this marginalized life of scrimping and scraping. Either that, or face the guilders of the workforce, which for both of them was out of the question. Even if they did, even if they dared try to settle into a more normal life, they might sooner get arrested for their various crimes of the past.

"I remind you," Fulgar patiently fumed, "that your last *initiative* nearly got us all killed." The blarkle heist, as they called it, had ended up a bust. Despite the fire in the cargo warehouse, Volk and his thugs had managed to load that wondrous, sparkling metal onto their ship and sail away overnight. That had been just over three weeks ago, and Binny still took the loss rather hard.

"Don't lose the forest for the trees, mate," replied Binny. He twitched his head toward Jinx. "You came out all right."

Fulgar smirked sheepishly, glancing at the lovely girl beside him as she admired the church's elaborate wall-carvings. They had obtained some better clothes for her than the tattered things they'd found her in, so now she had a clean, white button-down shirt and a red skirt. Obtained, that is, in the sense that the outfit had been easy to swipe from a fripperer's cart loaded with far too many wares.

She was an absolute charm, witty and clever, every bit a tomboy but also enticingly feminine. There was a natural attraction that drew them close, made them instant friends. Fulgar found that he truly cared for her, and he longed to find some way to help restore her lost memories.

They stayed quiet as they continued through the sanctuary. Clomping echoes from their footsteps blended with the tranquil babble of water, which flowed along the walls of the sanctuary in a raised waterway about the height and width of a horse trough.

Not a soul was in immediate sight. That wasn't unusual for a Whitesday afternoon, right in the middle of the week. Cathedrals of Elohism, the predominant religion within Tuscawny, were typically open to anyone who wanted to enter for prayer or meditation or private appointment with a spiritual leader. While no other citizens were in view, there was almost certainly a member of the clergy lurking about somewhere.

Fulgar and Jinx followed Binny down the heart of the sanctuary, their eyes roving over the countless intricate columns, spiral stairs, stone creatures, and marble busts placed alongside the rows of pews. Binny felt around the backside of each piece of statuary he came across.

"Binny," Fulgar finally said, "seriously, why have you brought us here?"

Binny glanced toward a stairway descending below the main floor. Every cathedral had such an area, and everyone knew it was off-limits—a space reserved for catacombs, treasures, and whatever secrets the church wanted to safeguard. Fulgar strolled over to it and looked down, seeing a barred door at the bottom of the stairs. Nearby, Binny turned with an "Ah!" and sauntered off toward an ornate stone column catty-cornered from the stairway. Based on his excited glances, he had chosen that column specifically because of its position.

Carved into the column were steps that spiraled up around it and, situated below those steps, a statue of an ancient, bearded figure in a crown. Binny reached behind the statue, running his hands up and down its backside. After a minute or so, he hopped back from the statue with a triumphant cackle.

A Borrowed Secret

"I brought you here, because of *this* little beauty." He held up his find—a key of yellow brass.

"Wha—" started Jinx. "Is that . . .? Is that what I *think* it is?"

Binny nodded toward the off-limits stairway leading to the inner bowels of the old cathedral and waggled his eyebrows. "*Oh* yeah, you bet it is."

Fulgar raised both his hands, palms forward. "No, Binny. I officially draw my line at stealing from churches. I've got enough enemies in the physical realm. Adding spiritual enemies is stretching me just a bit too thin."

"And *this* is why I didn't tell you before. Not *stealing*—just borrowing. Come on, Fulgar, I have standards, too, you know."

"Is that so?" asked Jinx with a wry smirk, hands on her hips.

Fulgar fixed Binny with his sternest glare. He, along with the others, remained careful to keep his voice low. "It's only borrowing if they willingly *give* it to you."

Binny shrugged. "Well, the chap in the tavern willingly *told* me where to find it. That's close enough for me." He took a step toward Fulgar. "Listen, mate, if what this guy told me holds true, then this is a big deal—the biggest yet—for *us*."

Fulgar rolled his eyes and squeezed at the bridge of his nose. "I *knew* it," he groaned. "What did this cost you, Binny? What did you promise in return for this *favor*?"

"Relax, Fulgar. He's more the associate of my associate, both of them in agreement that the church has been used to hide more than a few too many things over the years." He leaned in beside Fulgar's ear to whisper, "And the secret *we're* after is a real doozy. Few know how to get to it, including my associate's associate, some of the clergy . . . and me."

Fulgar gave a slight and disapproving headshake, whispering back, "You are very much in over your head." He leaned away, speaking again in his normal yet hushed voice. "What's your plan?"

From his satchel, Binny pulled a glass vial filled with black powder. "This is a high concentration of mineral sediment." He pointed toward the stream of water flowing along the inner walls of the sanctuary. "This water doesn't just flow in and out of this place at ground level—it flows *into* it, through very small ducts specifically placed within the waterway. I'm not sure how many there are. They're really hard to see, unless you know what to look for. The water routed down below is part of their system of hiding treasures."

"Excuse me," said Jinx, "but exactly how does a tube of sediment come into play here?"

"I'll be down below," continued Binny. "You guys will pour the sediment into the water, just a little before it flows over the correct duct. This stuff will sink to the bottom and flow into the duct, eventually blocking it. Once it's all silted up, the lack of flowing water should free the thingummy below so that I can get to our prize."

Jinx raised an eyebrow and circled her hands in an expectant fashion. She was often animated when she talked, something Fulgar found adorable. "And that prize is . . . what?"

Binny winked at her. "You'll see . . . assuming that my information is correct, that I'm able to get to it, and that we all get out of here without being arrested. Nothing to it."

"How do we know which duct to pour this near?" asked Fulgar.

Binny twisted his face in thought. "Let's see . . . right. It's supposed to be between two animal statues—one an amphibian and the other a bear or badger or something like that."

"Something like that?" Fulgar repeated with an edge of vexation.

Jinx nodded emphatically. "Yeah, there must be a thousand statues in this place!"

"You should know it when you see it," Binny replied. He pulled out a second vial and handed both to Fulgar. "I've got one extra—that's it. So, y'know, try to get it right sooner than later. I don't want to get eaten by a holy troll or whatever else might be down there."

He broke into a casual stroll toward the stairwell, eyeballing works of art as he went, convincingly like a sightseer. Moments later, he descended the stairs and disappeared from view.

Fulgar and Jinx approached the channel where the water entered through the wall to their right. From there, it flowed along the wall, around the semicircular apse behind the high altar, and eventually to where it exited, through the wall of the cathedral opposite from where it started.

They followed the channel, searching for any animal statues that resembled Binny's vague description. The sheer amount of art was staggering, such that it was nearly impossible to properly admire it all. That made Fulgar feel a little guilty, as truly every single statue and carving and mosaic and window and candelabrum was just as magnificent and detailed as the last.

Soon they were halfway around the church, rounding the apse. There were countless depictions of bygone patrons, past figures of royalty, angelic astrals of the Ethereal Realm, frightening images of the Gheol underworld, and plenty of art featuring all transcendients—collectively the world's three intelligent races: humans, grimkins, and the animalistic anthropods—but no common animals.

Jinx stared, hands behind her back, at one of the towering windows, which depicted saints undoubtedly important in the church's history, their names and deeds long forgotten by most. "Incredibly ornate, this place," she said.

Fulgar joined her in observing. "Church builders of old believed in giving the very best to the divine, both in craftsmanship and in the material used. It was their way of inviting Eloh to come in and dwell among them."

He observed a mosaic that depicted the prophet Aholiah, the Elohist savior figure said to have entered the world in three forms, one for each of the intelligent races of Eliorin. The scenes in the mosaic were as morbid as they were beautiful, showing the prophet's suffering and subsequent conquering of three deaths, altogether atoning for all inhabitants of the planet.

"Such powerful imagery and rich history," said Fulgar. "It makes a compelling case for belief that the greatness of Eloh is really out there."

"You don't believe it?" asked Jinx.

"I used to. I've wanted to . . . many times."

She came up beside him, close enough for their arms to touch. He breathed in her scent, something like creek water after a fresh shower of rain, a refreshing diversion from the church's spicy incense. "I like to think there's something out there," she said. "Wish I knew what my upbringing was, what faith or belief I might've grown up with, but I've always felt there's a touch of something bigger inside of us, y'know?"

"I am no authority on the spiritual, but I believe I know what you mean. There is a balance at the core of existence, a natural order. As I live and observe, I've learned that greatness is to be found from within, from one's place in that natural order, not from some realm in the sky. The sky is an impartial domain, from where we get both life-giving air and cataclysmic meteors."

"So sure of this, are you?" asked an aged, cracked voice from behind, causing a hop of surprise from both Fulgar and Jinx. Fulgar instinctively closed his palm around the vials.

A violet-robed clergyman with short, white hair came toward them. The garment pooled on the floor around him and gave the appearance that he was gliding as he approached.

"Only from your own inner strength can you find the best path through life, hm?" said the old man, his countenance friendly. Fulgar reasoned his dry voice was much the result of breathing far too much candle smoke and fragrances.

Fulgar exhaled a short laugh, allowing himself to relax. "It is merely personal observation. I mean no disrespect."

The clergyman gave a short bow. "To speak of the divine, even in doubt, I think is a form of honor. Unraveling the great truths of life is the task of us all. You are here, after all, and not by mere chance."

Fulgar grunted acknowledgement. "Of course. Thank you." He shuffled inconspicuously closer to the water channel.

"But I feel correction is in order, my young truth-seeker. Relying on oneself alone is not the path to your truest potential, for we are not meant to endure this life in isolation."

Disturbing thoughts of Binny suddenly hit Fulgar. He had already taken too long, he feared, to find the tiny duct positioned between the two animal statues. He imagined Binny lost in some labyrinth below, looking for something he couldn't find because Fulgar hadn't completed his task. Or perhaps worse, Binny might encounter another member of the clergy, if he hadn't already. At the least, Fulgar had to keep *this* clergyman from happening upon Binny.

"Perhaps," Fulgar replied, "but none will ever care about your needs and aspirations as much as yourself."

"An analogy, if I may," answered the old man. "Consider the duckling, navigating a lake much as we navigate life. Predators threaten from beyond, threats that the duckling does not even know about. On his own, he is prone to wander, and he is vulnerable to dangers. He is unlikely to cross the lake by himself. Alone he is small, much smaller than he knows or may even be capable of knowing, for the reality around him is unimaginably big. With the flock, however, he is protected. He can reach the other side with the help and guidance of others. Such is life."

Fulgar straightened his posture, a small internal flame ignited at the opportunity to engage this clergyman. It was a thrill few others understood, but Fulgar was loath to shy away from a good philosophical conversation, the sort that he rarely shared with Binny.

Jinx, meanwhile, was back to looking at the walls and into the water of the channel.

THE HEALER

"The flock provides a means of outward protection," replied Fulgar, "and outward protection can be achieved a number of ways. Even so, the duckling should not cross the lake until it finds the inner strength to do so. Until then, with or without protection, it lacks the confidence to achieve it."

The clergyman raised a finger. "Ah, but not only that! It needs something more. Guidance. Yes... guidance, such as from its mother or father, who sees and knows more than the duckling... and the wisdom to follow that guidance."

Fulgar allowed himself a light chuckle. "And then there's *mis*guidance, a thing as dangerous as any predator. There is another way—knowledge, achieved by the duckling's own careful efforts. A map, written directions, a developed sense of where things are—these an individual can attain by their own initiative without the need for the guidance of another."

"Well spoken," the clergyman assented. He seemed to enjoy the banter at least as much as Fulgar. "But are we—are *you*—so perfect that we make no mistakes? An outdated map can get you lost. Directions can be incorrect. If one who is fallible relies solely upon the guidance of the fallible, the results might not be perfect."

"When one cannot rely upon others, then one can only rely upon oneself."

The clergyman folded his arms, such that they became lost in the large sleeves of his habit. "In life we have ourselves, we have those close to us, and at the core of it all we have the guidance of Eloh."

"Ah, of course," replied Fulgar with a hint of smugness. "Visions, impulses, whispers, dreams—things that can be hard to distinguish from the imagination."

"Perhaps," said the clergyman with a large grin, "and present nonetheless. But it is not a forced guidance. It must be sought, discerned, accepted, and willingly followed."

Fulgar glanced at Jinx. She was focused on her search for the animal statues, trying to appear inconspicuous, but her frequent side-eyes and fidgety stance hinted at her sense of urgency.

Thoughts of Binny became forefront in Fulgar's mind, and he hoped his old friend was making progress in the lower level. He felt increasingly nervous that their timing would be off, or that Jinx and he would fail to locate the ducts, or that the whole plan would end in catastrophic failure.

He shuffled his steps idly away from Jinx and turned back to the clergyman. "To discern and willingly follow that which is ethereal—such faith is difficult for many to grasp, but I should like to hear more . . ."

Binny hated crypts . . . and graves . . . and sepulchres . . . and sarcophagi . . . and cemeteries. Basically, he hated anything that represented or even hinted at the concept of death.

All of it fueled his desire to find his talisman's shrine and attain the power therein.

A small flamethyst torch in hand, he navigated through ancient halls and archways composed of sturdy, unfinished blocks of stone. His main goal was to find the wall feature Afonso had described to him in the tavern, which served as a sort of vault for the artifact that would supposedly get them another step closer to the shrine of the talisman.

His secondary goal was to avoid any tomb or catacomb that might be down here, which some churches were known to have.

The area smelled damp and musty, and he heard the movement of water as if it were all around him, although he saw nothing but the occasional drip. Despite the moisture, his throat felt dry from the cool air. The environs reminded him of being in a cave.

He'd followed Afonso's directions exactly, but with everything looking about the same, it was hard to know if he'd taken a

THE HEALER

wrong turn somewhere. He also had the feeling that at least some of Afonso's information had come secondhand, which didn't give Binny an abundance of comfort. Not that Fulgar or Jinx needed to see any hint of doubt. With a goal and a plan of action, Binny found it was always best to fully commit.

Besides, Binny had a good feeling about this lead. Afonso seemed motivated enough, hoping to follow the talisman's clues himself after Binny and Fulgar finished with it.

Of course, thought Binny, *fat chance of him getting my talisman unless this artifact proves to be truly valuable.*

He paused mid-step at the sound of voices. Thus far, he'd gotten no indication that anyone else was down here. But these voices didn't seem to be coming from within the halls around him.

They were more . . . above. Binny looked up and realized with a start that he stood near a floor grate from the main level. He faintly heard Fulgar and someone else he didn't recognize. The grate was at least ten feet overhead, but what little he saw through it helped him to get his bearings. They were near the back of the cathedral, in the semicircular area behind the altar.

Binny continued a little farther, and then he saw it.

The wall feature stood a bit taller and wider than Binny. Its lower half and base were of stone blocks, but its upper half had six rectangular columns in its design, which alternated between solid brick and what appeared to be small, smooth river stones encased behind glass and submerged in remarkably clear water. Ducts ran from the feature's top to the level above. He could hear water flowing throughout the device.

And Fulgar's right there! he realized with a jolt of excitement.

Looking closer at the wall feature, he saw a recessed, grooved circular design in the middle of the center column. He grinned, all of his doubts suddenly washed away.

The circle mirrored the design of his talisman. Afonso had believed the talisman would be essential to unlocking this contraption. This all but confirmed it.

He pulled the talisman from under his shirt and placed it within the circle. It was just the right size, and its design fit perfectly among the grooves.

Glancing upward, he muttered, "Okay, Fulgar. Get those ducts blocked, and I'll take it from there."

Fulgar was getting near to escorting the clergyman outside and barring the door behind him. The man simply would not go away.

Suddenly, mercifully, Jinx looked up from the channel with a bounce that told Fulgar she'd found something. "There's a frog statue in the water here . . . and I think that's a . . . a beaver, just down there!"

Fulgar slapped his thigh. "Ha, a beaver!"

"A keen eye!" said the clergyman. "Those are, in fact, the only two animal figures depicted in this entire cathedral."

To Fulgar's dismay, the old man glided toward Jinx. His continued hovering would only make their task more difficult to complete without suspicion.

Thinking fast, Fulgar took long, hurried strides and crossed in front of the clergyman, so that Fulgar was directly between the man and Jinx. He placed his hands behind his back, his right palm—the one holding the vials—pointed toward Jinx.

"You know, the history of this place quite intrigues me. I've heard the structure predates even the end of the Foundational War." He wiggled his wrist, hoping Jinx would catch the gesture.

She did and quickly shifted to slightly behind and beside him.

"Oh yes, you heard correct!" replied the clergyman with a hop. Behind Fulgar, Jinx's deft little hand slid over his and snatched the vials. "In those days, Miskunn was but a small outskirt town in Soladrien, rightfully."

"Soladrien, all the way back then?" asked Jinx. "Fascinating!" She spun on her heel and returned to the channel, her back to them as she faced the water.

"Oh yes," continued the clergyman, "and in those days you could see far from here, even to Miskunn's great crater, before all the streets and arteries and buildings that arrived after our city was made the new kingdom's capital."

Fulgar swept his arm toward the vast array of artwork around the sanctuary. "Do you know the history behind all these amazing creations?"

"*Oh ho ho! All* of them? Would that I did, but I do know a great many."

Fulgar opened his mouth to speak but was halted by a loud gushing sound from behind. Water geysered upward, Jinx flailing at its base, her head drenching wet. She made something of a sweeping motion within the channel, and moments later the spout settled back into the stream.

"Um," she said, dripping on the floor, "there's a little hole down below, and I guess it didn't like me putting a finger over it."

The clergyman stared wide-eyed at Jinx and the water pooled on the floor around her. "Most curious."

"Are you all right?" asked Fulgar. He went up to her, his back turned to the clergyman.

She nodded. "Yeah, I'm fine. Just got a little extra bath, that's all." Discreetly, she showed Fulgar the empty vials. She had used them both. Fulgar hoped they hadn't just screwed things up for Binny. The sediment was supposed to block the duct, not create a dramatic spout. "It's done," she whispered, as if she had already sensed Fulgar's fear.

Fulgar turned back to the clergyman with a dismissive laugh. "We'll just be on our way. Get her out of here and dried off. Thank you, sir, for the lovely chat."

The old man merely gave a slow nod, looking mystified by

what had occurred. Fulgar and Jinx walked on ahead, back in the direction from which they'd come. The clergyman followed slowly and silently behind them.

"What happened?" Fulgar whispered to her.

"I'm not sure, actually," she replied quietly. "The first vial went straight down the hole and disappeared. I decided to try plugging it with my finger, and then it went all crazy. So I quickly dumped in the second one, and then it calmed down."

Binny rounded the corner ahead of them. He was soaking wet from head to toe.

"Oh my!" gasped the clergyman from behind.

"Hi there!" Binny waved cheerfully. "Sorry, old sport. Got a little too close to the channel back there and stumbled right in. Fancy that!" He glanced at Jinx. "Looks like I wasn't the only one."

"Let's just go," muttered Fulgar, feeling very ready to remove himself from this situation.

"So very, very curious," said the clergyman. He cleared his throat, seeming to compose himself. "Remember, my young friend, life is like the lake. Take care to find the right direction, or what you find on the other side might seek to devour you."

Binny gave a thumbs up. "Life, lake, direction—got it!"

With Fulgar practically pushing Binny out the door, they exited the cathedral.

Aside from the occasional cackle of glee from Binny, few words were spoken as they navigated the narrow, grungy streets of Miskunn's western slums, a true contrast to the broad, colorful arteries surrounding the inner city. Fulgar was focused on getting as far away from that cathedral as quickly as possible, and he was in no mood for conversation.

They were back at their campsite outside of town as the blue midday sky faded to dusk.

"Okay, Binny," said Fulgar in an ominous tone, "you'd better give us some answers."

Binny laughed out, something like maniacal triumph, as he sat upon his log and unshouldered his satchel. "Old churches always keep the juiciest secrets tucked away. Okay, you guys ready?"

"Of course we're bloody ready!" spat Jinx. By now, her hair was mostly dry though still well-tangled.

Binny reached into his satchel and pulled out a black, cylindrical case. From that, he extracted a scroll, clearly old but also in remarkably good condition. He handed it to Fulgar. "This, my dear quest-mate, is where the talisman belongs. *That* is what we've been looking for."

Fulgar returned a wry smirk. "After all this time, you tell me the talisman belongs to a scroll?"

Binny pointed at the old parchment. "Now we know exactly what to look for. *This* is what the ancient shrine looks like."

Fulgar unrolled it, holding it before him. Jinx leaned in from behind for a look.

It was illustrated in striking detail. A rocky, mountainous landscape stretched all around. In such a place, one might expect an important shrine to be at a high point. Rather, this gave the sense that one must go up to go down, into a deep, ominous cavity surrounded by jagged peaks. Within the cavity was the façade of a structure that sent a shiver through Fulgar's body. Sharp, imposing angles and crescent curvatures adorned the outer walls, with jutting tetragonal features like towers of black tourmaline. The shrine's tall entryway was tapered to an upper point, with a spike descending from the top, as though to indicate that the wrong person crossing the threshold could be impaled.

"What *is* that place?" asked Jinx, her voice something between amazed and mystified.

Binny showed her the talisman. "It's where *this* belongs." He allowed her to hold it. "That thing changes hands, over and over, generation to generation, until eventually the right person takes enough initiative to bring it to its origin."

"It came from his crazy uncle," added Fulgar, "the one estranged from the rest of the family. Naturally, it's around this artifact that we have oriented our dreams and aspirations since childhood."

Jinx handed it back to Binny. "Ooo . . . kay. So, what's the big deal about this?"

"There's a legend around it," said Binny. "You know what Aether is?"

"I've a feeling you're about to tell me."

Binny leaned forward, eager. "The king. The Throne of Light. Metsada Palace."

"So . . . you think this will make you like the king?"

Fulgar snickered. "Oh yes, he'd like that very much."

Binny shook his head. "No, no, you're missing the point. Every regular ol' person in this world has one thing in common: Someone is always above them, all the way up to the king and the supposed Aether power all around the Palace. Fulgar and me—it's not that we want to rule anyone. We just don't want anyone above *us*, ruling *our* destinies. What if, one day, the king isn't so benevolent? What if Aether's light isn't so brilliant? Wouldn't you want the power to overcome that? Doesn't have to be that dramatic, even, just power to gain an edge on life. Some of the legend even says this power can fulfill the basic essentials the simplest of us always need. Imagine never needing money, because you can provide for yourself all the things that money is needed for—food, shelter, clothing, influence—or you can even erase such bodily needs entirely."

Fulgar saw the hunger in Binny's eyes, the sheer passion. In Jinx's, he saw skepticism.

"Assuming any of that is true," said Jinx, "there's got to be a catch."

"The *catch*," replied Binny, "is that you have to be smart and good-looking and willing . . . but mostly willing."

"Willing to do what?"

"To commit. To be devoted. To keep the secret alive yet also replant the seed for others to find—those willing to earn it. Just like this talisman came to us, so it must circle to someone else."

Jinx stared at the ground, lost in thought. "Almost sounds like a lure to me, like something kind of dark and dangerous."

"*Looks* that way, too," said Fulgar, "now that I've seen this scroll."

Binny waved them off. "You have to know an opportunity when you see one. The powers associated with this thing are phenomenal, maybe even more than the Palace's Aether. It might even open the door to eternal life." Now even Fulgar gave him an admonishing glare. He'd always believed there was something special behind this talisman, but Binny was also one to sensationalize things that excited him. "Even if it's some kind of weird reincarnation or spirit thing, imagine never having to actually *die*. I find the whole notion quite ghastly—this *death* thing—and the sense of inevitability that everyone just buys into."

Jinx laughed. "Now you sound crazy. Why spend what life you have avoiding something you can't? Embrace it. Make it count. I rather fancy myself going down in a blaze of glory, satisfied that I've somehow made a difference in this world."

"That's noble, Jinx, really," said Fulgar. He dropped his own satchel upon the ground and sat down beside his log. "I really don't fancy this death thing either, if I'm being honest. I'm not sure why, but I've always felt a grave at sea would be the absolute worst."

Jinx squinted at something beside Fulgar. "What's that in your pack?"

The corner of a folded flaxsheet protruded from Fulgar's satchel. He pulled it out and unfolded it. It was an old picture he'd drawn of a white butterfly.

"Oh, this," he said. "I made this as a child on the last day my family was all together, before my mum was forced away with a band of merchants. I saw a butterfly just like this on that day, and it . . . stuck with me. There was something almost . . . ethereal about it. Of course, as a kid, I believed a lot of things." He still remembered healing the butterfly, reattaching its severed wing. Often, he wondered if that had been his imagination, yet the memory was ever vivid.

Jinx smiled down at him. "You know, I don't care what you told that old monk today, about belief in the self and all that. Deep down, I think you know there's something more. I rather think you *are* a believer, Fulgar. In what, I don't know—something bigger."

She leaned down, threw an arm around his shoulder, and kissed his cheek. "And I think it's adorable."

chapter 3

UNSCHEDULED DEPARTURES

6/8/3177 P.A.

F ulgar pulled a book about sailing ships from the library shelf, casting Jinx a look. "This could be promising," he said. Despite his words, he felt remarkably unconvinced.

She gave an appeasing, tired smile as he set it upon the nearest reading table. They leaned over the book as Fulgar thumbed through it, hoping to find something that might jog Jinx's lost memories.

Over the past two weeks, Fulgar had made it his mission to expose Jinx to as many different sights, sounds, and experiences as he could come up with. The effort had taken them throughout Miskunn, from the harbor to the surrounding fields and forests. If they could just find one thing to trigger a memory from her past, it could be counted a victory.

"How about this?" asked Fulgar, pointing at an illustration of a three-masted carrack. "Many voyages between nations are made in ships like this."

"I dunno," she replied. "A ship that size would have a big crew, right? Either I was the lone survivor out of a hundred, or no one out

Unscheduled Departures

of ninety-nine others managed to find me after the wreck."

"Yes, I see your point." Fulgar flipped some more pages. "Perhaps a brig, then?" She shook her head. "Right, still too big. Let's see... definitely not a barque... or a galleon. Ah!" He jabbed his finger at another page. "A light schooner seems quite reasonable. Smaller crew, perhaps a family with a few hired hands, could be tossed by rougher seas... or, hmm, maybe even something like this sloop here."

Jinx pushed away from the table with a groan. "I'm not sure. I don't think this is helping, Fulgar. None of these are familiar to me. I don't even remember ever sailing or even *how* to sail."

Fulgar snapped his fingers. "Jinx, that's it! You need to *sail*, to remember the feel of a deck beneath your feet, the smell of the sea, the bobbing of the waves, and ocean breezes in your face."

"It's just another swing in the dark," she replied. "What's it really matter, anyway? Maybe I'm better off not remembering."

"Memories are precious, Jinx. Where you're from, your heritage, friends and family you knew growing up, experiences you might have learned from. Maybe they won't all be happy memories, but otherwise you'll go through life never knowing and yet always wondering."

She stared at him for silent seconds, those gorgeous cinnamon eyes locked on his face. She sprang forward and embraced him around the neck, much like when they'd first met, except this time Fulgar felt no hesitation in hugging her back. Her shirt lifted, such that one of his hands pressed against the small of her back, smooth and taut with muscle. He drew an exhilarating breath, warmth radiating from his chest, the scent of her hair like fresh garden herbs.

When she pulled away, he grinned at her. "What was that for?"

"It's just that... since I came to this land, having no idea who I was or where I came from, no one has ever actually helped me. No one ever cared... until you." She blinked away watery emotion glistening in her eyes. "Okay, let's go sailing. But, Fulgar, if that doesn't work, then we're calling it, at least for now. It's just . . . too much to keep searching for something we don't know how to look for. Besides, I think it's getting to Binny."

"Binny will come around. He's just anxious to find that shrine. We've searched for so long, looking over every old map and book we can find, talking to every librarian and professor we can get access to, and that scroll remains our best clue yet. Really, it's the first and only validation we've received that the place even exists. Yet, Jinx, I desire very much to help you. I cannot help but care."

Their search for answers about the shrine's location had been so extensive that it seemed, if there were indeed answers to be found, they wouldn't be found in Miskunn. Binny had already started to talk of expanding their search to other towns, but Fulgar was loath to do that until he and Jinx had also exhausted their search for her memories. Binny didn't argue, just grumbled about finding someone to examine the scroll and walked off.

Jinx took hold of Fulgar's hand. "That's very sweet, Fulgar. Thank you. So, do you have access to a ship? Do you know how to sail one?"

With his other hand, he scratched behind his head. "Um, well, no to both . . . but leave it to me. I'll see it done."

And that he did. In just two days, Fulgar managed to persuade a merchant captain, Cedric Gotlieb, to sail them out far enough to put Miskunn just over the horizon and then right back. While Captain Gotlieb was overall generous to help them out, Fulgar having explained Jinx's situation, the short voyage still cost Fulgar a full set of platinum dinnerware they'd recently nicked from a convoy bound for Fort Morga.

Binny was displeased by both the cost and the diversion from their talisman quest, but Fulgar promised to give his full attention to finding the shrine as soon as they returned.

Jinx was impressed when they came upon the two-masted merchant brigantine moored in Miskunn's harbor. Her eyes alight,

Unscheduled Departures

she beamed at Fulgar with a sort of girlish excitement he had never seen from her before. "Wow, Fulgar, you really *did* see it done!"

Captain Gotlieb was a squat, bearded man with a sideways bicorn hat, its two corners spanning the breadth of his shoulders. He greeted them cordially upon their arrival. "Welcome aboard to the both o' ye. Master Fulgar, I thank ye again for the shiny new centerpiece o' me cabin. 'Tis just what I needed."

Fulgar gave a nod as he stepped from the gangplank to the deck. "And thank you, Captain, for your services on such short notice. We are truly excited."

The captain scanned Jinx up and down as though evaluating a barrel of cargo. "Yes, well, I sure hopes our little excursion proves to be of some help t' ye, Miss Jinx. A right awful plight it be t' lose your memories, t' be sure."

"Thank you, Captain," Jinx replied. "At the least, I'm sure it'll be a wonderful ride in your beautiful boat."

Gotlieb gave a short hop, placing his hands upon his belt. "A *ship*, me dear. This ain't some fisherman's rowboat ye be standin' on. A right pride o' Miskunn be the great vessel *Windsong*."

Two men hoisted up the gangplank, while longshoremen spread out along the pier to untie the dock lines.

"*Ready sails and braces!*" bellowed the captain. "Make it a swift jaunt, lads, t' the horizon in blue water and right back t' here." He turned back to Fulgar and Jinx with a tip of his hat. "Enjoy the little joyride, me hearties."

Fulgar and Jinx watched in fascination as the many sails were unfurled and secured like clockwork. Minutes later, they were underway. Sails bellied full, and the occasional flapping of canvas joined the smooth rush of the breeze. Seemingly eager for the waters ahead, the ship picked up speed and quickly put the harbor into the distance.

They made their way to the bow, where the view was nothing but cerulean water. Neither of them spoke for a long time. They simply enjoyed the experience of salty air, sea spraying off the hull below, and their hair streaming in the wind. From the bowsprit above, jib sails danced with the breeze. There was something harmonious in the way all these sensations came together as one. Fulgar had not sailed much in his life, but when he did, it was easy to see why sailors often became so passionate about it.

"This is amazing, Fulgar," Jinx said, her eyes closed as the wind caressed her face. "Thank you so much for this."

"Quite honestly," he replied, "there is nowhere else I would rather be than right here, sharing this with you." He waited a few minutes before the burning question in his mind finally reached his lips. "Does any of this feel familiar to you?"

Saying nothing, she took his hand and held it tight. He took the hint that she wasn't ready to speak of it quite yet.

Less than an hour later, Miskunn had slipped fully below the horizon, so that nothing but water encompassed their view. This experience was new even to Fulgar, as he had never before taken a long-distance voyage.

The captain made his way throughout the ship, bawling orders to turn the ship about for their return. At this point, Jinx sat and leaned against the front railing, arms wrapped around her knees.

Fulgar sat down beside her. "Jinx, are you all right?"

She nodded. "I've got nothing, Fulgar. This is all so amazing, but none of it is familiar. I'm very sorry for all you've given up to help me. It's completely unfair to you, that we've done all this and achieved nothing."

Fulgar laughed, and she returned a quirky expression. "Achieved nothing? I actually see it as one of the greatest achievements of my lifetime! Perhaps we haven't found your memories, not yet, but I have come to know you and like you more and more with each day we spend together."

Her mouth hung half open, but its corners were tugged upward with hints of gladness. "You know what, Fulgar? I fully agree with

Unscheduled Departures

you." She slid closer, so their bodies touched. "And I've also been thinking. Maybe there's a reason my memories are gone. Maybe I was just meant to start something new. Maybe it was the only way for me to find a new purpose and make room for certain things . . . like love."

"Love is a beautiful thing, so I'm told," said Fulgar. "I don't think I've ever truly understood that." He looked her in the eyes. "Until now, that is."

"You know, Fulgar . . . I thought finding my memories was the thing I wanted most in my life, but I don't think it is."

"Really? Then what is it you want?"

She nuzzled up against Fulgar, pulling his arm around her waist and holding it tight. "This."

He leaned back with an air of contentment unlike any he had ever felt, exhilarating and profound. He took a deep breath of the warm, salty air. "So then, after all this, is it safe to say that . . . we're a couple now?"

She grinned, showing brilliant white teeth, and gave him a kiss that seemed to rock the entire ship.

"Yeah," she answered, "it's safe to say that."

Having an illustration of the talisman's shrine hadn't bolstered their search as much as they'd hoped. Fulgar imagined, at times, that it was like being given a drawing of a special rock and asked to find it somewhere on a mountainside.

They'd exhausted every possible source of information they could get to. They'd asked around in taverns. They'd visited all the sketchier establishments specializing in artifacts of witchcraft and divination and mystic arts. They'd scoured all the libraries and museums and bookstores they could access. Their searches and inquiries all came up empty.

THE HEALER

Fulgar took to walking about Miskunn's harbor while Binny searched other areas. Sometimes Jinx went with Fulgar, but just as often he was by himself. Whenever he was alone, he tended to linger about the cargo warehouse they had just barely escaped a little over a month ago.

He had his reasons for being there. It was where he'd first met Jinx, and he liked that memory. Their relationship continued to thrive. They held hands while walking the streets. She frequently locked her arm in his. They always kissed each other goodnight before going to sleep in their campsite.

Binny seemed to pay little mind to their displays of affection. He was utterly focused on finding clues about the shrine's location, and every dead end only made him more obsessive.

Fulgar had another reason for spending time at the harbor. The feeling of that black, sparkling, wondrous metal stuck with him like an enchantment. He wanted to feel that again, to hold the metal and let its tendrils of warmth and energy flow throughout his body. By being at the harbor, he hoped he might again feel its presence. Alas, no matter how much cargo he wandered near, the feeling had not returned. It was like a long-lost part of him had sailed away in a crate.

Well into the month of Jervens, by wondrous circumstance, Binny came upon an instructor from Miskunn Vocational University. This was Professor Jira Dunkeld, who claimed to preside over the esoteric subject of historical arcana. Fulgar never knew such a subject existed at the university. From what he'd heard, it involved the study of seemingly magical phenomena recorded to have happened in the past, from any source and from any point in history, even including the world's ancient cataclysmic ages.

Upon rounding a shelf in one of the city's most prestigious public libraries, Fulgar and Jinx found Binny and the professor bent over a table, talking and pointing at something.

Binny had the illustrated scroll spread before them. The

Unscheduled Departures

professor's natural academic hunger was fully engaged. He was a wiry man, aged about fifty years by Fulgar's guess, bouncy with excitement as he asked Binny about the old parchment.

"This is on loan from an archive, you say?" asked the professor, scratching his pointy chin at the story Binny had just fed him. He had an accent reminiscent of a Whitelander, a bit nasal yet sharp and scrappy. "Why would they do *that*?"

Binny, ever quick on the mark, answered, "Because I have *this*"—he pulled out the talisman—"and we have a collective interest in finding out where it came from."

The professor's eyes widened. "These runes—this is an emblem of the Void, and a powerful one at that!" His eyes went from wide to narrow in admonishment. "I caution you, young sir, this search could lead you to meetings of a . . . very intense nature. That goes for whether this talisman—and this shrine, for that matter—is authentic or not. If it's not, it could be just a scam. If it's *real* . . . then I hope you're well-versed in your lore of the Shadow Age. Although obviously you haven't taken any of *my* classes."

A smirk was planted on Binny's face, the satisfied look that he was on to something useful. "How do we find where this place is located?"

"It's no place I've ever seen before," Professor Dunkeld replied, glaring at the scroll. "But there are those who might have records about this. Mind you, they're reclusive. If they don't want you to find them, it's possible you never will."

"Who are these people?"

"They are called the Order of Aether Diamond. They are an ancient order protecting knowledge, powers, and objects of an ethereal nature."

Fulgar, intrigued, leaned in closer. "And you know this order to be real?"

"Of course it's real! But, like I said, they are not easily found. They won't reveal themselves unless they have good reason."

"Would that I could take your class," said Binny. "If only your colleagues would let the likes of us in."

At this, the professor gave a wry smile. "Ah, but the pursuit of knowledge does not require a university." He glanced at the talisman. "Void energies are to be neither trusted nor trifled with. Just be sure, if you follow wherever *that* might lead you, that you do so under proper guidance."

Fulgar thought back to the clergyman he'd met in Glory of Saint Brinon Cathedral. *If one who is fallible relies solely upon the guidance of the fallible, the results might not be perfect. In life we have ourselves, we have those close to us, and at the core of it all we have the guidance of Eloh.*

"What sort of guidance?" asked Jinx.

Professor Dunkeld shrugged. "Someone from the Order, perhaps."

"You said this Order would not reveal itself without good reason," said Fulgar. "What sort of thing would give them good reason?"

The professor looked Fulgar up and down as though sizing him up. The man's eyes narrowed slightly. "People flaunting certain powers. Powerful artifacts. That's really their business, not mine." He started to turn away but stopped himself, facing them again. "If you *do* happen to find this place, I would very much like to know about it." He raised a finger. "But again, I warn you, *don't* go in unless you really know what you're doing."

"Of course," replied Binny. "Thank you, Professor!"

With a jittery nod to Fulgar and Binny in turn, the professor left them.

"What do you make of all that?" asked Jinx.

Fulgar paid particular attention to the smug look on Binny's face as he rolled up and secured the scroll. "Moreover, why are you smiling like that?"

Binny placed the scroll in his satchel. "Because the pieces are

Unscheduled Departures

coming together, and that old scholar just proved it."

"One thing he said was to be careful," Jinx pointed out.

"A piece of advice Binny is sure to ignore," said Fulgar.

"Oh, please," replied Binny. "Given the opportunity, that professor would jump at the chance to find this place."

"He has the immense resources of the university and probably countless contacts at his disposal, and yet, jumping he's not." Fulgar was toying with Binny, although a small part of him couldn't help but wonder if he was actually making a point.

Agitation flashed in Binny's face. "You know, sometimes I wonder if we're still on the same team here, old quest-mate. Maybe your priorities have shifted."

Fulgar held up a hand for calm. "I'm just bantering, nothing more. You said the pieces are coming together . . . ?"

Binny perked up, seemingly back to his usual self. "It all goes back to the blarkle."

Jinx stifled a chortle. "The what, now?"

Fulgar felt a surprising rush of indignation. "That, I am certain, is not what it's called."

"The blarkle," continued Binny, unfazed, "and the people I'd heard wanted it back when we first tried to get it. Remember the cult I mentioned wanting it, Fulgar?"

Fulgar's brow lifted. "I do."

"That, my good lad, was none other than the group we just heard named, the Order of Aether Diamond. Our search just got a new focus. We find some of that blarkle, we find the Order."

Fulgar's heart skipped, a variety of emotions colliding, and he remained speechless as they left the library.

Fulgar and Jinx grew ever closer. They took long walks in the woods, often ending up at a favorite creek, where they spent hours wading in the cool waters. Around the campfire, they sat side-by-side on the same log and kept their bedding close at night.

With fair regularity, often without a word, Binny would get up and walk off from the campsite. Fulgar felt the occasional pang of guilt, wondering if his own affection for Jinx might be causing Binny to feel more withdrawn. For the longest time, it had been only the two of them, with little on their minds besides survival and their dream of the talisman's power.

At least, that had once been Fulgar's dream. He wasn't so sure anymore. With Jinx, a certain hole in his life had been filled, and his drive to find that supposed legendary power seemed to recede. Other times, he found his excitement for the adventure and promise of their quest. Perhaps that power could still help Jinx and him to secure their best life together.

And, as Fulgar and Binny had mused about many times, their dream was not entirely selfish. Once obtained, the power carried with it responsibility. They would use it to help others rise above the kingdom's methods of assigning labor classes, empower people to be whatever they truly desired, regardless of their fates with universities, and fulfill their duty to pass on the talisman so that others might take up their own quest of discovery and devotion to the well of power held within the hidden shrine.

Still, doubt started to creep in for Fulgar. The professor's warnings brought to mind thoughts of black magic, shadowy incantations, and sorcerous beings such as the umbramancers from children's stories of old. He hadn't thought much about that before, that there could be such mystical dangers to what they sought, but it was easy to draw such conclusions from something so mysterious by nature.

Yet, he suspected he was fretting overmuch. After all, if there weren't challenges and tests along the way, the prize of their quest wouldn't be worth pursuing in the first place.

Binny seemed to sense Fulgar's wavering passion. Sometimes

he was his usual chipper self, and other times he seemed far more agitated than he ever used to be, more tense and irritable.

However, it didn't seem that way for long.

Binny worked his indelible charm once again, this time in the form of buying drinks at the Hobbly Horse Inn & Tavern for a few of the harbor's dockhands. He couldn't afford the drinks, of course, and worked around this challenge via some skillful pickpocketing within the very same establishment.

These particular dockhands happened to be especially familiar with the manifested details of shipments going in and out of Binny and Fulgar's favorite cargo warehouse.

And Binny believed a certain ship was sailing with blarkle onboard. They didn't know if it was the same shipment as before, traveling circuitous sea routes, or a different one entirely. It was blarkle just the same.

"Fate sometimes takes, and sometimes it gives," Binny told Fulgar, wearing his most roguish grin.

This was how, four days later, Fulgar, Jinx, and Binny found themselves traveling toward the town of Warvonia farther north and on the eastern coast, home to the kingdom's second-busiest seaport. Binny's intel pointed to Warvonia as the port where Volk Vorovka's ship was expected to make berth.

Their route from Miskunn kept the eastern coastline in sight most of the way. There was only one way to go to avoid treacherous mountain paths, and that was to stay near the ocean, passing along the rocky coastline that ended the chain of the Monarch Mountains. Fortunately, that particular road wasn't flooded out, as was often the case. A forced route via the nearest mountain pass would have added days to the trip under the best of conditions.

Binny managed to hire their carriage using some of the diamonds he'd previously nicked from the cargo warehouse. Otherwise, they'd have had to pull small thieving jobs for weeks just to afford the ride.

Fate sometimes takes, and sometimes it gives, Fulgar thought.

Even if they found Volk's ship docked in Warvonia, there was no guarantee any of that spellbinding metal would be among its cargo, but they were unwilling to let the opportunity slip away. This metal was expected to attract the attention of the Order of Aether Diamond, supposedly something they wanted.

"And this Order can be trusted to lead us to the location of the talisman's shrine?" Fulgar asked while in the carriage. One hand he kept on the sheathed sword on the bench beside him, and his other arm he kept around Jinx. They all had swords with them, simple single-edged blades that all could've used a good sharpening.

Binny turned from the window as though surprised Fulgar had spoken to him. "Yeah, mate, that's what I'm told." He turned back to the window.

"You're awfully quiet," said Jinx after some time.

Binny looked at her with a blank expression and blinked. "Just running through getting on that ship. That's trickier than sneaking into an enormous warehouse."

"And getting back out," added Fulgar, "this time with the actual prize. I find myself quite excited to find out what that black metal truly is. I think there's something very special about it."

Binny nodded silently.

For over an hour, he did little more than look out the window. Later, as Jinx napped against Fulgar's shoulder, Binny made eye contact.

"Hey." He tipped his head toward the peaceful-looking and pleasingly warm Jinx. "You two are good together, mate. For real."

Fulgar smiled at his longtime friend. "Thank you, Binny. I rather must agree."

Several hours later, they arrived at the southern edge of Warvonia's harbor.

Warvonia was renowned throughout the kingdom for its sea-trade operations and all the charm that came with it. Rough-

Unscheduled Departures

and-tumble sailors frequented its byways, taverns, and eateries, where, as Fulgar had heard, camaraderie reigned about long enough to finish drinks and get out the door. After that, once bounties were on the line, competition within their seafaring guild was famously fierce.

Unlike the more modern, colorful Miskunn, Warvonia seemed little changed since the Feudal Era and the days of the Foundational War, before Tuscawny and neighboring Korangar were kingdoms, when this slice of the land was part of the Sovereign Tracts of Kor. Old stones, timber, and red roofs comprised the buildings. Its maze of meandering cobblestone streets was enough to drive even the most devout and disciplined friar into fits of anxious rage.

Binny settled payment with the carriage driver, and they made their way to the docks. It took navigating a complex tangle of warehouses, service buildings, woodshops, and guildhalls to finally reach the lengths of timbered walkway that included the docks. The walkway stretched along the coast as far as they could see, dappled by the constant bustle of dockhands, sailing crews, repair workers, and merchant carts. Stacks of barrels and block-and-tackle arms were present at nearly every pier.

Jinx gazed around in wonderment. "Wow. This port might not be as large as Miskunn's, but somehow it seems more active."

"My sentiments exactly," replied Fulgar. He looked at Binny. "Do you know which ship is Volk's?"

"No," replied Binny, a deep scowl aimed down the docks. "To be honest, I underestimated how busy this place would be."

"Right. Then . . . let's just have a look around."

"Careful, though," said Jinx. "Volk and his goons might recognize us."

To mitigate this risk, they took frequent detours around the various buildings of the busy harbor, peering carefully around corners and carts. They slunk around overzealous fishmongers purveying their latest catch and wound their way back to the docks, passing ship after ship, with eyes open for any sign of Volk or his henchmen. They remained ever ready to spring back under cover of an awning or cart or building corner.

Then, upon passing by a ship with a crimson crescent on the mainsail, an image that looked like something painted in blood, Fulgar stopped in his tracks.

"Jinx. Binny," he said in a calm yet assertive tone. "This ship. This is it."

Jinx arched an eyebrow at the vessel. "Looks about right."

Binny nodded agreement but retained a skeptical expression. "How do you know?"

"I feel it," Fulgar replied. "It's faint, only because I'm not very near it, but it's unmistakable. That enchanting metal is here."

Jinx eyed two men trudging by with crates. "I think they're loading to set sail."

Binny smirked at the others. "Then let's give 'em a hand, shall we?" He jogged to the nearest storehouse, which left Fulgar and Jinx with the ongoing effort of trying not to be seen by anyone who might recognize them. Much to their fortune, they never saw any of Volk's men that they'd encountered before. Fulgar reasoned they were already aboard the ship. Of course, if current plans held, Fulgar and his friends would soon also be aboard that ship, right in the teeth of danger.

Minutes later, Binny returned with brown hats and overcoats just like the ones most of the dockworkers wore. Fulgar shook his head in amazement. It was as if Binny had planned the whole thing.

Fate sometimes takes, and sometimes it gives.

"Here," said Binny, handing out the newly attained accoutrements. "This ought to help us blend in. Put those on and grab a crate."

"Yeah," said Jinx, "and then what? A trio of dockhands wandering about the ship'll look a bit suspicious, don't ya think?"

"This kind of stuff goes down in the hold of these ships, doesn't

Unscheduled Departures

it?" Binny replied. "We'll just have to carry it all the way down."

Fulgar nodded. "And that's where the metal's also likely to be."

The tactic was remarkably effective. Their arms loaded with wooden, cubical crates, they all three went straight up the gangplank to the ship's main deck, where dockworkers and the ship's crew blended together in a dizzying flurry of activity.

"*Don't stop*," hissed Binny, gesturing with his head toward the stairs to the lower decks. He was right, of course. If they looked like they were lost or confused, they were sure to get caught.

Jinx ended up ahead of them, likely much to her dismay. With a crate in her hands, she stepped timidly between the rows of oarsmen benches below and hammocks above. She looked grossly out of place, surrounded by grimy-faced ruffians that each seemed to have a unique brand of physical disfigurement, from black teeth to nasty scars to strange piercings to missing eyes and appendages. Fulgar stayed as close behind her as he could manage.

About halfway through the rowing benches, she looked back at Fulgar and Binny and mouthed "Now what?"

In a deep and gruff tone he must've thought sounded more sailor-appropriate, Binny said, "Supplies in the hold, addle-brain, another deck down!"

Somehow, they made it down the steps and into the cargo hold without incident, even as other dockworkers were coming out. At the first opportunity, they dropped their crates with pronounced groans.

"Okay," said Jinx, "so the stuff should be down here somewhere, right?"

Fulgar stared down the dimly lit length of the ship's hold, which was packed with barrels, sacks, and crates, with a narrow aisleway running down the middle. He took a deep breath, sensing much more than just the scent of musty old timber. His head felt perfectly clear and his senses heightened, such that he could almost see the auras of anxiety and disquiet surrounding Binny and Jinx.

His body found energy that it didn't have before.

He walked down the aisle. "It's here. Look around."

Jinx looked inside crates, while Binny stayed near the stairs to search. Fulgar tried to follow his over-excited senses. It wasn't easy. He wasn't used to the sensation. He hoped he could home in on the source, to be led definitively toward it, as a sweet aroma might lead one to a warm berry pie. But it didn't seem to work that way. Instead, the power pulsed throughout the entire space. He didn't feel like it was leading him. The sensation felt less directed, more like being hit by an ocean wave.

"And we can just carry this stuff in our pouches, then?" asked Jinx.

"You just *now* thought to ask that?" replied Binny.

"What I saw before," said Fulgar, "was in shards, like slabs of shale. Some of those would fit, yes."

"Even one of those slabs would be worth it," added Binny. He stood up straight and gave Fulgar a serious look. "Just be careful getting off the ship with it, okay?"

Then Fulgar saw it.

Not quite what he'd expected, it was a faint, white glow coming from within a small chest right beside his leg. He made quick work of releasing the lock and opened the lid.

It was a roughly hewn weapon, seemingly chiseled and unfinished, what some might call a shortsword and others a long dagger. It sparkled like diamond dust upon polished obsidian, like a compact galaxy contained within a double-edged blade. Its hilt was of the same material, the grip itself with a grittier finish for better hold. The glow danced in Fulgar's eyes like something celestial and far too perfect for this world.

He removed it from the chest and stood, his hands like a mantelshelf for the blade. In the relative dimness of the hold, he could focus on nothing but that stunning glow. He was captivated, both by its beauty and by the surge of warmth that seemed to flow in through his wrists to bestow wholeness and strength in equal parts.

"So... that's not exactly slabs, is it?" said Jinx. "Is that the metal?"

"This is it," replied Fulgar. "Not in slabs or ore, but formed into a blade."

"*You!*" shouted a man from the stairs. Fulgar lowered the weapon and squinted. It was a lanky redhead, bearing a loaded crossbow. Recognition hit Fulgar like a slap in the face. This was the man he'd thwarted from shooting Binny back in the Miskunn harbor warehouse. Now he watched the man raise his crossbow again...

...this time at Jinx.

"*Jinx!*" Fulgar shouted. The man shot. Fulgar sprang forward, lunging ahead of Jinx in the aisle. He swung out with the glowing blade. He didn't hit the crossbow bolt.

Instead, it ricocheted, seemingly in midair, against a rippling anomaly right before Fulgar's eyes.

Binny tackled the man from beside the stairs and wrestled him to the ground. "Ladder in the back!" he yelled. "I'll see you up top. *Go!*"

Fulgar felt stunned, as much by the anomalous field as the idea of leaving Binny. "We're not going without you!"

"Don't be stupid!" Binny shouted as he grappled with the man and held him down. "Head up stern-side. I'll loop around!"

Jinx tugged Fulgar's arm from behind, and next thing he knew he was dashing with her toward a ladder in the ship's aft end. There was not a second to lose. If the rest of the crew became alerted to their presence before they could disembark, they were done for.

For no reason Fulgar could explain, the glow of the large dagger faded. There was no time to dwell on that now. He shoved the weapon into his belt and climbed, his mind and body in a state of panic over getting out alive, keeping Jinx safe, and ensuring they met back up with Binny.

The ladder took them into one of the aft chambers, likely a map room or officer's quarters. They barged through the door, perhaps with a bit too much gusto, bringing them back to the berthing deck.

"Hey!" shouted a bandana-wearing man, his mouth containing two gold teeth and little else. "Who're you two?" He drew a cutlass, and others nearby followed suit. So much for sneaking off the ship.

Fulgar could've pulled his own trusty old sword, as Jinx did, but he went instead for the celestial-looking dagger. He could only pray that Binny would somehow make it through from the other side.

He parried a swing from the gold-toothed man. The dagger's impact against the steel wasn't the typical clang expected. The sound was more like metal striking rock.

Fulgar and Jinx dueled with fervor, up and down and sideways in the tight space of the deck, pushing their way toward the stairs to the main deck above. Fulgar was as surprised as his opponent when his dull-looking weapon sliced right through the other man's sword, leaving naught but a stub on a hilt. Fulgar kicked the man in the gut and shoved him aside.

Jinx was a deft fighter, light and surefooted. She locked blades with another opponent, meeting his every swing. The man overswung high, giving her the chance to cut low at his leg. He screamed with pain, and she decked him to the planks.

Another of the crew lunged toward Jinx. She narrowly batted away his blade, pushing him aside, but he seemed agile as a squirrel. He whipped around and landed a cut to Jinx's left forearm. The injury could've been much worse than breaking skin, but it only fueled Jinx's battle fury. She scored a hard kick between the man's legs and pushed him into the rowing benches, so that he stumbled and fell indignantly backward.

They darted up the stairs, weapons still in hand. Fulgar soon realized that might not have been the smartest move. If they could've appeared more casual, they might have had the chance to make for the gangplank before anyone's suspicions were aroused. Any semblance of stealth had been cast aside, replaced by pure desire to be off the ship posthaste.

Every face near the stairs turned at their emergence, and every eye locked on their drawn weapons. Fulgar and Jinx froze. There were too many bodies between them and the gangplank to make a mad dash for it. A unified sound of drawn steel scraping against scabbards replaced the din of voices, and Volk's men advanced on their position.

Fulgar and Jinx backed up toward the starboard rail. He caught a glimpse of the blood-red streak on her arm and mentally noted that it would need attention soon. As the men shifted their way, Fulgar got a better sense of the scene, and it didn't improve his angst. Dock lines had been drawn in, and the gangplank had been pulled aboard. Men were ready at the braces on deck and the yardarm above.

The ship was already prepared to set sail.

A sharp *crack* rent the air, followed by an eerie, purple flash of light. There stood Volk, grinning like a madman and holding a whip. Centered within the whip's grip was a black, oval-shaped, purple-veined gem. "Yer not goin' anywhere *this* time, Fulgar Geth!"

The whip cracked again and snaked around Fulgar's right wrist with a terrible sting. With the purple flash came a searing, cold pain, like horrible frostbite. Sharp chills ran through his veins, as if the blood within had frozen.

"What *is* that?" shouted Jinx, sounding more distant to Fulgar than she really was.

"Some new tricks o' me own," growled Volk with a deep chuckle.

The dagger in Fulgar's hand regained its white glow. Like a comrade coming to his aid, the glow spread into his arm and countered the deathly cold with its warmth, extinguishing the whip's purple glow.

As Volk jerked back the whip, that beautiful dagger flew from Fulgar's hands and plunged over the side with a sickening splash.

Fulgar took one step ahead of Jinx, giving Volk the most scathing stare he could manage through his undeniable terror.

"Aaahhh!"

Binny swung across the deck from a sail rope, heading right for Fulgar and Jinx with impressive speed. Fulgar's eyes widened as his friend neared, showing no sign of slowing.

"Binny, look where—!"

It happened too fast. As Fulgar turned to shield himself and Jinx, Binny let go of the rope and rocketed into them, toppling Fulgar and Jinx over the railing. Everything was a blur for intense, awful seconds, and then all was water.

He and Jinx surfaced, gasping and utterly panicked. When he looked up, he saw Binny hanging halfway from the railing, his legs grappled by Volk's crew. They pulled him back to the deck, until Fulgar could no longer see him.

"*Binny!*" Fulgar shouted.

The ship's sail was unfurled, the vessel already moving away from the dock. Fulgar was powerless to stop it. All he could do was watch in horror as the ship sailed away with his childhood friend.

Fate sometimes gives, and sometimes it takes.

chapter 4

LOST AND FOUND

8/14/3177 P.A.

F ulgar's compass and best friend had gone, taken by the crew and Volk.
As soon as they got themselves out of the water, Fulgar fashioned a poultice for Jinx's arm. With some targeted application of his healing power, the wound was reduced to a light scar almost instantly.

The first few days for Fulgar were ones of disbelief. From that point on, Fulgar obsessed over losing Binny and how to find him.

Binny had always been his guide, the navigator over their bearings and direction. They had worked as a team to support their needs. True, it was largely through stealing, but it was all they knew, and always from those who could spare it.

It occurred to Fulgar how much he had taken Binny for granted. Fulgar could pull off a simple pickpocket or swipe an item without being noticed, but Binny was on another level. He could pilfer a meal from an eatery with not an ounce of shame and then employ his charm until the owner practically begged him to take more.

THE HEALER

And so, as days turned to weeks and weeks turned to over a month, Fulgar's desperation grew tenfold. Every day became a struggle. Along with the loss of his friend, Fulgar had also lost his purpose. Jinx tried to assure him otherwise, but it was never enough.

There had been no sign of Binny or his whereabouts. There was never any whisper, record, or rumor of Volk, his crew, or his ship.

Fulgar and Jinx had scoured Warvonia's harbor on an almost daily basis. They'd checked every merchant cart they could find, every warehouse they could get into. The goal had been simple: find any clue leading to Volk and Binny, including any trace of that mystical metal.

At least a dozen times Fulgar had tried diving into the harbor in search of the glowing dagger that had been lost to the water. Even when he managed to reach the murky bottom, he always came up empty. Almost worse, he no longer felt the weapon's presence. The loss was profoundly heartbreaking, its pain only amplified by the loss of Binny.

Dockworkers took notice of their constant presence and started running them off. Civic Force officers ordered Fulgar to stop diving into the water around the docks.

Fulgar rarely slept. He almost never bathed. With no alternative for income, he took some evening work, cleaning dishes in a sketchy tavern on the edge of town. He returned at least half his earnings to the tavern for drinks. For a while, he and Jinx lived off whatever leftover food the tavern had after closing, unsightly morsels often near to spoiling. Twice they got food poisoning, vomiting their way to exhaustion and near dehydration. After that experience, Jinx started finding her own food—from where, Fulgar wasn't quite sure.

As the days passed, Jinx seemed to grow lazy in her search efforts, unengaged and coy whenever they returned to the harbor

Lost and Found

to dodge the usual collection of dockhands, pry into manifests, and slink through the freight. Most nights, Fulgar returned to their campsite inebriated, passing out on the ground without a word. Then the sun came up, and their misery was reset for another day.

It was the fourteenth of Agust, a Soulsday, when Jinx awoke Fulgar with a hard smack in the face.

"Fulgar," she said firmly. "Fulgar, wake up."

He groaned and blinked awake. The sunlight hurt. "What is it?" he slurred.

"Listen to me, Fulgar. I know you're hurting. I know we've suffered loss. But we have to move on. We can't keep living like this."

He sat up, marginally more alert, his head pounding. "Living like what?"

She gestured around their camp. "Like *this*. Like what we've been doing for weeks on end." She struck a determined stance, hands on hips. "Fulgar, eating spoiled scraps and drinking yourself into oblivion every night isn't going to bring Binny back." He made a chore of sitting up, and she continued. "Maybe it's time we scout out a different port. We could go north to Stonehaven, give ourselves a change of pace. We could go back to Miskunn, maybe try to settle into some semblance of a normal life, more like we had before."

His fuzzy mind whirled on those words, causing him to scowl. "I think I know what this is. You're giving up. I've seen it for weeks. You don't believe we'll ever find him."

Jinx crossed an arm over her chest and cupped the elbow of her other, with which she touched her head and gestured as she replied. It made her appear guarded and like she was struggling to find the right words to say. "I don't want to lose Binny either, Fulgar. Our eyes will always be peeled for him, but what we're doing now is toxic."

Fulgar shook his head. "I . . . guess I shouldn't expect you to understand. Binny and I—we've gone through everything together. Our hopes and goals were bigger than either of us, bigger than all three of us together, the kind of opportunity almost no one ever gets. Now it's all gone, Jinx. It's gone, sailed away with Volk's ship, and I'm . . . I'm *scared*. I'm scared because I have absolutely no idea what to do with my life." His voice cracked, and his eyes welled with tears. "All our hopes for the future, chained around Binny's neck, are gone . . . unless I find him before it's too late."

Jinx dropped her arms, her expression now one of pity. "The *talisman*? *That's* your one hope for the future? Come on, Fulgar, that's bonkers! The future is . . . the future! Only *you* can decide what that looks like."

"You don't understand." He rubbed his sleep-deprived, bloodshot eyes. "I'm past hope for university, past hope for a respectable career, past hope for a fair shake in the workforce. We've lived a life of thievery, a cell in every jail with our name on it if we so much as look sideways at the wrong person."

Jinx scowled. "I'm not from Tuscawny—at least I *think* I'm not—but I've observed a lot. I think it's totally possible to have a good life without having gone to university. Call me naïve, but I still believe in things like redemption and optimism."

Fulgar snorted a laugh. "Whatever utopia you've dreamed up isn't Tuscawny, I'm afraid. My mother *died* and my father plunged into madness at the behest of this kingdom's labor system. Binny was right about this—he *always* was. Unless you're at the top of society's mountain, someone will always look down upon you. Someone will always dominate. If you can't be at the top, then all you can do is wield enough power to ward off those who would otherwise seek to control your destiny."

Jinx gave a deep sigh. "We're back at the talisman again, aren't we?"

Fulgar looked down, trying not to tear up again. "All I ever knew was Binny, what we experienced growing up, the misery of our parents, and our quest—"

"And *us*, Fulgar. You've not been alone since Binny was taken, try as you might to believe otherwise. What if *we* can make a good life for ourselves? Isn't that at least worth a chance?"

Fulgar felt a jolt in his stomach, a searing heat bubbling up like a volcano ready to erupt. Losing Binny had been his fault. He had gotten complacent, sidetracked. If he hadn't become so distracted by Jinx, he would have been right there with Binny, actively strategizing their plans of approach together. Instead, Binny had been forced to take the initiative, dragging the others along, and the result had been a haphazard attempt to steal from Volk's ship that failed miserably.

He looked up at Jinx, his face like stone, his eyes like steel. "Yes—*us*. That's what's happened here, really. We found *you*. I got preoccupied. I lost sight of the goal. And, because of my foolishness, Binny and the key we needed are both gone."

Jinx's jaw dropped, only for a moment. In the next moment, she was rolling up her mat and blanket and packing what meager belongings she had. With all that she owned strapped to her back, she faced him once more. "I know there is love in you, Fulgar Geth. I know it, because there was a time when I felt it. Maybe you'll find it. Maybe you'll find what can give you peace and healing. I hope so, I really do. But as of now, I can't do this anymore."

She lingered for long seconds, perhaps awaiting a response. Fulgar's senses were numb, dulled by liquor and hardened by a vague, blurry mixture of remorse, guilt, and grief.

"I know your belief in this . . . *power* is strong," she said. "Many people believe different things. They can't all be right, though, can they? Maybe it's time to listen to what someone *else* believes. Goodbye, Fulgar."

Fulgar said not another word, didn't bother to stand or look in her direction. He simply stared at the smoldering remains of the campfire as Jinx walked away and disappeared through the trees.

THE HEALER

The day after Jinx left, Fulgar awoke with quite a shock. No longer was she nearby when he opened his eyes, bidding him good morning or soothing him with an herbal tea brewed over the fire. All he saw was the profound loneliness that now enveloped him. His new reality, the cycle of loss almost complete.

There wasn't much left to lose.

Initially, he spent his days roaming the streets of Warvonia. A small, distant flame inside him kindled with the hope that he might see her, that he might do a more reasonable job of getting her to see things his way. Alas, it was hopeless. Like a fool, he had driven her away with his drunkenness—his weakness—and she deserved better than that.

Thus, he left the renowned port city of Warvonia. It seemed there was nothing to be gained by staying. Too many of the harbor hands wanted him arrested, Volk's ship hadn't docked there in months, and he hadn't felt the presence of the mystical metal in about as long.

At first, his wanderings were aimless, mostly on networks of rural roads and trails to the tiny villages that surrounded larger towns, collecting various medicinal herbs along the way. Occasionally, he offered to help with maladies encountered along the road and in villages, and he even found a few physickers in small towns that allowed him to assist for his academic betterment or, if he was lucky, even a little pay. He practiced and experimented with combinations of herbs and treatments, keeping a log of which ones he found most effective for different ailments, with and without the application of his power. He studied books about all methods of healing—accepted medical practice, rituals, herbs and plants, ancient crystals, charms, religious and spiritual traditions—

whenever he could get access to a library or bookstore.

Long gone as a career aspiration, his enduring pastime as a healer was more personally therapeutic than anything. It gave him something to think about and a way to occupy himself—something that wasn't depressing, desperate, or destructive.

He eventually ventured to other ports for any sign of Volk or Binny, sometimes on foot and sometimes hitching rides. He tried Stonehaven in the north. He went south to scout Cragport, giving Warvonia a wide berth along the way. He trekked across the province of Sharm to Freemantle, west of Metsada Palace, where he managed to review the entire manifest of docked ships from the past year. It was all for nothing. He managed to hitch a ride with a merchant convoy going from Ruca to Miskunn, where he stayed only long enough to evade the Royal Guardsmen that seemed to be stationed around every corner.

Rather than stay in Miskunn, he lingered around smaller outskirt settlements in the rural reaches of the Sharm province. Some of the friendlier innkeepers allowed him to sleep a night or two in an extra room or in the taproom afterhours. He spent some days lurking about the taprooms and taverns, much smaller than those of the city, usually more to hear travelers' tales than for the drinks. And the tales were plentiful.

There was talk of mayors and the clan-like, nobility-class kiths of Brumm cheating merchants, despite their already vast wealth, some even attempting to take the convoy travelers as personal servants. There were stories of an ambitious sailor who had lost his leg to the dragon-like terons of Aviania but had risen to become one of the most renowned seafaring merchants in the kingdom. Some spoke of spies from the neighboring kingdom of Korangar trying to pry into the military secrets of Tuscawny. A spice merchant told of his ascent up the star-shaped plateau of Alpha Makutu upon which sat Metsada Palace, where he passed through enough of the many gatehouses to look upon the Palace itself, a sight which nearly blinded him with its brilliance. One group of merchants spoke of receiving aid in the western forests from a tribe of kind anthropod badgers, while others told of rogue bands of the feather-covered grimkins that sought to pillage and plunder less-traveled roads.

One tale especially captured Fulgar's attention. An elusive, whip-wielding figure had been spotted in the vicinity of Warvonia, a man some described as a sorcerer of dark magic. As he heard this, Fulgar could almost feel the sting on his wrist from Volk's whip, back when the glittering black weapon had been wrested from him. It seemed far-fetched, but if Volk or one of his cronies had managed to regain the weapon, Fulgar imagined it might have given them sorcery-like powers. Of course, that part of the story could also have been the merchant's added flair. The man seemed to have few supporting details.

That's when Fulgar decided to return to Warvonia.

Over three months had passed since he'd last been there—since Jinx had walked away. By this point, he was a slovenly mess. Long past caring about appearances, his matted, unkempt hair had grown beyond his shoulders, his tangly beard reached down to his chest, and his clothes were soiled and tattered.

He could only hope for another opportunity to track down Volk. If not, he reasoned, someone within the town's exceptionally active seafaring guild could help him to find Volk's ship on the open waters. It was a bowshot in the dark, he knew, but it was more hope than he'd had in months.

After he arrived, his first inclination was to wander about the harbor, as he had done so many times in the past. He spotted a few familiar merchant vessels—the *Waveripper*, the *Epic Skipper*, the *Pilfer*, the *Iron Mermaiden*—none of them carrying what he wanted. It didn't take long for the dockworkers to notice his presence. Some simply warned him away with threatening glares. Others shouted him off. One pulled a three-pronged fishing spear and nearly skewered him in the side.

Lost and Found

That encounter hastened him into the meandering streets of town, where he wandered into the Old Bard district. Jolly as it might have sounded, it was a woefully dire part of town, the sort where brothels and sketchy trades and seedy taverns abounded. The ancient cobblestones of its byways and the bricks of its buildings were blackened by age, never properly cleaned like the façades in better parts of town. There was a generally sour smell in the air, likely no worse than the smell coming from him, and gaps in the streets tended to pool with filmy water.

Although he probably blended into the general riffraff of this district, his only intention now was to beeline through and get back to his woodside campsite just outside of town.

Suddenly he halted, as though he'd been tethered with a rope and walked full-speed to its length. It was that feeling—the gentle, energizing buzz of that sparkling, black metal that Binny had once called blarkle.

It hit him like air to a drowning man. It filled him inside and grew into a searing orb of invigoration, like a second heart that pumped long-lost vitality throughout his body.

Then it was gone.

He gasped, looking around with a sudden sense of desperation. The alley was drab and dreary, quickly darkening with the sun's descent. Nothing stood out to explain the feelings of appearance and sudden loss. Otherwise silent and reclusive figures common to this district took notice of him, some lumbering his way. These were not people to be trifled with, so he fled. He didn't slow his pace until back at his campsite.

It was a different location than where he had camped with Jinx. The memory of her still wracked his emotions. He had loved her, even up to the point of their final argument. He didn't blame her for leaving. He regretted his final words to her, but her lack of understanding still galled him. He often wished he could be different, that he'd never received the one hope for a future that was the talisman's power ... but he had, and so he didn't know how to be different. He would have to succeed and right his life's course—find purpose within that power and maybe win back Jinx's favor—or he'd have to die trying.

Unable to ignore the metal's pull, he returned to the Old Bard district two days later. It was the twentieth of Novashtay, and the chilly breeze coursing through the streets made clear that he would soon need to find warmer clothes.

In broad daylight, he reasoned, it would be safe here.

He reasoned incorrectly.

A burly arm like a tree branch appeared from between two buildings and clotheslined him to the ground.

His sudden view of the gray sky above blurred as he crashed onto the cobbles. For a fleeting second, he was reminded of his days of persistent drunkenness, one of the only things he had improved about himself in recent times. Of course, having no money made drinking easier to avoid.

"*Har*, Kotto, ye laid him down good!" cackled a rather thick voice.

"Course I did," replied a harsher voice.

Fulgar blinked, his vision returning just as he was yanked back to his feet by a strong, hulking wrist.

"And you was right about his hair havin' three colors! Black an' white an' blue, he has!"

Kotto, the bigger man, pulled Fulgar closer as he replied through a wicked grin, "Course I was right." His breath was like a blend of old onions and tomatoes rotting in the sun. "Grab his sword."

A hint of lucidity returned to Fulgar. "What do you want?"

"Just a nice payoff, old chap," replied Kotto. "There's folk 'round 'ere that'd find you worth some good dosh, I reckon. Always on the lookout fer three-colored freaks like you."

Fulgar felt the smaller man reaching from behind, and his

survival instincts engaged. He jerked his left elbow backward, jabbing the man in the nose and eliciting a yowl of pain. Fulgar spun out of Kotto's grip and tried to scurry away.

Kotto's fist was too fast. It pounded Fulgar's arm and smacked him into the building across the alley. Staggering a bit, Fulgar reached for his sword.

The sword wasn't there. A glance at the smaller man revealed why. He had yanked it from Fulgar's belt, perhaps as Fulgar was spinning away.

"Ye might as well come along quiet like," said Kotto, cracking his wrists. "Yer worth more alive than dead, sure enough, but that don't keep me from breakin' a few bones in the meantime."

"I might not look like much," Fulgar replied, "but you'll find I'm quite spry."

The smaller man hissed through his teeth. "Look more like a mangy toothpick. Ah, let's just cut his legs, Kotto, right in the hammies!"

Kotto chuckled. "See how spry ye are *then*, eh?"

Fulgar found there was a doorknob just beside him. It was locked, but the metal felt good. He grabbed it with his left hand.

"Just swing my sword this way," said Fulgar. "I should very much like to have it back."

"*Aaahhh!*" yelled the smaller man as he charged, bringing the sword in for a quick swipe.

Fulgar raised his right hand to block the blade. The sword, instead of completing its swing, jolted sideways, its blunt end attracted to Fulgar's palm.

His mouth turned up in a grin. He didn't always feel the power within him, but he had learned over the years that summoning it without the slightest doubt—a measure of confidence—ensured that it was there when he needed it. Almost as if to comfort him in the aftermath of losing Binny and Jinx, or perhaps because it was about the only feeling he had left, using the power had actually gotten easier for Fulgar over the past few months.

Mouth agape, the smaller man gave Fulgar a glance of confusion just before Fulgar yanked away the sword and shoved its pommel into the man's face. Fulgar turned just in time to duck Kotto's hook punch. Fulgar followed with a jab to Kotto's gut, then an uppercut to his chin, and finally a nasty slash at the man's legs.

Kotto fell, screaming and groping for his wound, a clean cut through a hamstring.

Fulgar reached down and grabbed Kotto's collar, yanking him close, as the man had done to Fulgar before. "A word of advice, *old chap*. Never mess with a man who has nothing to lose." He shoved Kotto back to the ground.

He sheathed his sword and walked away, Kotto's screams of rage and pain blaring in his ears.

"*Stop!*" bellowed Kotto. "I cain't walk—cain't move me leg! Maimed! I'll be *maimed*, you sick, worthless bastard! Ye cain't leave me like this!"

Fulgar closed his eyes, listening to the pathetic wails of the man who had just slammed him to the stones. In spite of himself, he turned around and walked back to Kotto.

Fear flashed in Kotto's eyes. Clearly, he thought Fulgar was coming to inflict more pain, perhaps slice his other leg. He recoiled, inching away, but he maintained a wary, unflinching glare at Fulgar.

Fulgar knelt down. "Hold still," he said.

He reached into his pouch and pulled out a large thorn.

Kotto's eyes widened. "What're ye doin'?"

"I said *hold still*, before I change my mind." He lifted the thorn. "This is a sanita thorn. The gel within accelerates the healing of lacerations. A little added flair of my own, and your wound will heal, at least mostly, with time."

He jabbed the thorn into Kotto's leg, ignored the resulting roars of pain, and placed his hands around it. A soft, orange glow spread around the wound. Kotto's expression changed from hysterical to something more like awe. Fulgar removed the thorn, and Kotto growled through a wince. He still looked as though ready to pounce on Fulgar.

"I hate to see a helpless animal suffer," Fulgar said. "The least I can do is help your immediate pain."

Fulgar blew a reddish-brown powder into Kotto's face and, two sniffs later, the man fell unconscious.

Then Fulgar jogged away, turning every street corner he came upon, until he lost track of the time spent navigating the maze that was Old Bard.

He halted midstride. There it was again—the metal's energy.

This was not the same area where he'd felt it before, not even close. In fact, he'd just stepped into a plaza that was outside the Old Bard district altogether.

Even as Fulgar stood there, the feeling wavered and diminished. He decided to continue to the harbor. Given his current mood, if anyone there crossed him the wrong way today, it would be much to their regret.

Walking about the byways of the harbor zone, everything seemed the same as usual—the usual bustle, the usual ships, the usual glares from dockhands who recognized him . . . and the usual lack of the metal's comforting energy.

Until the unusual occurred, causing him to stand board straight. He felt the energy again.

He glanced around, trying to be nonchalant despite his wariness. If his feelings were to be trusted, Fulgar felt certain he knew what was happening.

Someone had the metal, and that someone was following him.

He drew his sword and spun a slow circle, glaring at every rooftop and dock and pathway.

"Hey, you again!" shouted someone from behind.

Fulgar made a gradual, deliberate turn to face the man. It was a mere dockworker, someone he'd seen here countless times.

THE HEALER

The dockworker pulled a blade. It was just a plain knife, such as for filleting fish, and Fulgar felt nothing of the mysterious metal from this man. "Drop the sword," he said, "or I'll be callin' the Guard!"

Fulgar tightened his sweaty grip on the sword. Things were strange. He felt like he was being toyed with by some unseen force, and it galled him to the core.

"I mean it!" followed the dockworker, stepping closer, knife raised.

Fulgar channeled the magnetism within, raised his free arm, felt for the slight pull of the dockworker's metal blade, and jerked his arm to the right.

The knife jumped sideways from the dockworker's hand and plunked into the water. The man was left gaping, staring at his hand and then at Fulgar.

Fulgar sheathed his sword and ran away.

One night later, Fulgar strolled down the streets of a different part of Warvonia. It was the cleaner, safer Market Square district within the heart of town. Given the events of last night, he welcomed a change of environment. The sun had set during the twentieth hour, and since then Eliorin's full moon and rings cast a pleasant glow upon the notably brighter streets.

As the air took on a colder bite and he began to shiver, Fulgar decided to make his way back toward his campsite, where he could warm himself beside a fire. Avoiding Old Bard altogether required a much longer route through the town's meandering streets.

Few others were out at this hour. He nodded greetings to a few unassertive troops of the Civic Force, doing his best to look natural. They paid him little heed, although his untidy appearance did earn him some lingering stares.

Lost and Found

"Are you lost?" one of the troops asked.

"Not at all," Fulgar replied. "Just out for a stroll."

The trooper grunted in an unconvinced sort of way, likely one breath away from directing Fulgar toward the alleys of Old Bard. Apparently, he didn't consider Fulgar worth the effort.

Fulgar turned more corners and entered a straight length of street with a pronounced uphill slope. No one else was around, which was just as well with him. About halfway up this stretch, a blast of air gusted through with a shockingly frigid chill. He huddled himself together, rubbing his arms vigorously for even a hint of warmth. That campfire was beginning to sound very good. He would need to find himself warmer clothes or a decent coat, or the colder days ahead would freeze him into a grubby icicle.

Still, that wind. It was a staggeringly brutal gale, maybe not even half the temperature of the air before it.

Fulgar saw something ahead, at the apex of the sloping street. It was a person, but the light was such that Fulgar perceived little more than a silhouette. He squinted, still pressing through the icy breeze. The figure simply stood there, facing down the street toward Fulgar.

The figure wore a helmet of curved horns and a viciously rippling cape, but it was the thing in its hand that made Fulgar stop.

It was a whip.

Fulgar drew his sword. "Who are you?!" He had to shout above the wind.

The imposing figure did not need to shout. His voice carried over the soaring air, as though within the breeze itself. First came a dark, menacing chuckle, and then the words, "So, you're a Fielder." Within the air, his voice sounded deep and powerful. "That . . . and a pitiful, lowly street rat."

The whip in the man's hand contained a small black-and-purple gem in the grip, and it reminded him of only one person. "Volk?" It became increasingly harder to speak over the wind. "If that's you, Volk . . . I will chop you . . . slowly . . . into shark bait!"

Laughter swirled all around him, mocking from every direction. "Don't be ridiculous."

Fulgar heard the crack of the whip, and a purple, fiery blast exploded beneath a merchant cart standing between them. Upheaved and flying down the street, it turned three times before crashing near Fulgar.

Fulgar turned to run, but the breeze pushed against him, and his steps gained no ground.

Horrified, Fulgar doubled his effort. It was futile. Even against all his might, the wind blew him slowly back up the street, in the direction of the devilish fiend at the top of the hill.

Fulgar remembered the stories he'd heard about the figure roaming Warvonia, the wielder of dark magic. He'd believed that to be Volk, bearing the mystical dagger that Fulgar had so longed to reclaim. If this was indeed Volk, he had changed. Now he was something much more ominous and terrible.

He was something filled with darkness and cold, raw power.

Fulgar scrambled against the force of the gale, but his boots merely slid along the stones, taking him nowhere but backward. Violet explosions erupted in the street and on the walls of buildings all around him. In full desperation, he jabbed at anything and everything with his sword, until it found purchase in a gap between cobblestones. The wind whipped him around, so that he again faced the sorcerer above.

"*Stop!*" Fulgar screamed. He stood only about a spear's throw away. His entire body was nearly numbed by the chill swirling through him.

The sorcerer laughed all the more. "Now see *this*."

Another crack of the whip. Fulgar anticipated it. Purple flames lunged toward him like a predatory, ravenous tongue.

He acted on pure instinct, waving his arms and sword in a sweeping, circular pattern before him. A rippling distortion spanned the street's width, cutting off the wind and releasing its pull on Fulgar. The blast of purple fire slammed into the field and ricocheted back into the sorcerer.

Fulgar saw the explosion of violet and heard the mage's roar of surprise before he turned and sprinted, putting as much distance as he possibly could between himself and that demonic presence, even if it meant retreating through Old Bard.

Fulgar didn't leave his campsite or the reclusive shelter of the forest for a week. He spent the first two days struggling to believe that what he'd encountered was real. It was the first time he had ever harbored an especially thorough fear of Volk and the whip he now knew to be ensorcelled.

As the denial wore off, he spent the next two days in confusion. Ensorcelled by what? The tales he'd heard of dark magic now seemed accurate. Had that kind of power come from the mystical metal Fulgar had held, that same metal that had once so invigorated him? He hadn't sensed its presence. Still, the possibility prompted an unexpectedly profound period of self-reflection. What sort of person had he become, to feel invigoration from something capable of such dark, cold powers?

His encounter with the mage had been like walking headlong into a bone-chilling blizzard, whereas holding the metal had given him nothing but fulfillment and warmth. The feelings seemed diametrically opposed. Perhaps the metal's powers were more a reflection of the individual, in which case Fulgar was absolved, not quite the monster he feared he might be.

At least, the Fulgar of over three months ago was absolved. Now he was a mess, all alone, still a homeless thief, and cowering like a craven in the woods.

After another two days of deliberation, he decided to return to the harbor. He reasoned that, if Volk was back, then his ship must have come with him. If he found Volk's ship, preferably without Volk on it, he might also find that black metal he so longed for. He might find Binny or at least a hint about his whereabouts.

Not that, by this point, he really believed he'd be so fortunate, but the next day he went just the same. He was especially wary as he traversed the streets, like a cat slinking about unfamiliar territory.

He felt just about at the end of his rope. If this search failed, as every search before it had, he figured his life was destined for more of the desperation and down-spiraling that had accompanied him the past several months. He might finally be ready to give himself over to the officials for kingdom servitude and the general workforce of labor assigned by guilders. It was either that or descend to a hopeless point of no return. He wasn't sure which would be worse.

Taking twice as long as usual, he arrived at the harbor, expectations low. Sword drawn and held at his side, he ambled through the cobbled byways of the service facilities. Upon reaching the docks, he strolled along, gazing at the ships, seeing nothing new, as usual.

Eloh has truly forgotten me, he told himself. The utter meaninglessness of the life he'd lived struck him in that moment like a bludgeon. What a worthless pile of flesh he'd become, just an unwanted vagabond wandering the same old places for things he hadn't found after months of searching. Along the way, he had lost everything while achieving nothing but one disappointing turn after another.

He dragged himself to the edge of the wooden walkway, to a place mostly empty of dockworkers, most of whom were busy tending to ships farther down the harbor. He stared down at the rippling water. There was a certain raw rhythm to its liquid movement, a smooth pulse to the light swells that lapped against the docks. It was an eternal presence, an endless depth, a constant bearer of life beginning and ending.

There was a time when he'd thought a watery grave the worst, but perhaps there could be peace in it after all.

Eyes filled with tears, he raised his arms and screamed, "*Is this all I'm meant for?! TELL ME!*"

The lingering passersby cast him odd, glaring looks and kept walking, perhaps a little faster than before. Nobody tried to apprehend him. He wouldn't have cared if they had.

Still looking up, he saw movement. A white butterfly—the likes of which he hadn't seen since childhood—fluttered by, passing just in front of his face. It reminded him of home—not the painful way he often remembered it, but with a rare sense of fondness, from a time when hopes and dreams meant something, and when faith, even the faith of a child, was enough to bring healing.

Mesmerized, he lowered his arms, and then froze completely.

The feeling had returned.

"You're even more pathetic up close than from afar," said a firm, young male voice from behind. Fulgar turned.

The speaker looked to be an older teenager, with a black bandana tied around his head of spiky, white hair. His clothes were all black, with the exception of thin white piping along the sides of his trousers and white trim throughout his tunic, which was buttoned only up to his sharply defined pectorals. Heavy black boots planted his stance no more than twenty feet away from Fulgar. A shortsword of what appeared to be gold was gripped in his right hand, and at his left side was sheathed a second blade.

"And who are you?" asked Fulgar.

"Suffice to say, a person of interest . . . and a person interested in *you*."

"You don't see many swords of gold, unless it's something ornamental. The metal's too soft for combat."

The young man smirked. "It's also not magnetic."

Fulgar found himself unsurprised to hear the man allude to his inherent strength with magnetism. He nodded toward the golden sword. "Did you steal that from someone?"

"I know this might be hard for you to believe, but not all nice things are obtained by theft."

Fulgar cocked his head to the side. "That's not my experience, personally. And why am I of interest, exactly?"

"My name is Elcid Ursid, and I am interested in a real challenge." He raised his golden sword.

"You want to *fight* me? Look... you're, what, seventeen? Shouldn't you be studying and figuring out your life? You know, so you don't turn out to be some destitute wretch like me?"

"Eighteen," Elcid answered, "and don't worry, I won't turn out like you... at least, not like the man you are right now. My master thinks you're something better." He readied his stance and held the golden sword before him. "Now, prove it."

Fulgar raised his own sword, a meager, beaten thing in comparison, and stared into the young man's eyes.

Then he fled, sprinting down the wooden walkway, the youth's steps pounding after him.

He wasn't sure what about this Elcid man had spooked him. No abundance of thought really went into it. He just felt overwhelmed, too far in over his head to engage some cocky kid with a golden sword. Not that Fulgar was old at twenty-four, although he often felt much older.

Elcid was gaining on him. Fulgar overturned a barrel as he passed one of the warehouses, ignoring the angry shouts of a dockhand, and then knocked over a stack of crates as he passed a dock. None of that slowed his pursuer.

He took a hard left, back into the service byways of the harbor. Hollow thuds of his boots hitting wood changed to the softened skids of running on cobblestone. The thuds following him were gone within a second, Elcid in hot pursuit.

Fulgar shoved between two dockworkers, one of them dropping a crate of oranges and sending a torrent of curses in Fulgar's wake. Several other workers cried out as he dodged them in the path. Some of them likely would have given chase, had they not seen Elcid already on Fulgar's tail.

Up ahead, Fulgar spotted crates and barrels stacked to just below the window of a service building. Once within reach of them, he made a mighty leap and scrambled up the stack. It wasn't as stable as he'd hoped, most likely because the crates were empty rather than weighted down, but still he neared the window.

As he reached for it, a blinding light hit his eyes, wood exploded, and the stack tumbled beneath him. He cried out, first reaching to cover his eyes, then flailing to catch himself. He rode a small, cube-shaped crate to the ground. As he landed, his rump cracked through the wood. He groaned in pain, his sword somehow still in hand.

He tried to shake the bleariness from his head and saw Elcid tossing crates aside to get to him. This wasn't going to work. Fulgar would have to engage.

He pushed himself out of the crate, snatched it, lifted it overhead, and flung it at Elcid. Smirking the whole time, Elcid smashed through the crate with one swing, as though it were a tomato.

"Come on, Fielder," Elcid taunted. "Show me better than that!"

"I have *no* idea what you're talking about!" Fulgar replied.

Rather than allowing Elcid the upper hand, Fulgar lunged for the attack, which he figured Elcid wouldn't expect. Whether expected or not, the lad didn't falter. He met Fulgar's blade, the clash of steel against the golden weapon singing with a curious crystalline ring. Fulgar backed Elcid down maybe one step before the tide turned and Fulgar was the one stepping backward, thrusting his sword in every direction to parry Elcid.

Then, with one particularly good swipe, Elcid struck Fulgar's sword from his hand. It clanged to the street several feet away.

Blade still pointed forward at Fulgar, Elcid shrugged. "Eh, you're not *terrible*. Sloppy, undisciplined, desperate perhaps, but not terrible. Let's see how you do with better arms."

Elcid drew the other weapon from his belt. Fulgar's gaze was instantly drawn to it, and he sucked in a gasp of recognition. Sparkles danced in his eyes and captivated him like a trance. This was it—the mystical metal that beckoned to his mind and spirit—the weapon he had spent so many despairing months trying to find. If not the same exact one, this was its twin, looking just as unfinished and yet irresistible in Fulgar's eyes.

Watching Fulgar's reaction, Elcid freed it from its scabbard and tossed it toward Fulgar. "Now, let's see what you're *really* made of, Fielder. Go on. Take it."

Fulgar needed no second bidding. He snatched up the weapon, and profound clarity drove away the fog of emotion and misery and grief that had been his life for months. Warm strength radiated through his wrist, and what few good things Fulgar still saw in himself were amplified, wrested from the darkest corners of his inner being and thrust to the forefront.

He looked up from the weapon and locked eyes with Elcid, who looked back at him with hungry satisfaction, his sword grasped with both hands, held ready and eager to engage.

"What reason do I have to fight?" Fulgar asked. "I have no quarrel with you."

"Oh, you'll be coming with me," Elcid replied. "I just want to see for myself if you are what we think you are." He nodded toward the weapon in Fulgar's hand. "Also, you've been searching nonstop for that blade since you lost it months ago."

"Indeed . . . and you've just handed it to me."

"And you won't be keeping it."

Elcid lunged forward with blinding speed. Fulgar barely countered, swatting away at the golden blade. Bright yellow and white bursts of light erupted where the two blades clashed. Fulgar had forgotten how light and natural this weapon felt in his hand.

Crying out, Fulgar formed his will around the weapon and

channeled power into his every swing, easily matching the strength of his opponent. Bursts of light flashed all around them as their blades struck high, low, right, and left.

At first, the fight went much as before, with Elcid maintaining the upper hand and controlling the direction of the battle. Gradually, as Fulgar's determination grew, he riposted with increased vigor, and Elcid became the one backing down the alley.

In a moment of imbalance, Fulgar swung with his left fist. Elcid ducked it and landed a punch to Fulgar's back. It amounted to a push with little pain, so Fulgar spun around for a kick and another strike against Elcid's weapon.

A white glow surrounded Fulgar's weapon, although in his newfound fervor he barely noticed it. He struck with increasing command and confidence, Elcid continuing to back away until they'd nearly returned to the wooden accessway to the docks.

"Just let me know when you've had enough!" Fulgar roared.

Elcid went low for a leg sweep, taking Fulgar to the ground. In quick recovery, Fulgar rolled to the side, parrying the golden sword again as he regained his feet.

Elcid leapt back and put more distance between them. He glanced at Fulgar's weapon, which still maintained a soft white glow, and smiled.

"Okay," he said, "I think I've had enough."

Fulgar cautiously lowered his weapon, his shoulders heaving with heavy breaths. He hadn't expected that Elcid would actually yield. "Really?"

"Sure."

Elcid pointed his golden sword forward, and all Fulgar saw in the next moment must have been the brightest light in all the universe, aimed straight at his eyes.

"*Aaah!*" Fulgar screamed, slamming a forearm over his eyes. He felt the long dagger leave his hand, heard it land upon the ground. In his blindness, he heard its scrape against the stones as

THE HEALER

Elcid picked it up.

"Impressive, Fielder. Now, come with me."

Fulgar had no choice but to follow closely behind the now-blurry figure of Elcid. Their trek through town seemed to last forever as they turned countless street corners. His ability to see where he was going only got worse once they left daylight, passed through a doorway, and entered a much darker series of halls and stairways. Eventually, he was led into a room.

"Have a seat," Elcid told him, brooking no argument.

"Seems I have little choice," grumbled Fulgar, dropping himself into a large, well-padded armchair.

Elcid exited, leaving Fulgar to his indiscernible surroundings. It was a rather elongated space, judging by the footsteps to the chair, perhaps a large study or common area. A short time later, three people entered. Based on the black attire Fulgar had followed for the past hour, one of them was Elcid. Another was of a similar wiry size and stature.

It was the third man that approached Fulgar. He was heavyset in the burly sense, and the black blur on his face indicated a thick beard.

"Drink this," he said in a voice befitting his size. "It will help your eyes recover faster." His accent had the slightest Eidynite slant, perhaps northern Rocknee.

Fulgar took the mug handed to him and sniffed. "Bilwa, tamarind, and . . . fennel?"

"You know your herbs well."

Fulgar sipped and swallowed. It wasn't much for taste, but the brew felt wonderful as it coursed through his body. "Yes, well, believe it or not I've actually studied healing remedies quite extensively."

Lost and Found

The large man sat. Elcid and the other man lingered somewhere in the background. "Knowledge of this kind is well-suited for university pursuit. Yet, you are well beyond the age for declarations."

"You could say it was decided that the path of conformity wasn't mine to follow. I did try. The panel of professors decided it for me."

The man made a dismissive wave. "It is an oft-shortsighted system, and you are a man of independence."

"For all the greatness it's gotten me," Fulgar replied. "Have you brought me here, nearly blind, to discuss my career failures?"

"Please forgive my rudeness. My name is Zirion Tevet. Your past aspirations and your present way of... pursuing your ambitions... are not in question here. And yet, your interest is something I very much wish to address. You've taken a very keen interest in the ethereal."

Fulgar nearly snorted his fennel tea with laughter. "You're mistaken, I'm afraid. I'm the last one to have an interest in the ethereal."

"It is novidian—an ethereal material—that you seek."

Fulgar blinked upon hearing the name. "Novidian." The word felt like honey to his tongue, perfectly suited to the mystical intrigue surrounding the substance.

"Yes," replied Zirion. "You believe that finding it will mean finding your friend, Binny."

A shiver ran through Fulgar's body, despite the warm liquid he'd just swallowed. "What do you know of Binny?"

The non-Elcid skinny man came closer, and Fulgar realized he could now see well enough to make out a head of salt-and-pepper hair, a bit heavier on the salt. "Those who took him were illegally peddling novidian ore." He spoke with a slight lilt, sharp and crisp, and he sounded about as young as Elcid. "Of course, you and your friend knew as much, as you were just as keen to do the same."

Zirion raised a hand. "That is not quite certain, Silas. We had associates in contact with Binny. We had actually hoped he would be able to retrieve it and avoid our direct involvement."

Fulgar sat up straight, his attention piqued. "Wait. You're that group or cult or something that Binny got the lead from, aren't you?"

"We are of the Order of Aether Diamond, protectors of the ethereal in our world and keepers of the land's history."

"The ethereal . . ." Fulgar repeated wistfully. ". . . in our world?"

"The novidian you love so much," said Elcid, strutting nearer. "Because you're a Fielder."

"What does that mean?"

"A Fielder is someone able to tap into the ethereal powers of Dynamism, also called the Dynamics of Zophiel. For now, suffice to say that Dynamism is a form of ethereal genetics that resides inside you—what we call etheretics."

Fulgar frowned. "You're saying this is something in my blood. But . . . *ethereal* genetics?"

Zirion nodded. "Yes—passed into mortal bloodlines long ago by archastrals of the Ethereal Realm."

Fulgar felt his grasp on reality slipping and wondered if this might be a dream. "You can't be serious."

"It is a lot to take in all at once," said Zirion, "but we will show you, with time, and if you so desire. The Fielder capabilities awakened within you create a special connection with novidian. This is why you feel the way you do when in its presence. We are not sure that your etheretics are pure, but the presence of your power is unmistakable. Such power can awaken in different ways and in varying degrees. In you, it seems quite strong. You have felt it in your use of magnetism and your ability to heal."

Zirion gestured toward the man standing beside Elcid. "Silas is not etheretic but has an affinity to Dynamism. This means his body is receptive to novidian's energy, giving him some abilities as

Lost and Found

a Fielder, but these are limited compared to a true etheretic. Elcid is similar, with an affinity to Aether energies. I have felt a slight affinity to both but also lack true etheretics. Possessing etheretics is not a requirement for devotion to the Order, although historically we hold a very special place for those that do."

"The kingdom is most displeased that the novidian escaped their notice," said Silas. "We are displeased for different reasons. We believe Volk Vorovka had a buyer heavily intertwined with powers of the Void, potentially to corrupt the ethereal for their own purposes."

"They will not easily succeed," said Elcid. "Novidian's energy is very difficult to corrupt. It is even known historically as the Pure Ethereal."

Fulgar's head was beginning to ache, although at least his vision was now rapidly improving. "Powers of the Void . . .?"

"Shadow energies," replied Silas, "essentially in opposition to Aether."

"Aside from my wanting to find Binny, what does any of this have to do with me?"

There were elongated moments of silence as the three men exchanged glances. Elcid and Silas deferred any response to Zirion, their apparent leader. "There are always evils to be kept at bay—things that the typical Royal Guard alone cannot contend with. Many are minor, everyday offenses—someone's dabbling in sorcery and dark arts, not even realizing what they're getting into. Some problems are larger and require a more ethereal solution.

"Sometimes an actual ethereal, or an etheretic person, is found and must be protected. The kingdom itself houses stores of ethereal material that the Order is tasked to guard. Records and history are sacred—they must be read, absorbed, and always kept pure and free from hindrance. The Order keeps its own archives as part of our charge, separated from all public and royal libraries."

Fulgar shook his head, struggling to grasp the reality of such things as the Void and dark sorcery. Yet, he couldn't shake the memory of the mage he'd encountered, and the whip that reminded him distinctly of Volk. "I still don't know what you want," he finally said. "Why tell me all of this?"

"Because we need you, Fulgar," Zirion replied, "and you need us. We can help you unlock your potential, what you are truly capable of becoming. You can refuse, of course, and we can drop you right back into your life of petty theft and desperation. In my eyes, you are free to make that choice."

"What is it you want me to do?"

"Become part of the Order and learn our ways. As a true Fielder—a true etheretic—the world may one day rely on you more than it will ever know, just as with legendary Heroes of Time before you."

Fulgar fought an impulse to stand and leave. Running from opportunity to follow one bad decision after another had gotten him the life he had. He had only ever believed in one thing—the dream he and Binny had shared, the dream of empowerment that Fulgar had convinced himself could come from only the source of that talisman.

Then again, he had believed in something else for a time: Jinx. She was the one thing that had taken his mind to a different place. Binny had never liked that, but for Fulgar the days spent with Jinx had been some of the best he had ever known. She had been like a glimpse of the happiness that might be possible on the other side of their quest, with hopes and goals and dreams that felt different than any other he'd had. They felt like a real life.

And the life she had wanted, for a time, had included him.

Fulgar didn't know what to believe anymore. He was well and truly out of paths to follow. Although, in this moment, perhaps a new path was manifesting before him.

Maybe it's time to listen to what someone else believes. The last sentence he'd heard from Jinx played in his mind with resounding clarity. She was right. She had always been right.

Lost and Found

Fulgar looked at the broad, scruffy, yet not unkind face of Zirion, his vision suddenly so much clearer. "Okay, Mister Tevet. I accept."

"Oh, good," replied Silas. "Then let's start by cleaning you up."

chapter 5

FISHMONGERS OR SLIPKNOTS

6/35/3178 P.A.

A sudden flicker of candleflame and a stirring of air revealed that someone had entered the study. Fulgar paid little heed, his attention locked on the tome before him.

He was deep into the Order's historical accounts of the Foundational War, which had defined the borders of the Grandtrilia continent's three nations: Tuscawny, Korangar, and Holbrook. Warvonia was now within the Tuscawnese province of Rocknee, but in those days, Rocknee was part of the Sovereign Tracts of Kor, which would one day become the nation of Korangar. Fulgar, captivated by the account's portrayal of the conflict's primary warring factions, barely noticed when Zirion approached the table.

"Pleasant evening," greeted the big man.

Fulgar looked up. "To you as well."

Zirion glanced at the tiny flame beside the old book. "Still using candlelight, I see. Fulgar, these volumes are irreplaceable. This is why we only use the mineral-based lighting of flocalcite."

Fulgar stroked his clean-shaven chin. "I . . . apologize. You

Fishmongers or Slipknots

caught me in a rare moment. I do respect the Order's wishes and usually conform. It's just that I find a certain peace and calm from the light of natural fire."

Most of the writings here existed in copies elsewhere. The Order had painstakingly scribed multiple copies of countless accounts over the years. Still, one might have to travel a hundred miles or more to find another copy, and even then, only if that person knew where to find another Order safehouse.

Even before joining the Order, Fulgar had relished any opportunity to get his hands on reading materials of interest—histories, herbal remedies, healing techniques, medical theories, combat skills, power crystals, and just about anything else available. Back then, his access to books was limited to the occasional library. Here, the troves of knowledge were vast. He was compelled to read as much of it as he could.

"And how are you feeling today?" asked Zirion.

"Quite well, thank you. These accounts about Phos Kataneo of the Soladrien faction are *fascinating*. So revered by his followers, clearly to a fault when taken against other histories."

Zirion returned a gentle, almost fatherly smile. "Some of these accounts originate from Soladrien itself. They have long been considered reliable, many of them recorded directly by members of the Order."

"Yes, of course. It makes sense, knowing that the Order once served in Soladrien under Phos. Its allegiance only gradually shifted to Sumu Amor as Phos was exposed as the Great Usurper and overthrown—a shift, it seems, that came with much conflict, even infighting over legends and whom they deemed the 'Enbrightened One.' Just . . . fascinating."

Zirion nodded. He had been nothing if not patient with Fulgar over these many months. Fulgar's adjustment to the Order's disciplined lifestyle had not come easily at first. He felt, at times, like a caged animal, his feral instincts wanting nothing but to escape, despite having no idea what he'd do next.

Adjustment became remarkably easier with time. The more Fulgar gave of himself to reading in the study, combat training under Elcid, and coaching about his ethereal power under Zirion, the more the despondencies of his former life melted away.

Fulgar had tried to find information from Zirion and the Order's texts about the shrine of Binny's talisman, but he'd gained no answers. He had also spoken of Jinx periodically to Zirion, Silas, and Elcid, telling them of his many fond memories with her and how he had foolishly pushed her away. They had listened and sympathized, although Fulgar wasn't sure they'd really understood. Romantic attachment was not expressly forbidden in the Order, but exposing secrets such as the safehouse's location certainly was, which naturally led to fewer intimate relationships with people on the outside.

Fulgar had first opened up about Jinx after having spent roughly one month in the safehouse. He wanted to see her again, more than anything, when the time was right. Fulgar considered her the best reason for cleaning up his life. Despite not knowing if he and Jinx would ever again cross paths, she was his biggest aspiration.

In his time with Zirion, Fulgar learned more about the ethereals, all of them rare and some extinct, with special emphasis on novidian. The Order held that novidian had been brought into the world by Zophiel, an archastral of the Ethereal Realm, as a means of protecting the planet from catastrophic destruction. Zirion instructed and cautioned about a person's state of confidence, benevolence, innocence, shame, anxiety, or contempt and their power to influence an ethereal.

Zirion's instruction on etheretics was only to the best of his knowledge. Fulgar came to realize that, of their entire branch, he himself was the only true etheretic among them. Discovery of such people was exceedingly rare.

Fishmongers or Slipknots

Fulgar tapped his chin pensively. "Since you're here, perhaps you can tell me if you've heard of something. In the days of the Foundational War, some accounts speak of individuals who became overtaken by dark forces. It's like being possessed by bad spirits, I suppose, and it took ethereal might to remove the curse. More specifically, a strike at the heart with an ethereal blade." He looked up at Zirion. "Can this be true?"

Zirion squinted in thought. "Ah... the Strike of Faith. Aye, I've heard of it, and I recall it required the use of giamond, wielded by a true Lumineer. It required faith, because a strike like that would bring certain death in any other circumstance. In this case, the lethality of the blow is deflected by the energies involved."

"Yes, that's it!" Fulgar placed his elbows upon the book in front of him. "Different kinds of people, both with and without etheretics, became possessed by these dark powers. In the case of people *with* etheretics who also had giamond or novidian, there are writings which suggest that the ethereal itself was used to take control of its holder. I just wonder... how truly possible is this?"

"From that war come many stories. To take control of an ethereal would require the opponent to have exceptional strength and devotion to the Void. I don't know if this is truly possible. I've heard of no such occurrence since the days of that war many hundreds of years ago."

Fulgar nodded in understanding. "Of ethereal warfare, the handful of accounts I've read inspire awe as much as terror. I never knew people ever wielded such tremendous powers in the fight for this land."

Zirion smiled, letting a moment pass as the candleflame flickered between them. "Fulgar," Zirion said after a long moment, "the time has come for a different kind of learning, for not all things are learned through books and lecture. The other great teacher is *experience*." He paused, checking Fulgar's attentive stare. "I would like for you to join Elcid and Silas on a mission."

Fulgar flinched. "Me? Now? I am grateful, sir, but I fear I bring insufficiency. I have been within the Order's grace for nearly six months, yet the scars of my life before this remain fresh in my mind. To go suddenly back out into the open might see me woefully distracted."

Zirion chuckled softly. "Six months is not a short time."

"Perhaps for most, but it pales in comparison to all the years before it. I haven't even taken my oath yet."

"And yet you remain, and we do not turn you away. An oath is but empty words if not spoken from the heart, at the time of your own choosing."

Fulgar shook his head. "Zirion, please. I simply do not feel ready."

"You can always find a reason to doubt yourself, but you cannot hide from your past pains forever. Grief and loss are attributes of life we must all contend with. Find your confidence and make it a part of you. Acting upon all you have learned and your remarkable progress is the next logical step to reaching your full potential."

Forced into extensive self-reflection, Fulgar was astounded to realize how far he had fallen in life before coming to the Order. He spent much time in hindsight, wishing he had been the friend Binny truly needed, not by simply going along with his every ambition for the talisman's fabled power but by helping him to see past that.

Jinx had tried to do that for Fulgar, but he had been just as blind as Binny, believing there simply was nothing else for him to hope in. Fulgar remembered Jinx often, and those memories still brought a profound sense of longing for her companionship. He wondered what she was doing now, what she had become . . . if she had found someone else.

There he went again, his mind already reeling over Jinx. It wasn't just that. Isolation with the Order had marked a new direction for Fulgar. The outside world, whether in the town or the forests, would remind him of life before the Order, when desperation had brought him to the breaking point. His heart started racing at the thought. He wasn't ready.

"Please, give me another month," said Fulgar. "A few more weeks, at least, to prepare myself."

Zirion shook his big head. "Fulgar, it is of the Order to serve not merely yourself but that which is greater than the self. And you are now called to service." He turned. "Come with me."

Fulgar stood, blew out the candle, and followed without a word. They went to the long common area internally known as the Keepers Lounge. It was in this room that Fulgar, ill-tempered and blinded, had been introduced to the Order. With tables, an attached kitchenette, and benches spread along the walls, it was a cozy space—the sort of place where a group of university students might like to relax after a long day of classes.

In fact, that's almost exactly what it was, until recently. Elcid had finished his final university term under the knighthood discipline just over three weeks ago, while Silas had finished his final term under the blacksmithing discipline shortly before Fulgar arrived. This didn't make Elcid an official knight any more than it made Silas the owner of a smithery, but in the kingdom's eyes, they were both primed for service. Their work as part of the Order had so far kept them from the clutches of the guilders. Without hearing many details, Fulgar could tell there was some kind of working relationship between the Order and the kingdom that generally kept the officials out of the Order's affairs.

Fulgar could imagine no one more skilled at their crafts than Elcid and Silas, even if they had only just finished with university. Elcid had a natural talent for leading and training others. Silas had previously taken apprenticeship work from another Order member in the art of smithing rare materials, even those of the ethereal kind. He usually kept quiet about his projects, but Fulgar did eventually learn that the novidian dagger—what Silas more specifically referred to as an *anelace*—belonged to and had been made by Silas.

THE HEALER

He had decided to try it during a previous mission, which led to it being stolen by marauders, and ultimately it wound up on Volk's ship.

Fulgar's heart had sunk when Silas adamantly refused to give him the anelace. "Besides," Silas had said, "it's not even finished yet."

Silas was the only one in the room when Fulgar and Zirion arrived. He offered a lopsided smirk and a searching look as Fulgar made for a bench.

"Ready for a real test, are we?" Silas asked.

"So I'm told," replied Fulgar, trying not to sound overly seething.

Fulgar and Silas sat in silence for several long minutes, whilst Zirion busied himself with a tea kettle. Elcid finally strode in with a conspicuous shove on the door. He halted midstride for his usual entry ritual.

This involved a rock with a small, golden dagger lodged inside, which Silas had mounted just beside the doorway. It was fabled that whoever could pull that dagger from the rock was destined to become a great legend. Naturally, having quite the legendary view of himself, Elcid made it a point to tug on this dagger each time he entered.

As usual, the dagger remained stubbornly in place. Foiled again, Elcid snapped his fingers and continued his march into the room.

"So," he said grandly, "we have a mission before us."

"That we do," replied Zirion, turning from the stove with a tray of steaming teacups. He made his way around the room, handing them out to each person. Only after returning the tray to the kitchenette and taking a cup for himself did he further elaborate.

"It appears that our old friends, the Misty Marauders, are back in town, and I have good information from Wilcox where they'll be."

Elcid snorted a laugh. "That old clod? You sure he didn't get a better deal to mislead you?"

Fulgar took a sip of his tea. It had been infused with spearmint

Fishmongers or Slipknots

and sweetened with honey, very refreshing. He listened in silence to the others.

"Of course, I'm sure," Zirion replied with a touch of indignance. "Reasonably sure, anyway. He has more to lose by lying to me than he has to gain from the likes of those buggers, and he knows it."

"Doesn't matter," said Silas. "If they're around, we'll find them. Most importantly, Zirion, have you qualified our involvement?"

"Based on what he told me of their shipment, the description checks out. We must confirm it, though, and that's where Fulgar comes in."

Fulgar looked around at each of them over the rim of his teacup. "Am I supposed to have the faintest idea what this is about?"

"Probably not," replied Silas, "seeing as how you're always hidden behind a book."

"What business have we with marauders?" pressed Fulgar. "This sounds more like something for the Royal Guard rather than the Order."

Elcid sat his teacup upon an end table. "When it comes to ethereal matters, we prefer to beat the officials to it."

Silas raised a placating hand. "That's also a way of saying that there are those even within kingdom rulership that entrust such matters to the Order." Elcid rolled his eyes and sat back in his chair.

"What's our interest in these marauders?" asked Fulgar.

Silas raised an eyebrow. "Novidian, of course. The very stuff you failed to capture from Volk Vorovka in Miskunn."

Fulgar frowned, feeling both anger and anxiety at the mention of that name. "You act as if I was there to follow some mandate of yours. I knew nothing of novidian or the Order back then."

"To be fair, Silas," said Zirion, "our associate in Miskunn had only spoken with Fulgar's friend. Fulgar might not have known the details."

Fulgar managed a small laugh. "Binny only said it would make us rich. That's about all we were concerned with. Binny saw the Order as little more than a cult."

Zirion gave a nod of understanding. "Aye, rich indeed, but that was not the extent of your path. What matters now is the opportunity to get this novidian into the Order's keeping. You three are to go to the marauders' hideout and confirm they have the novidian. Secure it immediately, if you can, or report back here so we can further develop a plan."

Silas rubbed his hands together. "Just a small amount of that would allow me to finish my anelace. I've finally managed to get it properly fullered. A bit more ore would allow me to complete the form just so."

Zirion cleared his throat loudly. "Yes, Silas, you may get what you need—*only* what you need."

Fulgar eyed the others, still unsettled that they expected him to come along for this. "What exactly do you need me for? I thought Silas had Fielder affinity. So, he would be able to sense novidian as well, right?"

"Of ethereal energies," replied Silas, "I have the greatest sensitivity to novidian. That is not the same as having strong etheretic power like you have. However *sensing* novidian works, that's not something I've ever done."

Zirion nodded. "Even non-etheretic persons can have sensitivity to ethereal materials to varying degrees—what we refer to as an *affinity*. You, Fulgar, are a true Fielder with a much stronger connection to novidian. Your bloodline need not be pure for you to have great power."

"I . . ." Fulgar started. "I still don't feel I'm ready for this."

Zirion stood. "Get ready. We make our move tonight." He met Fulgar's pleading stare. "I have faith you will do well, Fulgar."

He exited the lounge, leaving Fulgar, Silas, and Elcid to stare searchingly at each other. Most notably, the others both stared at Fulgar.

Fishmongers or Slipknots

"Why do you look at me like that?" Fulgar finally asked.

"Trying to decide if you're the sort we can depend on," Elcid answered. "Or, in a pinch, when really backed into a corner, if you're the sort that might get us killed."

"Well," said Silas, "he's not getting *me* killed."

Elcid got up and walked toward the door. "We shall see." He yanked on the golden dagger again to no avail, grunted, and left without another word.

Cloud cover concealed most of the sky's nightglow, shrouding Warvonia's streets in more darkness than usual. A halfmoon floated above, which along with stray rays of ringlight peeked occasionally through rifts in the blanket of clouds.

Fulgar, Elcid, and Silas had waited until after sunset to exit the Order's discreet brick-wall doorway to the outside world. They wound through the alleys of the Old Bard district, Fulgar's anxious heart racing.

Even accompanied by two warriors, he felt more skittish than in any of his prior days as a lone wanderer. Isolation had pulled Fulgar from the quicksand of desperation, but it had dulled him in other ways. He felt disoriented, a sensation probably not helped by the dark night, and his instincts felt clouded and shaky.

Dressed in shades of black and gray, the three of them traversed major streets, plazas, and alleys in a generally northward direction. Zirion's information pointed them toward the opposite side of Warvonia, usually considered one of the more affluent districts.

Each of them had a sword sheathed at their side, beautiful weapons of Silas's own making. Elcid had left his golden blade behind.

"I've been thinking," said Fulgar, keeping his voice quiet for no particular reason. "Why would they have brought the novidian ore to Warvonia? More than a year has passed since Volk had it in

Miskunn, and it really hasn't gone far, assuming it's the same stash."

Elcid shrugged. "Whether or not this is the same shipment we were after before, novidian is only easy to sell to the right buyer. It might be highly valuable to those who understand what it is, but it also makes you a big target."

"Especially if you happen to have a connection with it," Silas added. He followed that with a dry chuckle. "Imagine being the thief who's managed to steal novidian, only to find that it glows white in your grasp."

"But that glow comes with great power," Fulgar replied.

Elcid turned to Fulgar with a smirk. "It didn't help you enough to beat me, though, did it?"

"Even if you can channel its power," said Silas, "you must know how to use it."

"Competent in using it or not," said Elcid, "it still makes you a target."

Fulgar frowned. "Being a target doesn't explain why the Misty Marauders bought it from Volk or why they would bring it here to Warvonia."

Silas exhaled a short laugh. "Who said they *bought* it? Perhaps they raided Volk. They *are* marauders, after all."

"They could be expecting to meet a client here in Warvonia," ventured Elcid. "People of all stations come and go from this port. The Order is especially wary of those who seek ethereals for purchase. They could be attempting a form of vile sorcery, they could be seeking influence, or it could be some vain noble looking for a rare collector's item. Any of those things only makes our mission that much more important." They turned another corner, and Elcid halted them. "I think we're here."

True to the stately nature of this district, with its fenced, perfectly spaced trees and streets so bright they seemed white-washed, the buildings were tall, regal, and immaculate. Many had vines growing up designated trellises, as though in an attempt for a more rustic look.

One abode stood out in subtle ways. Sandwiched between two taller buildings, it was a slightly darker, dingier color. Vines, many of them brown and dead, grew unchecked up its walls. Old grime blackened the stone steps to its front door, and moss and grass filled in gaps and cracks. A small front yard mottled with patches of dirt and weeds separated the building from the street.

Elcid led them to the front of the structure, where they remained on the street, looking the place over. They saw light behind some of the windows.

After a minute, Silas turned to Fulgar. "Well, do you feel anything?"

Fulgar furrowed his brow. "I feel you pressuring me."

"Focus, Geth," Elcid replied in a commanding tone. "This is why you're here."

"I don't feel anything *yet*," Fulgar replied. "I might need to get closer to it."

Elcid growled under his breath. "Then we'll need to find a way inside."

Silas scratched his chin. "Well then, shall we just . . . knock?"

"They'll likely try to kill us on sight. We need to find out where the novidian is located and aim for a swift extraction."

They crossed the yard and searched around the front of the structure, moving as quietly as they could manage. Silas and Elcid checked the corners for any kind of access around the foundation. Fulgar examined the yard itself.

Feeling about with his feet, Fulgar pushed aside a growth of tall weeds. Beneath them was a metal door flush with the ground, thoroughly rusted and secured with a padlock. "What about this?" he asked, keeping his voice hushed.

They joined him. "Could be something," said Elcid.

"We'll have to get past this lock without anyone noticing," added Silas.

Fulgar grinned back at them. "Leave that to me."

He took the small lock within his palms, closed his eyes, and channeled his magnetism. He concentrated deeply on the lock, every click and movement of its internal components. Within moments, it popped open.

Silas stared at the lock with wide eyes. "That ... was something."

"Nicely done, Geth," said Elcid.

"Please, just call me Fulgar. I'm not some soldier in the field, and you are *not* my superior." Elcid quietly huffed and managed a curt nod in response.

"*Hey!* There's people down there!" someone yelled from one of the upper windows. Fulgar immediately straightened up, well-spooked.

Not missing a beat, Silas cupped his hands around his mouth and shouted back, "Ahoy there, old boy! Might you chaps be among the group known as the Misty Marauders?" Elcid flashed him a scowl.

Another man appeared in the window, a tall and dark silhouette before the lit room. "Who are you and what do you want?"

"Business, my good sir. Shall we come in for a chat?"

Fulgar's heart skipped a beat. "Silas, is that really such a good idea?" he whispered.

"They've already seen us," he hissed back. "We might as well get right to it. Keep your senses keen."

"It's like they were watching for us," muttered Elcid. "Stay sharp."

The man in the window remained still, keeping everyone in suspense. Finally, he nodded to the smaller man beside him, who promptly retreated from the window. "Come to the door. Leave your weapons."

"Naturally," Silas answered. "Of course, you'll do the same."

"Of course." The man turned away, and moments later the room went dark.

Fishmongers or Slipknots

"We need a codeword," said Elcid, "some way for you to let us know the novidian is here." He dropped his sword belt to the ground.

Fulgar's anxiety was near the breaking point. Removing his own sword belt didn't help. "Shall I just shout *magic metal* and point you toward it?"

Elcid took a large step toward Fulgar. "You think this some joke?"

Silas pushed between them. "Oh, stop it! Fulgar, say 'frisky fishmongers' if you feel it. After a while, if you don't feel it, then say 'slickery slipknots.' Got it?"

"Are you *serious* right now?" Fulgar replied. "How in Gheol-fire am I supposed to utter gibberish like that without raising suspicion?"

Dim lights came on in the building's ground level.

"Work it in *naturally*," said Elcid, already moving toward the door. "Come on!"

"You're both going to get me killed," Fulgar groaned.

Silas gave his shoulder a pat as they made for the door. "Hopefully not before you've given us the codeword."

"Fine," said Fulgar through gritted teeth, "but I'm just going with 'fishmongers' or 'slipknots,' not the rest of it."

"Fair enough," Silas conceded.

Just as they reached the steps to the front door, it opened. A gaunt, half-bald man with matted brown-and-yellow hair and sunken cheeks looked them over carefully, likely confirming that they had indeed left their weapons. Once satisfied, he gave a wordless jerk of his head and moved aside to let them in.

They stepped upon a grayish hardwood floor into an empty atrium, with stairs leading up just ahead. Arched doorways led to rooms on their left and right. The area was softly lit by flocalcite lamps. Fulgar's nose twitched as it sucked in air that seemed old and dusty.

Fulgar checked his senses, probing remotely for the novidian, trying to focus his sense despite his nervousness.

THE HEALER

"In there," the man said, pointing to the archway on their left.

Three other men were seated inside the room, including a particularly tall and burly lout who must have been the one they'd spoken with outside through the window. His black hair, streaked with strands of white, was slicked back with pomade.

Even better, Fulgar thought. *Now we're outnumbered.* From the looks on Elcid's and Silas's faces, he figured they might be thinking the same.

The large man wore a pinstriped suit with a black tie, somewhat odd attire for this late hour.

That is, unless one was expecting visitors.

The other men seated were dressed more casually, with various shades of brown and gray shirts and trousers. One was stout, with a round head and thin mustache, while the other was old, with rheumy eyes and thinning, grizzled hair. They sat on either side of their leader, all of them in old-looking armchairs.

The leader gestured toward a line of opposite-facing chairs, separated only by a rectangular tea table. "Please, have a seat. My name is Mikhail." His voice was husky and ruggedly accented. He waited for them to sit. "What business is it you wish to discuss with the Misty Marauders?"

With every moment, Fulgar checked his senses, not really sure he trusted them. He tried his best to look relaxed, certain he was failing.

"We'll get right to it, then," said Silas. "We are part of an order trusted under special circumstances by kingdom officials."

Mikhail bounced with a laugh. "Aren't we all, from time to time? It very much depends on those circumstances, doesn't it?"

"Indeed. We're looking for a rare and highly valuable material, one that we believe your band has recently come into possession of."

Mikhail steepled his fingers. "We come into possession of a great many materials. You will have to be more specific."

"You would know this one. It is a mineral ore, quite unique,

Fishmongers or Slipknots

usually in slate-like slabs, black with pinpoints of sparkle."

Fulgar leaned forward. "You might find it sometimes glows to the touch. It is fully unmistakable."

Mikhail raised an eyebrow. "Most interesting. It sounds extremely valuable."

"The glow is inconsistent," Elcid interjected with the slightest glare toward Fulgar. "It's our understanding you retrieved this cargo from the smuggler Volk Vorovka."

"I do not discuss other clients," said Mikhail, "unless, of course, I have enough to gain by doing so."

"The amount of payment is not a concern," replied Elcid. "Right now, our mission is to confirm that you have it, and then we will discuss terms for its transfer to us."

"Might be that we have what you're after. So happens we have some commodities with us in this very building. You are welcome to take a look . . . under our watchful eyes, of course."

"That would be splendid," said Silas.

Mikhail nodded. "Shall we begin upstairs, then?"

Elcid and Silas stood. "Of course," replied Silas, "and thank you for your hospitality." Fulgar remained seated as they approached the door. "Are you coming?" Silas finally asked.

Fulgar had checked his senses long enough to determine what he was feeling. He spun words together in his mind, which tumbled out of his mouth before he had much time to regulate his tone or speed. "Have you experienced the riffraff of our harbor, especially in the *lower levels* of the storehouses? Fishmongers everywhere. It really is quite the disturbance."

Mikhail stared at Fulgar, narrowing his eyes. Feeling every bit as awkward as he'd anticipated over their codeword, Fulgar rose from the chair.

Silas sighed through an eyeroll. "There he goes again, on about the harbor. Do keep your head in the here and now, if you could so manage."

"You know," said Mikhail, "I think he has an interesting point." He took large, imposing steps toward Fulgar. His piercing gaze caused Fulgar to tighten his grip on the top of the armchair, his fingers digging into the cushion, as if somehow the chair might save him from a surprise attack. Fulgar felt himself breaking into a nervous sweat.

Mikhail stopped about a step away, his form looming over Fulgar. "There is always something about the lower level, isn't there? That is where you find the best-kept secrets, whether it's something of immense value or simply a fishmonger cavorting where he does not belong. Wouldn't you agree?"

Fulgar forced himself to keep his eyes on Mikhail. "Yes, very much."

Silas cleared his throat from behind Mikhail. "Right, well, I believe we were about to search upstairs . . . ?"

Mikhail spun around. "You go ahead." He nodded to his men. They shoved Silas and Elcid through a nearby doorway and slammed the door. A series of shouts and thuds followed.

Mikhail grabbed a coatrack standing against the wall and pulled it like a lever. A trapdoor opened in the floor to reveal stairs leading down. "So, you're the one who can sense it, the one they call a *Fielder*, yes?" He followed this with a deep, throaty chuckle. "Funny thing is, valuable as that sparkly ore is, we're getting even more for *you*."

Fulgar couldn't get a single word out before Mikhail yanked his arm and threw him into the stairwell, slamming the trapdoor after him. He landed hard three stairs down, so that his knees buckled and he tumbled the rest of the way into total darkness.

He hurt in at least a dozen places, but his nerves had given way to a potent blend of desperation and fury. He sprang up from the bottom step and raced back to the top, where he banged with all his might against the door.

It was no use. The door was thick, heavy wood and wouldn't

budge.

Back down the stairs, he felt about for any source of light, a weapon, or any other way out. He felt the wood of crates and banged into various unidentifiable items. The darkness was maddening.

After a period of fervent rummaging, he began to see vague outlines. At first, he reasoned that his eyes might be adjusting well enough for minimal vision, but then he realized it wasn't because of his eyes at all.

A soft, white glow had appeared from within one of the crates. He grinned and made his way toward the source. His senses had been right after all.

The crate was much smaller than the one he'd fallen into back in Miskunn. This was one small enough to be carried by hand.

Fulgar stood still for a moment and blinked with realization. All of this was for *him*. He had been baited. Somehow the Marauders had known that Fulgar could sense the novidian. If Zirion's informer had been paid off to specifically lead them here, then whoever was behind this had also calculated that Fulgar was involved with the Order. He shook his head. There wasn't time to dwell on that matter now.

He found a crowbar and forced the crate open, and the glow spilled into the room. That allowed him to find a light switch. Upon flipping it, a sparse scattering of flocalcite fixtures cast the basement in muted, yellowish light.

Fulgar frantically dashed back and forth throughout the basement, dodging crates and tools and other junk covered in cobwebs, hoping to discover some secondary access.

As he made his way across the space for the umpteenth time, a metallic thud halted him. Then another, and then a third. He turned toward the direction of the sounds.

Something like steam drifted from behind a crate against one of the walls. Moving it aside, he saw three holes blocked by gratings, from which the steam was emanating.

Immediately he felt tightness in his lungs and coughed. This wasn't merely steam. It rose from three rocks that had been dropped into the basement from above. *Some kind of mist rock,* Fulgar thought. Apparently, the Misty Marauders wanted to take Fulgar to their client without a fight, nice and quiet and unconscious.

He shoved the crate, along with a few others, back in front of the mist, which of course did nothing to stop it from entering the space. Lifting his shirt over his nose and mouth, he ran to the opposite side of the cellar.

Then he saw it, half-hidden behind another crate: an access door, rectangular, metal, and flush with the stone wall. He remembered the door he'd found and unlocked outside. For the first time in months, he thanked Eloh, and he prayed that this door led out to the yard.

He wrested the stubborn door open, using his magnetism for extra pull. He saw steps going up. Looking at the position of the steps he'd tumbled down, he roughly calculated that these steps could lead where he wanted. At least, it was a hope.

He started through the door but paused and looked back at the crate from which the novidian's white glow emanated in heavenly brilliance. Sucking in a deep breath, he raced across the space and grabbed the crate. It was heavier than he'd hoped, but he managed to move it back to the access door. By the time he got there, he was coughing and struggling for breath.

Obsessive determination willed him through the access and up the steps, even as he gasped for air and his vision grew fuzzy.

He shoved through the door at the top of the steps with the very last of his strength, mist curling into the air around him. The crate dropped to the ground as he fell upon a carpet of grass. A cacophony of men shouting, glass breaking, and a door slamming was the last he heard before finally passing out.

chapter 6

THE WHIP AND THE DIAMOND

6/36/3178 P.A.

F ulgar awoke in his chamber within the Order's safehouse. His head felt weighed down by a sack of bricks. He slung his legs over the side of the bed and, with a groan of exertion, forced his unwilling body to stand.

His small room was simple and cozy, housing the few possessions he owned, mostly a meager variety of outfits, his sword, his satchel, his old drawing of the white butterfly, and very little money saved from his thieving days. As his activity increased within the Order, he would begin earning actual wages, rather than merely existing as an etheretic vagrant they cared enough about to house.

He still wore the black clothes from their mission. Realization slowly dawned on Fulgar that he had survived the Misty Marauders' attempt to capture him. His hands absently felt up and down his body, as though skeptical that he could still be in one piece and unharmed.

Groggily, he shuffled toward a basin in his room. The pitcher beside it had been filled with fresh water. He splashed some of the sleepiness from his face and glanced at the clock on his nightstand. Its hands indicated half past the fourteenth hour. He had slept well into the next day.

Feeling halfway human again, he made his way from the chamber into the halls of the safehouse, which itself was a winding labyrinth of the Warvonian underground. The only things that ran deeper than these passages were the secrets of the Order itself. This very safehouse harbored vaults and passages that Fulgar had no access to, many of which he had never even seen after months of being isolated here. Such secrets neither surprised nor concerned Fulgar. They were to be expected, considering that the Order safeguarded countless original historical records and objects of power, especially those of an ethereal nature.

He entered the Keepers Lounge with the gazes of Elcid, Silas, and Zirion all locked on him. Elcid stood and approached him, the others silently watching.

Fulgar searched Elcid's expression. It was stern and stony, and Fulgar began to wonder if something had gone horribly wrong. Had *he* done something wrong? All he could remember was desperately trying to escape from the Marauders' basement.

Elcid stopped in front of Fulgar, facing him, fixing him with an unyielding stare. "Well, it's about time you showed yourself."

Fulgar opened his mouth to reply, but he was drowned out by laughter. It was from Elcid, a great hearty chuckle, and he clapped Fulgar's arm hard enough to push him sideways.

"You did good, Fulgar!" He laughed some more. "Sure better than I ever expected."

By now Silas and Zirion had joined in the laughter, filling the room with mirth. Elcid went back to his chair, Fulgar following dumbly.

"But . . . what happened?" Fulgar asked as he sat, taking a cup of tea from Zirion.

"To start with the obvious," said Silas, "you passed out."

The Whip and the Diamond

"And the timing couldn't have been better!" Elcid bellowed.

Silas nodded. "The Marauders had us subdued, swords at our throats. We were likely seconds from having our wrists bound." He pointed at Fulgar. "They thought you were as good as theirs. They prattled on and on about their greatest bounty ever—you and their services to deliver the novidian, while Elcid and I would be bonus hostages for further ransom."

Elcid laughed again. "And then there you were, popping out of that door with those mists rolling all around you. Those Marauders couldn't help but turn their heads, completely flummoxed, and that gave Silas and me all the room we needed. I shoved one of them right through the window, and we took down the others hand to hand."

Zirion beamed as though his own son had just been named the mayor. "And you got out of there with the novidian to boot! Suffice to say, Elcid and Silas managed to get both you and the crate back here to safety."

Silas held a rectangular tea biscuit before his eyes, appearing to examine it. "*That* was a most unpleasant venture." He broke the biscuit in half. "I think I'd have preferred taking on a few more marauders rather than dragging your etheretic hide across town."

Fulgar felt a fantastic sense of relief. "Really, all I did was escape."

"Ah," said Elcid, "but even that wouldn't have happened if you hadn't unlocked that door beforehand. Your instincts were well-honed."

"You did much more than escape," added Zirion. "To bring any amount of a lost ethereal to the Order's protection is a massive victory. That novidian is now safe, away from those who might seek to corrupt it."

"And it might serve to protect other people and ethereals, as well," said Silas. "It should give me just what I need to finish my anelace, what I believe will be my finest work yet."

Fulgar's jollity faded, however, as his memory drifted back to last night. "Fortunate and successful as we were, it was shocking to learn that I was their main target. They had planted the novidian specifically to trap me." He shook his head and stared into his teacup. "*Me* . . . and I'd never even heard of the Misty Marauders."

Silas scratched his chin. "Yes, they had already pegged you as a Fielder."

"But how?"

Zirion's stern face exuded concern. "This is not something we would expect simple marauders to identify. Hmm." He looked sideways, thinking. "This could mean that whoever informed my contact also knew about you, Fulgar. Who else might know of your abilities?"

Fulgar recalled a number of thugs over the years who had received the business end of his abilities, but he didn't believe any of them would have linked it specifically to novidian. Only a very few names came to mind. "The friends I lost, Binny and Jinx."

His encounter with the mage just before joining the Order stormed into his mind, giving him a shiver. "Volk," he said, the name like acid to his tongue. "Volk quite likely knew about it."

Elcid nodded. "That could explain it."

"This must be watched closely," said Zirion. "Fulgar, I will not take your freedom, especially when you have already deprived yourself of that for so long, but I recommend you remain nearby and alert. That goes for all of us. Report anything suspicious immediately. If we have someone seeking a Fielder, it could be for purposes of the Void, and that could mean great danger."

"Void . . ." repeated Fulgar, staring in thought. He had heard Zirion speak of it before. "You mean . . . forces of the Shadow Age? Forces that would seek to overthrow the Throne?"

"Yes," Zirion answered, "and to twist and corrupt all ethereals in the process. This is why, for millennia, the Order has sought to bring all ethereal materials and those who connect with them

The Whip and the Diamond

under protection. The Order's allegiance is to the Throne of Light above all, for it is the divine right by which this land exists, and to the lineage of kings ordained to sit upon it."

"To protect *all* ethereals," said Fulgar, "how can it be done? How much ethereal material exists?"

"How much gold is in the world? Or emeralds or sapphires or onyx?" replied Silas. "The answer, of course, is no one knows. We are ever on alert for hints of more."

Zirion shifted in his seat and continued, his eyes on Fulgar. "Any ethereal, such as novidian and giamond, must be under care of the Order and always in safekeeping. There is one exception, but an important exception. An ethereal, such as one forged into a weapon, may remain in the possession of anyone who will use it for good and who bonds with it, much like the legendary Heroes of Time."

Elcid snorted lightly. "Who is to say what is *good*?"

"Trusted and senior members of the Order," Zirion answered.

Fulgar understood, having seen this legend referenced many times in the annals of the Order. "It is by these Heroes that the forces of Shadow have been kept at bay."

Zirion gave him a warm, almost fatherly smile. "You have learned well, Fulgar. It is said that there are always such Heroes among us, those who would arise at the time of greatest need, answering the call in service to the Light and all that is good. It is perhaps the grandest part of the archastrals' plan to protect our world."

Fulgar stared blankly ahead, pensive. "Archastrals of the Ethereal Realm . . . of Eloh."

"Of Eloh," Zirion repeated, his big voice remarkably gentle.

That struck a chord with Fulgar. Since the loss of his parents, he had spent so much of his life spurning the divine. How small he now felt. How petty and selfish, so much of his life wasted on folly and denial. When he spoke, his voice felt weak. "Many long years have passed since I paid any heed to Eloh."

Zirion placed a large hand on Fulgar's shoulder. "It is easy for us to forget, but we are never forgotten. In this life, it can be difficult to see beyond ourselves and the fragment of world around us. We are part of something greater than ourselves. We often feel we must find our own way, but really it is more about finding our place in the everlasting chronicle of time and legend. Divine purpose is a blessing, and we must all strive to be worthy of that blessing."

Fulgar returned a half-smirk. "Does this mean I'll be getting a novidian weapon?"

"Of the stuff we brought in," replied Silas, "I'm afraid there won't be enough left to craft an entire weapon after I use what I need to complete my anelace." At this, Fulgar scowled.

"Focus more on yourself than on extrinsic things," said Zirion. "With time, the right weapon for you might yet present itself. The use of certain ethereals can be a highly personal experience."

Fulgar kept his eyes on Silas as he replied, "I agree."

"And there's another matter to be aware of," said Zirion. "A few of my informants have witnessed a female warrior, bearing what some have called a glass sword. There've also been increased sightings of rogue grimkins and other criminals stirring chaos. Mostly, they make a mess of things, perhaps a bit of looting and petty theft, and then they retreat. It appears this warrior has rescued many citizens from harm . . . and, based on descriptions I've heard, there might be a Fielder with her."

Fulgar cocked his head with interest. "*Another* Fielder?"

"I am not certain, but this bears watching. It seems, of late, there is much stirring in the shadows."

Elcid stood and began pacing, his brow furrowed. "Whoever's behind this plot to capture Fulgar will almost certainly strike again, perhaps with greater strength in the wake of their failure."

Silas chuckled. "They probably didn't expect to lure Fulgar, only to lose both him *and* the novidian."

The Whip and the Diamond

"The fish got away with the worm," said Elcid, "but there's always a bigger fish hoping to get them both."

"I agree with Elcid," said Zirion. "We must be watchful throughout town and look for signs that anything is amiss."

"We could just parade Fulgar through the streets," said Silas. "That should get their attention. He's what they want, after all. They like him as bait? Then very well!"

Fulgar's scowl deepened. "You can't be serious."

"Actually," replied Zirion, standing, "I was just thinking the same thing." He saw the concern in Fulgar's face and seemed to find it amusing. "Don't worry, Fulgar. You might seem alone out there, but you won't be."

Fulgar couldn't help feeling unconvinced, but he was in the Order's service now, a Fielder with a key role in their mission. It was time to get to work.

A week of aimlessly roaming the streets of Warvonia had transformed Fulgar's mien from anxious to bored.

Sure, it was all according to their plan to draw out the mage, and his Order companions occasionally popped around nearby street corners to check on him, but this did little to ease the tedium.

Sheer monotony brought him to the point of hoping to see something—*anything*—more exciting than regular people doing regular things. Witnessing a crime, for instance, perhaps with the Civic Force giving chase, would've provided a welcome change of pace. Not the type where someone gets hurt, of course, but maybe a good petty theft or a barfight between two sozzled twits. Basically, the exact sort of shenanigans he would've been arrested for.

In his idle time, he thought often of Binny and Jinx. With each street corner turned, he gazed at every face in sight, although with only the slightest hope that he might happen upon one of them. His hope, of course, was always quickly dashed, returning him to that same state of boredom that followed him the whole week.

Then, on the sixth of Jovidor, Fulgar left his post after long hours of watching a rat sneaking in and out of an alleyway. Sometimes it darted across the street with a morsel of food, and sometimes it came back empty-pawed. Given the past week, it was an activity that bordered on exciting.

As he made his way down a hillside street, he heard screeching sounds from behind, as if large birds were chattering. He stopped in the street and turned to see what it was.

Up the hill stood three grimkins, the race of feathered, birdlike beings with beaks and taloned feet. Originating from the island nation of Akkadia, grimkins were typically rare visitors to Tuscawny and trusted by few. Just as with humans and anthropods, not all grimkins were bad. In fact, Fulgar had befriended a couple of them during his travels between Ruca and Miskunn, even making a splint for one of their talons following a bad stumble.

Dressed in black-cowled uniforms, these grimkins ignited three barrels with an eerie, purple fire and sent them careening down the hilly street. The barrels headed straight toward Fulgar and enflamed everything in their path.

With a yelp, he dodged the rolling death-barrels in favor of an alley. Clearly these grimkins were not the friendly kind.

Once the barrels had passed, he stuck his head out from the alley and watched two of the barrels crash into buildings on both sides of the street and the third into a merchant stand. Despite the stone construction of the buildings, the violet flames licked up the sides. Within seconds, people emerged from the buildings screaming and running. It was a miracle none of them were caught by the fires.

Fulgar shuffled to the end of the alley, closer to the trail of purple fire. He felt no heat from the flames nearest him. In fact, the air felt colder. Even so, he sensed this fire was every bit as dangerous as the hot kind, probably more so.

Like a flash of light in his mind, he remembered the bursts of cold, purple fire that he'd experienced more than half a year ago, back when he'd encountered that mage of dark sorcery. His heart did an unpleasant, fluttering dance in his chest.

Up the street, the grimkins cackled in screechy noises and dashed away.

Fulgar emerged from the alley, leapt a trail of fire—if it could be called fire—and ran in pursuit of the grimkins.

Knowing the Marauders had gotten involved with novidian, this time Fulgar and his companions were prepared for encounters of an ethereal nature. Fulgar was armed with his sword as well as a small rod of novidian to help bolster his Fielder abilities. Meager as it seemed, its warm flow of energy did much to boost Fulgar's confidence.

At the street corner, he skidded to a halt just in time to avoid barreling into a wide-eyed Silas, who had just rounded the corner of a bakery, sword in hand.

"Did you see the grimkins?" shouted Fulgar, panting.

"There's plenty more where they came from, I assure you! And not just grimkins but also men, all of them wearing black. Either our plan to lure out fiends worked, or this is quite a fine coincidence." He looked down the street, and his eyes widened. "Fulgar, you can't just leave all that darkfire! We must put it out, or it will continue to spread!"

Fulgar looked back at the purple flames. "What *is* it?"

"It's a product of Void. They're using byrne to conjure it."

"They're using what?"

"Byrne! It's like the Void's version of novidian."

Fulgar glowered. "In all fairness, how am I to know that? I've only read hints about things like this in the Order's histories. I've never *seen* it!"

Silas pulled out his own rod of novidian, a bit larger than

Fulgar's, more like a small staff. "I suppose you must learn some things by experience."

"And have you brought along buckets of magic water, or how else do you propose we extinguish it?"

"Novidian, you lackwit! Watch me!"

Silas took off down the street, aiming his novidian staff at the flames and using his Fielder affinity to blast them with white energy. Fulgar rushed to join him, following suit with his own smaller rod.

"Why don't you have your anelace?" Fulgar asked.

"It's not ready yet!"

Fulgar rolled his eyes whilst snuffing another flame. "With your enduring perfectionism, it'll be a miracle if you ever finish it!"

Silas flashed him a glare of warning. "Even once finished, it's still mine, you know!"

Fulgar doused a ten-foot trail of flame in one blast. "Yes, I know, damn you!"

Silas and Fulgar turned their gazes up the street as something dashed across. Fulgar recognized the digitigrade posture of running grimkins, likely the same three he had seen earlier.

"I see them!" shouted Silas. "I'll go. You stay on these flames! You're stronger against them than I am."

"Silas," Fulgar prompted. Silas stopped, looking at him. "Do you think they have to do with the Marauders?"

Silas nodded. "Yes, Fulgar. Yes, I do."

Anxiety and rage roiled like acid in Fulgar's gut. That could mean these were minions working for Volk. Whatever the case, Fulgar would be their primary target.

Silas seemed to sense Fulgar's worry. "Be careful. Stay confident. I'll see if I can find Elcid and circle back to you." He gestured his head down the street. "Hurry with those flames, now. They spread quickly. And don't touch them!" With that, he was off.

Silas was right about the flames. They were spreading rapidly, making the street look like a corridor straight to Gheol. Fulgar wasn't sure he could extinguish them fast enough.

Just in front of him, a man in a robe bolted from an apartment entrance, paying too little heed to the trail of darkfire. He stumbled and fell, and his right arm contacted the flames. Wild with shock, he flailed his arm in every direction.

"Stop!" called Fulgar. "Hold still!"

The man continued waving his arm, crying out like a wounded animal. He was too panicked to hear Fulgar's calls. As carefully as he could, Fulgar aimed the white energy from his novidian rod at the man's arm. Where it connected, the darkfire disappeared, and this caused the man to stop and notice Fulgar. Fulgar removed the rest of the darkfire.

"My arm!" the man yelled. "It's turning white! And . . . and I can't *feel* it!"

Fulgar took a closer look. Indeed, the skin was white and steaming, and the pallor was spreading farther along his arm, even with the fire gone. It was like some kind of intense frostbite. Fulgar wracked his brain. He knew of no remedy for something like this.

So, he did the only thing he could think of. Pocketing his rod, he placed his hands just over the wound, shaping his will and power around the spot. The whiteness of his energy seemed to pour into the wound, but the pallor stopped spreading. The arm's frostiness transitioned to a scar-like pink, and the man calmed down significantly.

"I'm starting to feel again," said the man through a wince, "but it stings horribly."

"I hope it will fully heal, with time," Fulgar replied. His response felt grossly inadequate, but he knew nothing of darkfire or the potential effects of exposure to it. "And please," he added, "if you see a street burning with mystical, purple fire, stay away!" He dashed off to blast more darkfire, concerned about its continued spread.

By the time he got halfway down the street, his worries

increased. Purple flames lapped hungrily up the buildings where the barrels had crashed, and by now the ghoulish fire had nearly reached the tops.

He was contemplating how he might reach the upper flames when black, rectangular, white-glowing plates slit through the air and passed over many of the highest flames, snuffing them upon contact.

Spooked, Fulgar looked around frantically for the source. A moment later, he saw a gangly man—about his own age, with long, silvery hair—sprint past, heading up the street. "You're welcome!" was all the man said, not even bothering to stop. The cards he had flying all about—they looked suspiciously similar to novidian—returned to the man's hands as he ran.

Maybe this was the other Fielder that Zirion had heard about, although clearly he was alone and not with the rumored female warrior.

This left Fulgar with only a few more gouts of fire to deal with at ground level. He made quick work of those and bolted back up the street, pausing for a moment to consider his direction. Silas had chased the grimkins to the right, where he might rendezvous with Elcid. The man with the flying cards had gone to the left.

Fulgar decided to go left.

He reasoned Silas and Elcid could handle themselves. Meanwhile, if this new individual had novidian, Zirion would want to know about it. Whoever he was, he didn't seem to be on Volk's side, or else he wouldn't have put out those flames.

At least, that's what Fulgar wanted to believe.

Fulgar broke into a dash, as fast as his legs would take him. The streets were eerily quiet, most citizens likely in hiding by now, and he saw no signs of the card-man, rogue grimkins, or anything else out of the ordinary.

He stopped at an intersection, panting and listening, trying to focus his senses on any kind of activity or presence. Silence. Such a strange, haunting silence for what would normally be an active time of day in Warvonia.

A distant crash caught his attention. He took the street to the right, heading uphill and toward the western fringes of town. Once far up the hill, a very unsettling reality struck him like a blow to the face.

This was the same area where he'd previously encountered the mage.

He turned a corner and continued up one of the curving streets so uniquely Warvonia's. It eventually straightened and broadened until merging into a plaza with a tall and rounded fountain in its center.

As soon as Fulgar entered the plaza, the entire fountain exploded into a sundered mass of stone and watery sprays. He staggered and flung himself to the ground behind a fruit cart, narrowly avoiding a shower of stone shards. Apples, pears, and a melon rained down upon him from the cart.

Cursing under his breath, he peeked around the edge of the cart. Black-garbed men and grimkins darted in and out of businesses and apartments to the sounds of breaking glass and splintered doors.

Propelled by a surge of anger, he leapt out from behind the cart and grappled one of the passing cretins by the neck, swinging the startled man into the outer wall surrounding the fountain. The man held his head in reflex for a moment and then fell unconscious.

Fulgar drew his novidian rod and blasted an unsuspecting grimkin as it emerged from a shattered window. The white energy sent it sprawling back into the lobby of the raided establishment.

Another man sprinted toward him. Fulgar widened his stance and dodged a kick. He pushed the attacker's leg aside and returned a hard jab into the man's shoulder.

Fulgar's sword was at the man's throat in half a second.

"Who are you people?" he shouted, sweat spraying from his

lips. "Who are you working for?"

The hooded man grinned through blackened, crooked teeth. "Stick around and you'll see. Then you'll be *his*." He followed this with a grating cackle. "His, his, *his*! *Ah he he ha!*"

Fulgar ended the cackle with a hard kick to the man's jaw, laying him flat.

Across the plaza, Fulgar saw two small flashes of white in the air. It was the man with the flying cards.

Another explosion occurred before he had the chance to pursue, this one just about a pike's length away. Pieces of the fountain's wall and cobblestones of the street soared from the impact. Dust clouded the air. Fulgar lifted an arm to shield himself.

Tiny purple flames danced about the impact site, rippling with the gust of an icy breeze.

As the dust drifted away, Fulgar saw the horrifying figure with the helmet of curved tusks and that terrifying whip of doom, which dangled from the mage's hand like a black cobra, radiating a glow of deep purple.

The whip cracked, and its fangs caught a man dashing from a building, his arms loaded with bread loaves. The victim screamed and fell, the loaves scattering before him. Fulgar watched in horror as the man convulsed and then became still, as if paralyzed. Some moments later—Fulgar lost all sense of how long—the man's body burst into a violet flash, and he was gone, vanished completely.

Fulgar's right hand raised his sword in a white-knuckled grip, while his left hand tightened around the novidian rod, now flaring a white glow.

"*Volk!*" he roared. "Today your madness ends!"

A thunderous laugh followed, its deep and resounding echo such that it made the plaza sound more like an empty atrium. "Volk? Volk is no more. What stands before you is one much greater." It didn't sound like Volk's voice, or anyone's voice that Fulgar knew. This was booming, imposing, and even the accent Volk once had seemed lost in its resonance.

As if the whip wasn't bad enough, the mage pulled from behind his back a black broadsword that glinted like polished jet.

"Now, Fielder," said the mage, "you will come with me."

"I think not!" Fulgar yelled. With a thrust of the rod, he shot a stream of white energy directly toward the mage.

The black sword absorbed it easily, not affected in the slightest.

Fulgar charged, ignoring all sense of danger. He got his first glimpse of the mage's face. Although it was concealed by the helmet, he saw a rim of blackness surrounding hard, ruthless eyes, as if the skin were ash. If this was Volk, he was barely recognizable.

The mage cracked his whip. Fulgar repelled the attack with another white blast and raised his sword to strike. The black sword parried against him. Fulgar rebounded with a neat spin and struck his foe's leg. His sword clanged harmlessly, indicating armor beneath the mage's cloak.

That did not bode well for Fulgar.

Volk—the only name Fulgar could ascribe to this thing—reached for the novidian with his whip-bearing hand. Fulgar managed to protect his rod with a field, a slight ripple in the air, which repelled Volk's hand.

Growling, Volk brought his sword around. Fulgar blocked it, to the detriment of his own sword. The black broadsword cut through Fulgar's blade as if it were molten from the forge, its severed tip now a mess of melted metal.

Before Fulgar could even register his shock, a mighty gust of freezing wind blew him backward. He fell upon his rump and lost his grip on both the sword hilt and the novidian.

He looked up as the mage approached with powerful, heavy steps. Fulgar knew he was dead if he didn't reclaim his novidian.

Even then, what could a little rod do against *this*?

Someone leapt between Fulgar and Volk, a figure covered in a blue cloak and wielding a sword that appeared like gold-flecked crystal. From behind, Fulgar could not see the person's face due to the cloak's hood. But the body was that of a woman, thin and agile, and she raised her beautiful sword to trade blows with the mage.

Still on the ground, Fulgar scrambled back, found the novidian rod, and snatched it. Without a second thought, he aimed another white blast at Volk. This time it caught him in the chest and threw him back.

The woman turned and helped Fulgar up, giving them their first good look at each other.

"Fulgar?" she exclaimed.

"*Jinx?*" he replied even louder.

Volk was already up and coming back toward them. He was delayed by two glowing cards from the man Fulgar had chased here.

"Come on!" shouted Jinx. She tugged him forward by the arm, and they ran to the cover of a side street.

"I can't believe it's *you*, Jinx! What are you doing here?"

She smiled, melting Fulgar on the spot. "I'm something of a vigilante now. You know, helping the little guys when the little guys can't help themselves." Then she frowned. "What are *you* doing here? The big-bad have a shiny bracelet or something?"

"I . . . guess you could say I'm sort of a vigilante myself."

Jinx shook her head. "Well, fancy that. If only I'd known you might finally come around."

"Jinx, look, you should come with me. This order I've joined can provide shelter and support"—he jerked his head toward the plaza—"and perhaps a means of dealing with *that.*"

"My partnership days are over, Fulgar. I work alone."

Fulgar pointed out to the plaza. "Then who is this man with the flying cards?"

She rolled her eyes. "That's just Dolion. Probably fancies himself a vigilante too, actually. Guess we're all just doing loads of good in the world now, aren't we?"

Fulgar was amazed at how much he had missed Jinx's wit, even

The Whip and the Diamond

in the midst of extreme danger.

They heard another explosion in the plaza and saw a fresh line of purple fire trailing along the ground.

"*Fulgar!*" roared the mage, his voice reverberating as though through a megastone funnel. "Or should I say *Fielder*? Listen well! Surrender yourself to me." He extended a hand, as if inviting Fulgar to a dance floor. Fulgar, too stunned from hearing his name, said nothing. "Do it! And let your little *powers* fulfill a new purpose by my side." His words were laced with derision.

"I'm not coming with you!" Fulgar shouted back from the side street.

A deep growl reverberated throughout the plaza. "I shall give you one more chance to join me willingly. Or I promise you this: Every town, every city, every village where you go will burn until I have you. Every person you know will become *mine*. You have three days. Where the River Helkath ends, there will you come to me."

The mage retreated.

Jinx raised her eyebrows. "Just like old friends, huh?"

"Not exactly," replied Fulgar, his voice a little shaky. It was about all he could say through the fear struck in him by the mage.

Jinx nodded, looking distant. "Listen... good seeing you again, Fulgar. Good luck to you and... this order thing you're in. Hope it goes well, truly." She bolted off down the street.

"Jinx, wait!"

She stopped, her back still facing Fulgar. She turned her head slightly, listening.

He took a cautious step toward her. "You're up to something—something to do with that mage—and I'd really like to know what. What is this glassy sword you carry? Whatever it is you're trying to do, perhaps we can work together."

"Oh, really? And why should I work with you?"

Right then and there, Fulgar wanted to launch into an elaborate monologue about how much he missed Jinx, how foolish he had been in the past, how much his life had changed, how he still loved her and hadn't stopped thinking about her a single moment since their last parting, and that she should give him a second chance.

That didn't happen. Instead, when he opened his sorry mouth, all he said was, "I believe we have common goals."

She turned around, half-smiling. "That's the worst pickup line I've heard since 'We can't just leave her here.'"

He stared at her agog. "You . . . remember the first thing I said after we met?"

"Back when you convinced Binny to rescue me. Yeah. Hard to forget, actually." Her expression hardened again. "I told you—I'm on my own now, and I intend to keep it that way."

"Then why, Jinx? Why did you come, just as that sorcerer was ready to attack me?"

"I *came* because I saw someone who needed saving. I didn't know it would be *you*."

Fulgar held up a finger. "But you've been tracking them, haven't you? The mage and his followers. Why?"

Her eyes became ominous slits. "Don't concern yourself with this, Fulgar." She turned again to leave.

He reached out his arm as if he'd be able to grasp her hand, calling back, "The concern is there, whether I want it or not! You heard him. There's a countdown on my head. Three days."

She stopped again, arms at her sides, her fists clenched into tight balls. "This order you're in. Is it the Order of Aether Diamond?"

He blinked in surprise. "Yes. How did you—?"

She spun around and stopped almost within reach, pointing a stern finger at his face. "Dolion warned me about them. They call themselves *protectors*, right? They collect every object of power they can and take it under *their* control, under *their* watch, so only *they* have access to it. Maybe even something like this sword." She held up the gold-flecked, crystalline weapon. "Sound about right?"

Fulgar lifted a hand for calm. "They concern themselves with objects of divine energy, in particular materials known as ethereals. One such material is novidian, what Binny once called *blarkle*. I don't know what their interest might be in that sword, if any."

Jinx backed away a pace and exhaled a breath. "Listen, Fulgar. I actually think we *can* help each other. I've got a little job tomorrow, and I could use your skills."

Fulgar felt a little flicker of excitement at the idea of adventuring with Jinx again. "And this leads to stopping the mage?"

"That's the endgame, yes. But there's one thing you must promise, and this is *very* important."

"What is it?"

She looked him straight in the eyes. "Promise that you won't involve the Order—that you won't even breathe a word about what we're doing."

It was several long moments before he realized his mouth was hanging open. "That is a difficult request, Jinx, for they are my comrades . . . but I agree." They shook hands, Fulgar relishing even that simple, amicable touch. "May I know what it is we're doing?"

"Tomorrow," she said, turning away, this time with a thin smile. "Just before the twelfth hour. Find me outside the nearest blacksmith's shop."

She walked away, leaving Fulgar wondering very much what he'd just gotten himself into.

chapter 7

THE SHARPEST CUT

7/7/3178 P.A.

Fulgar held up a hand to shield his face from the blinding Jovidor sun. Its bright and hot rays beamed with vigor upon the cobblestones, making his trek through the streets and alleys of Warvonia much like navigating a blazing firepit.

Braving the heat was more than worthwhile for the opportunity to help Jinx. Although, he would've felt better knowing what the job was.

Seeing Jinx again evoked a range of emotions. There was excitement, naturally, but there were also pangs of intimidation, as he wondered how much she might resent him for the past. A not-so-small part of him worried that she would use him for this job and then simply leave, and that was a level of rejection his heart was not prepared to take.

He found some relief from the sun beneath the awning of a merchant hawking fresh produce. In the day's heat, it didn't take long for flies to hover about the diverse spread of fruits and vegetables. Despite the pests, he favored the shade and remained awhile, indulging in two apples and a handful of strawberries.

The Sharpest Cut

Fulgar gulped down his last strawberry and wiped the juice from his palm, taking up a brisk walk of pursuit. He soon came up behind her. "Business with a blacksmith? The vigilante trade must be doing quite well."

She stopped and turned to face him, eyebrow arched. "Fulgar. You showed up."

"Of course I did. Did you really think I might not?"

She shrugged. "I'm sure I don't know *what* you're inclined toward these days."

"It's so good to see you again, Jinx."

She gave him a sideways look, her face tightening. *She's got her guard up*, Fulgar thought.

"Right," she said through a sigh. "You've said nothing to the Order, then?"

"Not a word." He glanced behind them. "What were you at the blacksmith's for?"

"Had to get my sword sharpened." She patted the steel by her side. "You did bring your sword, right?"

"Yes. Why do you ask?"

"Well, hopefully you won't need it . . . but there's a chance you might." She gave a tittering laugh. "But there's really always a *chance*, isn't there?"

"Perhaps," he replied with hesitation. "Sometimes more of a chance than others."

A horse-drawn, red-topped wagon crossed the street about a spear's throw away. Jinx's attention was instantly drawn to it. "Quick," she said. "This way." She took off in the direction of the wagon, Fulgar following.

"Are we coming to the part where you tell me what we're doing?" Fulgar asked from behind. She simply gestured for him to keep up.

They rounded the corner and saw the wagon stop far down the street.

"Friends of yours?" Fulgar asked.

She whipped around to face him, her face showing no nonsense. "Okay, quick rundown. That wagon's got what I need—a moissanite wheel from an old gem preforming machine. It's black and gritty and sort of prehistoric looking."

"Is this a new hobby you're purloining for?"

"It's not for me." Her eyes narrowed. "And I'm beyond petty theft now, thank you. So happens *these* guys stole it from someone who stole it from someone else, and I mean to get it back. Is there anything else you'd like to judge me for?"

Fulgar took a quick breath, maintaining calm. "Realm knows I'm in no position to judge you for anything, Jinx." He cracked a faint smile. "And I'm not nearly brave enough to try."

She exhaled a laugh. "Well, you've got *that* much right, at least." She turned back toward the wagon. "Come on."

Rushing in too fast would draw suspicion, so they adopted a hurriedly casual pace down the right side of the street, their eyes fixed doggedly on the wagon ahead. Two men disembarked and entered the nearest establishment—an eatery specializing in seafood and crowded with patrons dining alfresco.

"I wonder what business they have in that place," said Fulgar. They were almost halfway there, about to pass a pedestrian alleyway.

Jinx shrugged. "Maybe they're hungry."

"What's so special about this wheel? More importantly, what does it have to do with the mage?"

She sighed. "Are you going to help me, or are you going to ask a bunch of questions? I didn't exactly *beg* you to come along, you know."

A man appeared from the alleyway ahead and stood directly in their path. Jinx and Fulgar stopped in their tracks. The man had a wiry build, wavy locks of silver-and-blue hair, and a thin mustache. He wore a brown leather jerkin over a lavender shirt and gray trousers, and a brown sword belt encircled his waist.

The Sharpest Cut

The man strutted toward them. "You really think this coarse wheel thingummy will appease Smeltier?" said the man in a lilting, nasal, almost lazy-sounding voice. He gave Fulgar a bucktoothed smirk. "Along with the wheel, that is."

"What are you doing here, Dolion?" said Jinx.

"Merely looking after our interests."

Fulgar narrowed his eyes at Dolion. He sensed the presence of novidian, which evoked a somewhat irrational feeling of defensiveness. "You're the one I saw running through the streets after those grimkins—the one with the flying cards." After a breath, he added, "I suppose thanks are in order for helping to control that darkfire."

Dolion raised an eyebrow while taking Jinx's hand. "My darling Muriel, you could do *so* much better than"—his eyes scanned Fulgar up and down—"*this*."

Fulgar reared back, looking upon Jinx with surprise. "*Muriel?*"

Jinx rubbed at her forehead as if warding off a headache. "A . . . lot has happened since you last saw me, Fulgar. For one, my past memories came back . . . so, you know, *yay* for that."

"Sweet mercy of Eloh, Jinx! That's . . . amazing!" He gazed at the street, processing this new enlightenment. "Then, Muriel is your name—your *real* name?"

Jinx swayed a bit, looking coy. "Yeah. I still mostly go by Jinx, though."

Fulgar delivered a fresh scowl to Dolion. "Except with *him*, it seems."

"Look," said Jinx, "this lovely conversation will have to happen later. I've got work to do." She pushed between them and kept walking.

Dolion took off after her, Fulgar a step behind. Dolion pointed back with his thumb. "Then, *he's* still coming?"

"Yes, Dolion, *he's* coming," she answered, not looking back.

"The name's Fulgar." He extended a hand. Dolion reciprocated with a firm shake, although his expression radiated something between suspicion and annoyance.

They stopped at the edge of the eatery's outdoor seating area, which gave them a good view of the wagon from the right side and behind.

"There's still someone in the seat," Fulgar observed, craning his neck to see better. The driver, the reins resting lazily in his hands, had greasy black hair and a round face.

Dolion rubbed thoughtfully at his chin, then pointed at Fulgar. "You, provide a distraction. I'll hop in and retrieve the thingummy." He looked immediately at Jinx. "It'll be heavy, like a big rock."

Fulgar sized him up. "I'll wager I'm the stronger one, whilst you'll make a better distraction."

Jinx nodded. "Fulgar probably *is* the stronger one."

Dolion grunted. "Do you even know what moissanite is? What it looks like?" Fulgar opened his mouth but stalled, and Dolion pounced on his hesitation. "I think we'll go with *my* plan."

"Shut it, both of you!" Jinx hissed. "*I'll* distract the driver. Dolion, you go inside the wagon and then hand the wheel outside to Fulgar."

Dolion looked her over through squinted eyes. "On second thought, you *do* make a much better distraction."

Groaning through an eyeroll, Jinx made her way down the wagon's side. Dolion walked toward the rear opening, while Fulgar took position at the back corner, where he could observe both directions.

He barely heard Jinx as she started asking the driver for directions to the harbor. The man was unfriendly and dismissive, but his demeanor soon softened as Jinx charmed him with the dulcet tones of her voice and a subtle batting of her eyelashes, all accentuated by the smooth sway of her hips. Fulgar had to resist running to give her directions himself.

He heard rustling inside the wagon, which, thanks to Jinx, the driver didn't notice.

The Sharpest Cut

Fulgar took a step toward the wagon. "Do you have it?" he said, keeping his voice hushed.

Dolion's head popped out between the canvas flaps. "A moment, please. Bloody thing's got locks on it."

He heard Jinx give the man an overly adorable *thank you*. She started back toward the rear of the wagon. Fulgar attempted to signal her with a shake of his head.

"You don't have it?" she said discreetly. "He finally told me to move away."

"You both were right," said Fulgar. "I could not have been half as good a distraction as you. And, no, Dolion's still in there."

Her shoulders sagged. "Great."

Two men emerged from the eatery with food sacks. One was short, with a thin, gnarled face and brown hair with streaks of bright green, probably about twice Fulgar's age. The other was a bit younger and about Fulgar's height, with short-cropped blond hair and a square jaw. Both men stepped up to a bench seat behind the driver.

"*Dolion!*" Jinx hissed. "We're out of time!"

Up front, the driver took the reins and urged the horses forward.

"*Dolion!*" she tried again.

The wagon started to move.

There wasn't time to think, only to act. Fulgar ran and flung himself up into the wagon, glimpsing Jinx's wide-eyed expression for only a moment before passing through the flaps. He was surrounded by rattling cargo and the smell of musty canvas.

"What's happening, Dolion?" Fulgar asked in his loudest whisper.

"Told you, didn't I? Locks . . . and no bloody key in sight."

Fulgar moved beside Dolion, struggling to remain upright as the wagon bounced along with increased speed. He saw what had to be the moissanite wheel—a sandy-looking black cylinder flecked with sparkles in a way that vaguely resembled some unrefined form of novidian, although Fulgar knew it wasn't. Those feelings of fondness and connection simply weren't there. The item was secured by two lock-chains placed crosswise and bolted at the ends to a heavy wooden plank.

"Let me have a go with that," said Fulgar.

Dolion staggered back, looking grumpy. "What are you going to do, pick it with your fingers?"

Fulgar ignored him, took the first lock into his hands, and concentrated on its internal components. The thing was a little rusty and stubborn, but after a couple of minutes the lock came loose.

"Well," said Dolion, "that's a nice trick. Magnetism?"

Fulgar looked up from the second lock at Dolion. After a moment, he nodded.

"You're a Fielder, then." He gestured toward the lock. "A remarkable skill, even so."

"You're also a Fielder," Fulgar replied, taking the second lock into his hand. "And those cards you carry—novidian, aren't they?"

"Well, you *are* the observant one, aren't you?"

Fulgar felt the lock move in his hands. "Got it!" He had to steady the moissanite wheel to keep it from rolling freely. A new predicament dawned on him. They would have to escape from a moving wagon with this thing in hand. "Now what?"

Dolion rubbed at his chin in thought. "Patience. Wait for them to stop, and we'll slip out the b—*ack!*" he yelped as the wagon took a hard jolt, knocking him onto his rump.

They heard voices from the front of the wagon. "What was that?"

"Get back there an' check, Ruford!"

Fulgar scowled at Dolion. "That's *wonderful!* Now they're going to find us!" Dolion dropped to his hands and knees and crawled toward the front, keeping himself concealed by the assortment of barrels and crates in the wagon.

The Sharpest Cut

A sword-bearing hand appeared through the front flaps of the canvas, followed by the face of the blond-haired man. He scanned the area, looking vexed and confused, his gaze passing over the cargoes of the large wagon.

He stepped fully in, and his eyes landed on Fulgar.

Fulgar waved to him in greeting.

"Hey! Who're you?" the man bellowed.

Dolion popped up from behind a barrel and punched the man in the mouth. Any man of a smaller size, or perhaps punched by one of greater strength, would've fallen from such a direct hit. This man simply stumbled back about half a step and spat blood in Dolion's face. He grappled Dolion by the shoulders and tossed him toward the end of the wagon. Fulgar's eyes widened as he watched from beside the moissanite.

"That didn't go as hoped," Dolion muttered as he stood, right hand in his pocket.

His hand emerged, gripping three novidian cards rimmed in a faint white glow.

Snarling, the man was upon him in a trice, his sword whirling toward Dolion's side. Dolion blocked it, not with his sword, but with a raise of his hand, repelling it with magnetic reversal. He pushed the blade back with invisible force and landed a fist into the man's side.

The man pummeled Dolion again with his other fist, knocking him sideways into a barrel. Dolion ducked another swing and slammed his card-bearing hand into the man's torso. With a white burst, the man soared to the front of the wagon, crashing just behind a row of crates.

"We've got to stop this wagon!" yelled Fulgar.

"I'm on it! You just stay there, doing the easy job." He sprang forward, hopping cargo toward the wagon's front.

Fulgar looked down and noticed one of Dolion's novidian cards lying on the wagon bed. With a furtive glance at Dolion, and

THE HEALER

while keeping a hand on the moissanite, he stretched as far as he could go and snatched it.

Once it was in his grasp, those feelings of familiarity and renewed strength pulsed within, fueling his confidence. He breathed in deeply, as though waking from a long and satisfying nap.

Dolion made it past where the man had fallen, with a sigh of relief from Fulgar, and reached to push through the front flaps of the canvas.

Fulgar saw sudden movement. The fallen thief was back up. "Dolion, behind you!"

Dolion turned just quick enough to evade a right hook, but the man managed to lock his arms around Dolion's neck and shoulders from behind.

The man with brown-and-green-streaked hair appeared through the flaps, grinning behind a dagger that was pointed at Dolion's chest.

He didn't get the chance to thrust it.

A white zap blasted him back through the flaps and over the front of the wagon. Fulgar couldn't help but wince at the pronounced bump that followed from the forward wheels, then the back.

With the other man stunned, Dolion wriggled free of the stranglehold. Fulgar blasted that man too, granting him the same fate as his accomplice.

Dolion turned to Fulgar. "You almost hit me!"

"But I didn't!" Fulgar yelled back.

Dolion flung himself through the flaps and dispatched the driver. Fulgar couldn't see exactly what happened, but he heard the driver's yelp whip past the side of the wagon and, looking out the back, saw him rolling away like a log.

The wagon bounced along down the cobblestone streets, gaining distance from the unlucky band of thieves, Dolion now at the reins.

The Sharpest Cut

Fulgar and Dolion left the wagon behind in a southside plaza with grimy walls and weeds pushing between old, cracked stones. They took only the moissanite wheel with them. Fulgar, after much dispute, had been granted the displeasure of bearing it. Dolion argued that he had done all of the fighting. Fulgar countered that he had done all of the saving. Dolion had driven the wagon to safety, but Fulgar had released the locks.

When it was pointed out that Fulgar had only saved them by way of Dolion's novidian card, Fulgar had to relent.

"Fine," he grumbled. "I'll just prove that I'm the stronger among us anyway."

"You feel obligated to prove that to her, do you?" Dolion replied through a toothy grin.

Fulgar ignored the comment. "I trust you know where we're going with this."

"I know where your fair Jinx will be." He rubbed his chin, arching an eyebrow. "Jinx—a rather unlucky name, isn't it?"

"A play on her former plight, cursed as she once felt by the loss of her memories."

"Well," said Dolion, "I suppose the weight of that plight depends on the memories themselves, doesn't it? Sometimes a clean slate is the greater boon."

"Perhaps, but how can one know without remembering in the first place?" replied Fulgar. "Besides, whether good or bad, we are all shaped by our past. Light shines brightest in the darkest of moments, after all."

"A right spiritual guide you are, mate."

Fulgar had to admit he even surprised himself. He would never have uttered such words of wisdom in his past thieving days, unless he was actively making it all up to deceive someone, back when life was all about climbing a step above everyone else, Binny's talisman as their guide.

"I suppose I have my friends in the Order to thank for redirecting my own path," Fulgar replied.

Dolion scratched his mustache thoughtfully. "Got picked up by the Order of Aether Diamond, did you?"

"Ah, that's right—you're familiar with them. Jinx mentioned you were."

"O' course I am. Hidden, reclusive, sitting atop countless mysteries from before the kingdom even existed—indeed, I find them *very* interesting. Not interesting enough to pledge my troth, mind you. A certain . . . vagrant self-governance suits me well."

Fulgar chuckled knowingly. "I understand that better than you may realize. When going my own way didn't work out so well, the Order came to me when I needed them most."

"I hate to break it to you, but they wanted you because you're a Fielder. Been after me for quite some time. O' course, with *these* little beauties"—he flashed one of his novidian cards—"I'm quite irresistible."

"No one from the Order's pursued your novidian yet. Perhaps you should speak with them. Find out if there are any synergies."

Dolion lifted a finger. "*Yet* being the key word there, me bucko."

It felt like Dolion was leading him across the entire town in the most roundabout way possible, the bulky wheel increasingly heavy in Fulgar's arms. After about half an eternity, they entered a distinctly sketchy-looking series of narrow, winding alleyways.

Fulgar shifted his grip on the wheel for the umpteenth time, past the point of finding comfort. "I really hope she's getting something good in return for this thing."

Dolion stopped and faced Fulgar. "Doesn't really matter what she's getting, so long as you get the girl." He followed this with a wink.

Fulgar blinked and stared dumbly back at Dolion. "You are

quite a difficult man to read, Dolion. What's your role in all of this? What do you hope to gain?"

"I'm just an okay man trying to do okay things. If that warlock fellow gets too far along, won't be a whole lot left for the rest of us, will there?" He started forward but stopped again, as though a thought had just occurred to him. "Besides, I hope to make out with your lovely lady's lovely sword when all's done."

"You're hired help, then?"

"I agreed to help—that much is right. The sword . . . more of an incentive."

They rounded a few more corners, deeper into what felt to Fulgar like an outdoor labyrinth. He was about ready to drop the wheel and start rolling it.

"*There* you two are!"

Fulgar felt a surge of strength to pull him through the pain of his burden. It was Jinx, approaching from the other direction.

Jinx's face lit up when she saw the wheel. "And you got it!"

"Yes, and it's not pleasant to carry," said Fulgar. "Where are we taking it?"

"Smeltier's place is just down the way here." Jinx gave his shoulder a pat. "I'm impressed, Fulgar, truly!"

"I do hope this has something to do with your plan for dealing with the mage, because I've only got two days before . . . *something* happens—likely something quite bad."

Dolion snapped his fingers. "Ah, of course! So *you're* the Fielder that ruddy spellcaster was talking to. I heard it. Didn't think he was talking to me, but gave me the shivers just the same."

"You're likely next," said Jinx. "He really seems to like Fulgar, though. Come on—we'll talk on the way." They stepped into the narrow byway of what felt like the side alley of another side alley. "Believe it or not, Fulgar, this all works right into the plan."

"Then, you *do* have a plan?" asked Fulgar, keeping his voice down by instinct.

She gave the diamond sword a pat. "That's what *this* is for . . . but it's not ready, not quite. To stab him successfully, it needs to be sharper."

"And Smeltier's got a blize furnace," said Dolion, "one good enough to form up diamond alloy."

"In *this* dreary part of town?" asked Fulgar. Only the best and wealthiest among those skilled in lapillurgy—the art of producing and perfecting metal-gemstone alloys—had blize furnaces for reaching exceptionally cold temperatures.

"Well, he's not exactly *supposed* to have it," Jinx answered. "What matters is he *does* have it . . . and the skill to use it."

"Why this diamond sword, though?" asked Fulgar.

"Diamond and *gold*," Dolion corrected. "Kelau diamond, at that—the world's oldest, wisest, purest, most complex crystal structure. Not quite a gift of the Ethereal Realm, but reasonably close . . . we hope."

"Your plan is to *stab* the mage?" said Fulgar. He shook his head adamantly. "No, Jinx, that's far too dangerous."

"That's cute, Fulgar, really," she replied, "but I've faced plenty of dangers in my time." She stopped at a door appearing black and grimy from neglect. "Ah, here we are!"

They opened the door to a curious fragrant blend of molten metal and flowery candles. The man named Smeltier did not look like the typical blacksmith. He was short and well along in years, with a ring of grayish-black hair circling a mostly bald head.

Smeltier raised his head from what appeared to be a golden arrow on the table before him. He wore an eccentric pair of glasses with built-in jeweler's loupes. They made his eyes look enormous.

He soon spotted the moissanite wheel. "Is that what I think it is?"

Jinx rested her hands on her hips proudly. "Yes, it is!"

"Oh, fantastic!" He swept his arm across a workbench, scattering tools and metallic debris. "Here, put it on this table." Fulgar was thrilled to be rid of it. Smeltier immediately began examining the object. "Core mineral still intact . . . no loss of diamond fleck . . . Yes, perfect!"

"That was *not* easy to get," said Jinx.

"You can say *that* again," muttered Dolion.

"You should really take precautions," Jinx continued. "The people who stole that might come back here looking for it."

Smeltier waved her off. "Yes, yes, I know."

Jinx drew the diamond sword from her side. "Now for *your* end of the bargain."

The curious old smith watched her for a long moment and then gestured to the same table that held the moissanite. "Of course. Sharper'n steel this'll be, when I'm done."

"And when will that be?" asked Fulgar.

Smeltier returned an impatient glare. "Soon! Maybe in a week."

"No good," said Jinx. "We need this done *today*."

"Today?" Smeltier protested, sweeping a hand about his untidy workspace. "Can't you see I'm busy?"

"It's important. *Today*."

"So, what, are you the grand vizier now, more important than my other clients?"

Jinx leaned in a bit closer. "If you want to live much longer, we just might be, and that's actually *not* me threatening you."

Smeltier grunted. "Tomorrow—best I can do. Come back then."

"I will," Jinx replied. Dolion exited. Fulgar was halfway out when Jinx turned to add, "*Tomorrow*, Smeltier, and razor-sharp, or I'll lead those thieves right back here by the hand . . . and that *is* me threatening you." She walked out, slamming the door.

"That last part seemed a bit harsh, don't you think?" said Fulgar.

"That's the kind of talk people understand round here. He'll get it done."

"Smeltier knows what's best for him," said Dolion. He extended a hand to Fulgar. "A pleasure, Fulgar."

"Oh!" piped Fulgar, digging into his pocket. "I almost forgot." He pulled out the novidian card that Dolion had dropped in the wagon and held it out.

Dolion's eyes flicked to the card and back to Fulgar. "Hold on to it . . . for now. You never know when it might come in handy."

Fulgar placed it back in his pocket. "Thank you."

"Now that you're quite the hero, best of luck with fair Muriel." With a pronounced wink and a half bow, Dolion left them.

Jinx shook her head. "Don't listen to him."

Fulgar laughed. "He is rather dramatic . . . isn't he, Muriel?"

She glowered and wrinkled her nose. "You're pining for a bit of drama yourself." Then her expression softened, and she took his hand. "It really *is* nice to see you again, Fulgar. Can you meet me at the docks tomorrow night, after I've got the sword back? Twenty-fourth hour. Things're quiet then."

"I'll be there . . . of course, with one day to spare."

"Don't worry—that magical bugger won't be getting anything."

"I'm not worried. Even if it's my last day alive, I'll be happy knowing I got to see you again."

"Good. See you then, Fulgar." She smiled, released his hand, and disappeared to the alleyways.

A chaotic array of emotions within left Fulgar feeling mostly numb. Tomorrow would be the third and final day of the mage's ultimatum. Fulgar tried not to imagine what would happen if he ignored the demand. He equally struggled to imagine why the mage wanted him in the first place. Clearly it had something to do with him being a Fielder.

Being a Fielder meant he had powers and abilities, and those powers had only grown since he joined the Order and spent more time exposed to novidian. Terror still writhed within him, with an ever-suffocating sense that his powers were far overshadowed by the mage's.

But he was about to see Jinx again, and they had a plan to stop the mage's terror. It was like they were a team again, like they used to be, and that was enough to comfort him.

It was a clear, cloudless night, placing Eliorin's rings on full display across the southern sky. On nights like this, the rings' whites were extra bright, and the muted hues of teal and copper in some of the orbital rocks were especially prominent. The harbor was one of the best places to view it all, where the sky's tapestry was reflected in the rippling mirror of the ocean.

Fulgar found Jinx sitting at the very end of one of the docks, her legs dangling over the side and her gaze lost to the horizon. She wore a burgundy halter top with dark shorts. The small white patches in her black hair glistened like snowflakes under the glow of the rings.

Just as Fulgar was about to step upon the dock, he drew back and sucked in a breath of realization.

It was the same dock where Volk's ship had been berthed the day they lost Binny.

Keeping his eyes on Jinx helped him to push aside the painful memory of that day and continue down the dock. So still was the harbor at this hour that his boots clomped resoundingly with each step on the wooden planks.

As he neared Jinx, he saw that the diamond sword was sheathed at her side. She must have successfully retrieved it from Smeltier—sharpened to her satisfaction, or she'd almost certainly still be there driving in him the fear of a long, painful death until he got the job done right.

She said nothing as Fulgar approached, keeping her eyes to the sea. Fulgar sat down beside her.

"Thank you for coming," she said.

"I wouldn't have missed this for anything. It's a perfect night to be out—probably the most beautiful I've seen in a long while. And you... well, you look stunning as always, Jinx."

She smiled—a tired, placatory, yet no less adorable smile. "I suppose you know which dock this is."

Fulgar paused for a breath and blinked at the ocean. "Of course."

"I loved Binny, you know, as a true friend. You I loved as something more. I believe it was right here, after losing him, that you became a different person."

He kept his eyes on the gentle ripple of the water as he answered. "I... lost my way, my compass, my future. At least, that's what I thought. I hope you can forgive me, Jinx. I was a very misguided man, but all that aside, I had still lost my best friend since boyhood."

"I don't blame you for that." She laid her right hand atop his left, which was resting on the dock between them. "I don't even blame you for the things you said the night I left. I mean, of course I did in the moment, but after some time I realized I'd acted on instinct—an instinct that knew you needed the space to make room in your heart for more than the hopes and dreams you shared with Binny."

Fulgar turned to her with a smirk. "You knew all of that, did you?"

She shrugged. "More or less. Sounded good, didn't it?" She gave an airy chortle. "I've had plenty of time to dwell on things too, you know."

He took hold of her hand. That one simple touch flooded him with memories of happiness, pain, elation, heartbreak, love, and anger. The anger, he realized, was never really directed at her but rather at himself for a past fraught with bad choices. Jinx remained still, looking at him as he said words that were long overdue. "I'm sorry, Jinx... for everything... for the way I treated you. I've regretted it every day since."

Her eyes glistened with a watery sheen. Exhaling, she looked away at the ocean. "Curse you, Fulgar." She sniffled and wiped her nose with her arm. "I haven't cried since that day I left your sorry hide in the woods."

"I was such a fool. Binny and I were so consumed by the pursuit of power, so determined that no one could control us the way our parents had been, that we became controlled by the pursuit itself. When he was suddenly gone, I completely lost myself."

She gave his hand a squeeze. "I understand. You needed time, painful as that was for both of us. But, over this time, you *have* become more powerful—I saw you fighting in that plaza, even before I realized it was you—and you seem more sure of yourself."

He nodded. "Power has its blessings and curses. Like money, power tempts people into a never-ending pursuit, even people who have the most. Now I find myself a target of forces I never even knew existed until recently."

"Yeah, well, we'll deal with that bugger."

Fulgar looked down at the diamond sword sheathed at Jinx's side. "But why, Jinx? Why are you risking yourself to go after this warlock?"

There was a long pause as she thought. "I remembered. My memories returned. I had gone out to the western coast of Sharm, the earliest place I could remember being. I just . . . stared. Stared at the beach, at the waves, at the horizon. Then I just . . . remembered. It was nothing dramatic at first, but then with those memories came the emotions. Fear . . . betrayal . . . loss. It was real fuzzy, at first, but it all came back like a storm.

"I'm from the Coral Ash Islands, as people often suspected. I didn't like my parents. They were pirates. Some people in my life showed me kindness, but not them. They made me help them with bad things that I'm not happier remembering. We were often at sea. While sailing west of Grandtrilia, we were attacked by grimkin hitmen. That's when I saw that eerie, cold, purple fire—the same as the mage used here in Warvonia. That same devilry was used to attack our ship. I'm not saying it was the *same* mage, but of the same kind of dark power. I thought I was a goner. Turns out I managed to ride some driftwood all the way to the shore, where I woke up completely clueless. Maybe it was too long in the cold sea, but I think it was something else.

"I think it's possible for the mind to become so overloaded with strife and conflict and turmoil that it shuts itself down completely—locks out all memories associated with those feelings. That's what mine did—shut out everything from before that moment, right down to my given name, Muriel."

"Muriel," Fulgar repeated. The dulcet moniker rolled gently off his tongue. "It is a beautiful name."

Jinx seemed lost in a thousand thoughts as she continued watching the water. "Keep calling me Jinx, though," she said. "My real name is of the past, of all those painful memories." She raised her head. "You, Fulgar"—she looked down again—"I don't want you calling me by that name."

He took her meaning, and it warmed his heart. She associated Fulgar with her life as Jinx and wanted to keep it that way—to keep him apart from the more painful memories of her youth. Rarely could people compartmentalize their life experiences in such a way. Fulgar's own transformation since joining the Order was different, but it helped him to relate. It was just one more thing that made them perfect for each other.

"You will always be Jinx to me," said Fulgar in his most sincere voice.

She spluttered in laughter. "That's me, the great curse!" They chuckled together for a few moments, and then she spoke again. "The mage—I do believe he has ties to Binny."

Fulgar felt the air empty from his lungs. Of course, he had already suspected as much, but to hear it so bluntly from Jinx

The Sharpest Cut

brought a certain gravity. "How so?"

"I don't know if he's still alive and captive or long gone. Maybe a couple months after you and I separated, I managed to track down Volk." Her eyes snapped up to his, the sort of look that warned him not to take her words too seriously. "I had to stay far away to keep from being seen, but I saw others with Volk—some of his lackeys but also, I'm almost sure, Binny among them. They went to a cavity in the mountain—maybe that shrine you guys wanted to find." She paused and looked away, seeming to struggle with the weight of what she was about to say. "I've not seen any of them since—not Volk, not his men, not Binny... but one time I *did* see that mage come from the same place." She shivered. "And he saw me. I was lucky to escape from there with my life."

"Did you get a good look at him?"

"Not really." She sighed, looking exhausted. "I think it might be *my* fault that he started targeting Warvonia."

"Do you think the mage is Volk?" asked Fulgar.

She shook her head. "I really don't know. It's possible. If so, something about that shrine made him much more powerful in dark magic."

Fulgar scratched his head in thought. "Then, you're after this mage because you feel responsible for his threats to the town."

"Yeah, but also because those cold flames connect with my past. Those are sinister, awful powers. The Civic Force won't stand up to it, and the Royal Guard are never around when it shows up. I'm telling you, Fulgar, things are *weird*... like something bigger is brewing all around us."

Fulgar wondered about one last thing, which Jinx had not yet touched on. "What is the significance of this diamond sword? How did you come by it?"

"In the islands of Zoar, there's an old legend about Kelau diamond warming the 'flames of midnight.' I followed the path within that legend. When that became difficult, I sought help. I found Dolion through a series of tavern contacts, and we managed to find *this* one." She patted the sword by her side. "It's not entirely one of a kind but still very special and supposed to hold some of the world's purest energies.

"After Dolion got involved," she continued, "the mage only got more interested in Warvonia. Of course, he almost seemed to forget about Dolion entirely once *you* came around. Probably because you're a more powerful Fielder, and he could sense that."

"Yes," said Fulgar pensively. "I *had* noticed. And Dolion is helping you in exchange for the diamond sword?"

She unsheathed the weapon, which sang a subdued crystalline note as it emerged. Jinx laid it across her lap and ran her fingers along its smooth, glassy surface, which reflected the ringlight of the sky. "He claims to have business with it in Zoar, and he assured me his client or associate or whatever he called them would cause us no trouble in Tuscawny. Knowing Dolion, his payment is probably some blend of money and influence. He's usually too clever to seek only money." Lifting the sword, she looked up at the rings through its blade. "Kind of a shame, really. It's such a pretty thing to give up." She slid the sword back into its sheath.

"Yes—it looks striking enough to be an ethereal."

Jinx lay back on the dock and folded her arms behind her head. "And that brings you up to speed, more or less."

"What you've accomplished is amazing," he replied, "and it seems promising. But please let me help, Jinx. Don't try to attack the mage on your own. We must work together."

She smiled up at him. "Seemed to have gone well enough yesterday."

He glanced over Jinx's supine figure stretched along the planks. From where her shirt had lifted just above her midriff to her trim legs, even in the soft nightglow her skin was radiant. He leaned back to lie beside her. Together, they stared up at the rings that coursed the sky in celestial brilliance, and Fulgar told her about his own

The Sharpest Cut

struggles after they'd separated and about how quieting his mind and reflecting within the Order had changed his life.

It was peaceful, staring up into the infinite vastness of the sky with the glow of the rings and moon, and he found the conversation with Jinx therapeutic. As much as Fulgar fancied himself a capable healer, he'd come to learn that not all healing was the physical kind. Sometimes you just needed to talk to someone who cared enough to listen.

He was well into describing his friends and colleagues in the Order when an explosion reverberated in the distance. They sat up in unison. They heard faraway chaos but saw nothing unusual from their location.

"What was that?" asked Fulgar.

"Maybe your friend's decided to come back a night early."

They stood, drew swords—Jinx her sword of steel—and bolted down the dock, listening for more signs of disturbance as they made their way through the harbor zone and into the city.

The sounds were erratic, but after a short while of roaming streets the cacophony grew, leading them toward the main market square in town.

Black-garbed grimkins and men—minions of the mage—dashed to and fro wreaking havoc. They slashed and punched holes through awnings. They shattered windows. They set market stands ablaze. And, of course, it wasn't mere fire that they used.

It was cold, purple darkfire.

Fulgar and Jinx sprang into action, tearing into the vermin. Fulgar punched one man square in the nose, while Jinx hilt-butted a grimkin unconscious. Fulgar raised his steel against the dark-gray cutlass of another grimkin, while Jinx landed acrobatic kicks into a duo of foes who clearly hadn't seen her coming.

This grimkin was tough, and his feathery biceps bulged with muscle. Fulgar wasn't certain his skills with the sword would be enough.

Fortunately, he had more skills than that.

Giving himself as much distance as he could, he snatched a broken metal pole from one of the merchant carts and tossed it to the grimkin. The additional metal would make the move easier... he hoped.

Focusing on reverse magnetism and forming it around the pole and sword, he propelled the grimkin like a ballista, slamming the foe into a brick building.

"That was a neat trick!" Jinx cheered.

"Thanks, but I'm afraid my luck ends there. All this darkfire must be extinguished, and I left the safehouse without the novidian. You should leave here to safety. I'll retrieve the novidian and possibly others from the Order."

Jinx pointed toward the other side of the square. "I don't think you'll have to!"

A swell of white energy confirmed her words. Moments later, Fulgar saw Silas working on the darkfire, while Elcid pulled aggressive combat maneuvers against a group of enemies.

"Ah, yes!" Fulgar cheered. "These are my comrades! Come on!"

Jinx looked suddenly worried. "From the Order?"

Fulgar locked eyes with her, keeping his voice level and sure. "It is now time for you to trust *me*, Jinx. Nothing will happen to you or your weapon. I'll see to that."

"How can you be so sure?"

He gave a small, amused smile. "Well, it so happens I am the only etheretic among them. When it comes to the Order, that carries some sway."

After a moment's hesitation, she nodded.

They ran to join Elcid in the battle. He spared Fulgar a sideways glance. "Where have you been the past couple of days?"

"Oh, you know, getting out for some fresh air." He grappled a grimkin around the neck and slammed its beaked face into the side of a produce stand.

The Sharpest Cut

Silas had just snuffed a nearby trail of flames. He glanced at Jinx and then at Fulgar with an arched eyebrow. "Fresh air, you say?"

Elcid didn't appear amused, but then again, they were in the middle of a battle. "Do you have any idea of the reason for this attack? What are they after? There's not even anyone around during this time of night!"

"I have no idea," Fulgar answered. Although, he thought he might have *some* idea. "Be on the lookout, though. That mage of the Void could be looking to spring a trap."

"Maybe this *is* the trap!" replied Silas.

But the assailants, whose number had notably thinned, were already retreating down various side streets.

One especially ugly-looking grimkin turned and glared at Fulgar. Gold and silver earrings dangled from his ears, one eye seemed more closed than the other, his beak was chipped in half a dozen places, and his head-feathers were ruffled. He pointed his cutlass and stared down the length of its blade, a straight line to Fulgar's heart. When he spoke, his voice was screechy and harsh. "Remember, Fielder! By the third day—*tomorrow*—or this town will burn!"

"Be gone, vermin," shouted Elcid, "or we'll float you back to Akkadia in a bed of your own feathers!"

The grimkin ran off to join his comrades.

Fulgar sheathed his sword. "Well, I'm glad you two showed up when you did." Jinx came up beside him. "Gentlemen, I'd like you to meet my very dear friend, Jinx. Jinx, meet Elcid and Silas, my friends and comrades from the Order."

Silas nodded greeting. "Ah, the famous Jinx."

"That's me—the famous bad-luck charm," said Jinx. "And you're the famous . . . Order . . . people."

Elcid's attention seemed elsewhere, his hard gaze aimed at the damage around them. So intense was his expression that Fulgar felt suddenly uncomfortable.

"Thank you, both," said Fulgar. "I'll see Jinx safely off and meet—"

"What did he mean?" asked Elcid, cutting off Fulgar with his sharp tone. "The grimkin. What did he mean about the 'third day'?"

Fulgar licked dry lips. "That refers to the Shadow Mage. He seems to have taken an interest in my Fielder powers and insisted that I turn myself over to him by the third day. That was . . . two days ago."

"Sweet Realm above," muttered Silas. "Then, this little attack was to lure us out, so they could drive home their threat."

Elcid sighed, glaring at Fulgar. "And you didn't think to tell us about this?"

"Of course, I did . . . but Jinx and I have already formulated a plan for dealing with this mage. I believe this connects to men of *my* past—Binny and Volk."

Elcid looked furious, but he kept his words calm. "It is not only *your* well-being and life at stake in this. We must report this to Zirion. Come along, both of you."

There was no arguing with Elcid. Fulgar didn't dare. Jinx, looking furious, took Fulgar's hand in a firm grasp, and they departed from the market square at once.

chapter 8

BEHIND THE MASK

7/8/3178 P.A.

Stillness reigned in the streets of Warvonia as Fulgar, Jinx, Elcid, and Silas navigated their way to the Order's safehouse. The quietude bestowed a sense of isolation, their steps loud as horse-clops, and it felt as if they had the entire town to themselves. This was not a typically bustling hour of night, but the raucous presence of the mage's minions had kept even the most obsessive pub crawlers self-confined.

"Why should we need to drag Jinx into a matter of the Order?" asked Fulgar, feeling defensive.

"You know why," Elcid answered. "She clearly has an interest in this mage, much like you. I saw her in the streets during the last grimkin attack, actively joining the fight. She must be this female warrior we heard about. That she is close to you strikes me as no coincidence, not to mention the very unusual weapon at her side." He gave Jinx a sideways look. "I should hope we are fighting for the same side."

Jinx met the look. "I should also hope so."

"We are," said Fulgar in a forceful tone. Knowing how strong-willed and assertive both Jinx and Elcid could be, Fulgar preferred to avoid unnecessary suspicions.

"Is there another Fielder working with you?" asked Silas.

"The other man is independent," she replied curtly.

Elcid halted them a short time later, before they entered the Old Bard district, and proceeded to blindfold Jinx.

"Is this really necessary?" Fulgar asked.

Elcid, unsmiling, raised an eyebrow. "Do I really need to explain the reasons?"

"So much for unnecessary suspicions," Fulgar muttered.

"It's fine," said Jinx. "Not like I couldn't find the place anyway, if I really wanted."

"I think not," replied Silas. "Even if you did, you wouldn't get in." Jinx only smirked in response.

They continued into the grimy, narrow, darker byways of Old Bard. Fulgar took care to guide Jinx, notifying her of every potential trip hazard and kicking away minor obstructions.

She seemed amused at his fussing and walked with certainty in her bearing. "I see there *are* still some gentlemen left in the world," she said, Fulgar having just led her around a patch of damaged street and missing cobblestones.

"Why establish the safehouse in slummy outskirts such as this?" seethed Fulgar. "It seems obvious—just the kind of place someone would choose to hide. Why not pick somewhere right around the market square or mayor's manor? No one would suspect the safehouse of an ancient sect of underground protectors there, in the middle of town."

"Oh!" chirped Jinx. "Old Bard. We're in Old Bard, aren't we?"

Fulgar clamped his mouth shut. Elcid rubbed at his temples and groaned.

"Doesn't matter," Silas insisted. "She still wouldn't find it."

"Sorry," said Fulgar insincerely. "Was it the 'slummy outskirts' comment that gave it away?"

Jinx shook her head. "Nah, it's more that acrid smell. You really don't forget that."

A few street corners later, they arrived.

Zirion let them in through the heavy brick-wall-façade door. "I expect there's a good reason for this," he said, motioning toward Jinx.

"Yes," said Elcid. "It appears there is a matter of urgency pertaining to these two"—he pointed at Fulgar and Jinx—"and the Shadow Mage. We believe she's the mysterious warrior you've been hearing about."

"Let's get to Keepers," Zirion replied. "We'll talk there." He looked at Jinx. "Please, remove the young lady's blindfold." Fulgar did so. "Welcome. I am Zirion, master over this safehouse of the Order of Aether Diamond."

"I'm Jinx."

"Pleased to finally meet you, Jinx. Fulgar has spoken very fondly of you. I hope you'll forgive the . . . method . . . by which you were brought here. We like to limit knowledge of our locations as much as possible."

"I get it," she replied through an airy laugh. "I've known plenty of people with plenty to hide."

"Plenty to *protect*, in our case," said Zirion.

Fulgar ran his hands absently along the ancient stone walls, enjoying the cave-like chill of the Order's passageways. "Ancient histories and knowledge, as much as artifacts."

"Yeah, I could still find your place," said Jinx. She gave one of Zirion's big arms a pat. "Don't worry, though, your secret's safe with me." Zirion arched a thick eyebrow.

"Drivel and tripe," grumbled Silas under his breath. "Even if she did find it—"

"She wouldn't get in," Fulgar interrupted. "We know."

They arrived moments later to the Keepers Lounge. "So named because those of us who commune here are all keepers," Fulgar explained.

"How adorable," Jinx replied, claiming a cushy chair for herself. Fulgar sat beside her.

Elcid gave the golden dagger a firm tug to no avail and joined the others in finding seats. He then cast a hard look at Fulgar. "Tell him."

"What has happened, Fulgar?" asked Zirion.

The events of the past two days flashed through Fulgar's mind—the encounter with the mage, the moissanite heist with Jinx, the other Fielder named Dolion—and with these memories came an unexpected pang of guilt. It was a strange feeling, almost as if he were a child that had just undermined a parent. Zirion had, Fulgar realized, become the closest thing to a father in Fulgar's life since his own father had been lost to guilder-induced madness.

Fulgar swallowed and took a deep breath. Beneath the emotions, his convictions were still intact. Jinx had already thought this through with a plan bolstered by a legendary sword, and Fulgar had not wanted to jeopardize it by breaking his promise to Jinx and involving the others.

Perhaps that hadn't really been for the best. Perhaps Jinx's worries were unwarranted and the Order could help their plan to succeed. It was just too uncertain, and there wasn't time to sort out how to satisfy everyone.

He also realized he could no longer keep their efforts a secret.

"During our fight with grimkins and wielders of Void two nights ago," Fulgar began, "I encountered the mage. I was alone, with only the novidian rod to protect me. Jinx suddenly arrived and distracted him long enough for me to fight back with the novidian. She had someone else with her—another Fielder, a man named Dolion."

"Dolion," repeated Zirion, rubbing his beard. "Yes, we are familiar with him."

Jinx leaned forward, looking annoyed and guarded as she aimed a glare at Fulgar. "Just putting it all out there, are you?"

Behind the Mask

"It's okay, Jinx," he replied, hoping he was right. "We took a chance to get to safety, and the mage issued an ultimatum. He wanted me, as a Fielder, to turn myself over to him within three days. He threatened to destroy Warvonia and everyone I care about if I don't. I . . . do not mean to alarm you. This mage . . . I feel certain he is connected to people of my past—the gangster Volk and my old friend Binny, who was taken by Volk. I had hoped not to drag the Order further into this conflict. We have a plan—Jinx and I—that per Zoar legend we believe has merit."

Zirion's expression became like stone. Even his skin seemed to lose its color. "Fulgar, you should've come to me with this immediately." Fulgar was struck by his lowered, almost growling tone of voice. "And this was two days ago now?"

Fulgar nodded. Zirion turned his back to Fulgar and faced the wall. An ominous silence swept over the room. "You . . ." said Zirion in the same rumbly voice. Then, as he turned back around, his tone morphed into something much more terrifying. "You have no *idea* what you are dealing with!"

Everyone in the room flinched. All they heard next was the sound of Zirion's heavy breathing.

When Zirion spoke again, he was a bit calmer. "Fulgar . . . when you came here, you were utterly lost, hopeless, living a purposeless life of thievery and sin. We took you in, nurtured your skills, set you on the path to your true potential. We asked nothing from you and never pressured you to take the oath expected of those who belong to this Order. It is now time, young Fulgar, to decide in whom you will place your trust . . . where your allegiances lie."

Fulgar remained still in his chair, stunned, and said nothing. The room remained silent for several long moments.

"You said you have a plan," said Silas. "What is it? What of this strange sword she carries?"

Fulgar and Jinx spent the next several minutes describing the sword of gold-infused Kelau diamond, the Zoar legends around its ability to neutralize powers of the Void, and their ultimate goal of using it to stab the mage. Fulgar was glad for Jinx's cooperation, for her trust. Once they had finished describing the plan, the room fell into a pensive silence.

"Is there any precedent for this?" asked Elcid. "Any evidence that it will work?"

Silas frowned at the floor, knitting his fingers in thought. "Well, I don't know of the Order ever trying any such thing, but there are countless energies that can be harnessed from the world's minerals and ores. That often comes down to the way the materials are processed. Not every powerful element is of the ethereal. Gold and diamond have particular merit. They are, after all, part of the very alloy which comprises the Light Ethereal from which our kingdom's Throne of Light is made."

"Perhaps this matter warrants the sword of giamond," said Elcid, glancing at Zirion.

"Maybe," Zirion replied, "but it's dangerous. We don't know that weapon's purity . . . and would that we had a Lumineer to wield it."

"And clearly we don't," said Silas.

Elcid pounded his fist on a small table beside him. "I am Lumineer enough to wield it!"

Zirion sighed. "Even for you, it is dangerous. This is why you must use it sparingly, only at times of true need, or the energies within the giamond could overwhelm you, despite your Aether affinity."

"The Kelau sword *will* work," said Jinx. "I've *seen* it work . . . against those cold, shadowy flames . . . against users of byrne."

"No." Everyone looked at Zirion.

"No?" said Fulgar. "What do you mean *no*? There is evidence of this sword's power against the Void. We have the accounts of the people of Zoar, who endured through the Shadow Age just like the people of Grandtrilia."

Behind the Mask

Zirion shook his head. "I am sorry, Fulgar, but I must ask that you and Jinx shelter yourselves from this matter. This mage carries the signs of one who follows a certain Void mysticism, steeped in mystery—yet, by Order accounts, extremely dangerous. I was blind to it before, but now I see it. The mage's methods of attack, his hunger to take etheretic captives alive—this all hearkens back to wars of the Shadow Age, when powerful forces of the Void were at work. If I'm right, you are not ready for this, not an enemy of this magnitude. It is too risky. I am not willing to gamble the safety of Warvonia and even the kingdom on the merits of a weapon we of the Order know nothing about—a non-ethereal one, at that."

Jinx sat up straight, defiance etched in her face. "Yeah, so, here's the thing: you don't really control me, so . . ."

"Jinx, please," said Fulgar, raising a hand. "Zirion, I am sorry for not telling you about this sooner. I meant no disrespect, and I ask you to understand that this matter is an extraordinarily personal one to me. Going at the mage could be my one and *only* chance to find and save Binny. And I know Jinx. She is of a sound mind and spirit. If she believes that this sword of Zoar legend has the ability to dispel this power of Void, then so do I."

Silence reigned in the room as Zirion seemed to consider Fulgar's words. "I cannot condone it," Zirion finally answered. "There is far too much danger, Fulgar, and far too much that you do not yet understand. As a true etheretic, facing an enemy of this magnitude while inexperienced is even *more* dangerous. He could very well have the ability to siphon and steal your Fielder energies, which would make him even more powerful. This is why you must stay back, at least until we can better assess what we're dealing with."

"There isn't *time* for that! And you can't expect me to sit back when the lives of those closest to me are at stake!"

Zirion drew a deep, resounding breath. "As lord of this conclave, I can, and that is precisely what I'm doing. It seems your personal attachments in this matter are a shroud over your judgment."

While Fulgar kept his voice calm, his heart raced, and a spark ignited inside him. He stood and faced Zirion. "I did not seek you out. It was *you* who brought me here! I am, in fact, grateful for that. However, it is worth asking why. *Why* did you bring me here? You don't have to answer. I know the reason, and it's not because I needed help. You found out that I was a Fielder. You wanted me here, a part of the Order, for my powers as a Fielder. Maybe it's to help me, maybe it's to help me reach my potential, maybe it's to keep me from hurting others, or ... maybe it's to *control* me, just one more person with etheretics added to the Order's roster, just as you stand there and try to control me now. In that light, are you really so different from this mage, who seeks me out for those same powers?"

In his peripheral vision, he saw Silas shake his head and Elcid stare unmoving at the floor. Zirion was a frightening sight to behold, the scowl of his large face boring into Fulgar, his shoulders rising and falling with deep, heavy breaths.

"Have you learned nothing," rumbled Zirion, "to deem our brotherhood and the vices of this Shadow fiend as one and the same? This is *precisely* why you are not ready."

"This is *my* fight!" Fulgar shouted. "You cannot deny me the closure I am due!"

"Elcid," said Zirion, "please assist Jinx back to the market square."

Jinx released a pronounced sigh. "Good riddance." She got up, Elcid approaching with the blindfold. "It's been real, Fulgar. Till next time."

As they exited, Elcid said, "Upon my return, we'll get some people on watch outside for signs of the mage." He gave a nod to Silas. "We need to discuss how we plan to deal with this."

"I'll find you later," Silas replied.

"And what do you mean to do?" Fulgar said to Zirion, huffing, fists tightly balled.

Behind the Mask

"An ethereal problem requires an ethereal solution. *We* will handle this. You, Fulgar, will remain in your chamber."

"He *is* a powerful Fielder," said Silas.

"Which adds to the danger. We will not allow this *thing* to capture him."

"Yes, I suppose there's *that*." Silas glanced at Fulgar. "However, that's not what I meant. I meant that, as a powerful Fielder, he could easily escape his room, and I'm the best one to ensure that doesn't happen."

Zirion sighed deeply. "I do not mean to make this place a prison, especially for our own ... but for this moment, I agree." With that, he exited the room.

Silas looked at Fulgar, and Fulgar glared back. "Alright, then," said Silas, "let's get you to your chamber."

"I'm perfectly capable of getting there myself," Fulgar shot back. "If you know what's good for you, Silas, you'll stay out of my way." He made for the room's exit.

As he passed the doorway, he heard Silas mutter, "Yes, that's the ticket."

Fulgar entered his chamber, where he would be alone with his thoughts and anger, and pulled the door shut with a slam that echoed throughout the safehouse.

Fulgar snapped awake.

It was the fourth hour of morning, still nighttime. As he remained on his back, staring up at the old, stony ceiling, his mind took off again.

This mage had been a bane in his life for months. Fulgar remembered the whip in Volk's hands the day he and Jinx fell from the gangster's ship. Volk had dabbled in Void powers well before the Shadow Mage revealed himself.

Fulgar remembered the mage's words. *Volk is no more. What stands before you is one much greater.* He wasn't sure if the mage had overtaken Volk or if the mage *was* Volk. By now, he didn't feel it much mattered. Either way, the mage had deemed Fulgar his primary target.

Twice Fulgar had escaped before the mage could take him. Both times, it had been the might of his own innate Fielder powers that saved him. Jinx had been there the second time, but she couldn't have taken the mage alone. It was little wonder the mage—and the Order, for that matter—wanted their grip on his abilities.

And then there was Binny. To Fulgar, all of this revolved around his long-lost friend.

If the mage was indeed Volk, it could only mean that he had used Binny and perhaps the talisman to acquire his power. If the mage wasn't Volk but some other device or manifestation of the Void, then Fulgar was confident Binny's talisman had been involved, and Volk had been behind it all.

Fulgar was tired of the questions, tired of never having the answers. He would not be the mage's gateway to powers of the Light. He was not some puppet of the Order's to be shut away when unwanted.

He was so much more, and he finally allowed himself to see it. Within him flowed energy of the ethereal, a light from beyond this world. He was the thing everyone wanted; with but the palm of his hand he could control the tide of this conflict. It was he who would decide, once and for all, who could be trusted and who must be stopped. The time for action was upon him.

He would not sit here in a bedchamber, becoming the very sort of pawn he and Binny had sworn they would never be. His significance was greater than Zirion's distrust. He was defined by more than the many pains that resided in his past. He was more than the totality of old failures and wounds. Wounds were beneath him—he had healed them in both creatures and people alike.

Behind the Mask

He was Fulgar Geth—Fulgar the healer—and it was finally time to find healing for himself.

Standing, he secured his sword belt and satchel over his black outfit. Zirion had left him without access to novidian, knowing it would've been a temptation for Fulgar to get involved.

What Zirion didn't know was what Fulgar still had in his pocket: Dolion's novidian card.

He took the pitcher from beside his in-room basin and used it to fill a canteen with water. Then he shouldered the strap, along with his satchel of supplies, and made for the door.

He exited his chamber and eased the door closed with a nigh imperceptible click. Silas was nowhere in sight. Silent were the passages of the safehouse, and he took great care to ensure his own steps were equally quiet. He veered toward the kitchen, where he grabbed a few rations of venison jerky, bread, and husked ground-cherries and stuffed them into his satchel. It would be enough to get him through the day's journey.

There was still no sign of Silas or anyone else. He accepted that as a gift of fortune and remembered an old line from Binny: "Fate sometimes takes, and sometimes it gives."

The excessively heavy door out to the streets of Old Bard gave him the most concern about being detected, but he managed to squeeze through, secure it, and scurry down the street without any stir from those of the Order.

Where the River Helkath ends—that was where the mage had told him to meet. It would mean traveling out of town to the west. From there, the land gradually inclined into the forest where he used to camp with Binny and Jinx. He knew a path through those woods, not heavily trodden but by far the most direct, although with the hills and uneven terrain it was bound to take most of the day. Other roads existed, used mostly for agricultural conveyance, but they veered in many directions to make the journey easier by horse-drawn wagons and were far more circuitous. Time was of the essence.

THE HEALER

Fulgar was highly attuned to any sign of motion as he skittered through town, wary of being followed by someone from the Order. Every shuffle, every drip of water, every pitter-patter of rodents in the alleys piqued his senses.

Dawn broke just as he exited Warvonia and entered the forest path. Despite the increasing daylight, his nerves cued him in to even the smallest noises of the forest, whether woodland chatter, the fall of a nut, or the rustle of leaves. He had to continuously reassure himself that no squirrel, rabbit, bird, or raccoon was trying to catch him from behind.

It was so peaceful in the forest. The air was full of the rustic, resinous scent of conifers mixed with the damp odor of decaying wood, all of it a fresh, welcome contrast to the stale, sour alleys of Old Bard. A light breeze conducted the green and blue canopy overhead in a steady whispering symphony of leaves in motion, harmonized by birdsong. An old Elohist priest had once told him, "Only the fool can look at the transcendent fabric of nature as existing by chance, when all the skill of art and industry cannot create a single acorn." He took this to heart with each deep, invigorating breath.

He did not allow himself to stop. Anything he ate or drank he took only while treading the woodland. It was a long, arduous walk, and with twilight came the swift depletion of light within the forest.

After a grueling trek of what must have been close to fifteen hours, he reached the other side of the forest, where the line of trees nestled against the farmlands that supplied crops throughout the Rocknee province. Here, rolling knolls and low-lying floodplains yielded rich pasturage all around where the River Helkath ended.

Fulgar expected the river's end to be just beyond the forest, where it was reduced to barely a stream at some times and a dry riverbed at others. Much of its volume disappeared into a network of subterranean caverns before its aboveground end, and overuse of its water had already caused the river to recede from within the forest. Many believed the river's flow would only continue to diminish. Some newer maps had already shortened its length. Wherever it ended today, Fulgar had a feeling he would know when he found the right place.

Fulgar set out into the fields, keeping his eyes peeled for whatever watery zone might comprise the visible end of the river. Only a faint glimmer of sunlight remained from below the western horizon ahead of him, giving way to soft, white nightglow from the rings in the southern sky.

The sharp crack of a stick back in the woods caused him to turn around. He drew his sword and glared at the forest long enough to dismiss it as harmless. Now was the time to be ready for anything.

He turned back toward the field, and then he saw them in the distance—a gathering of dark figures beside a watery valley which snaked off beyond sight. There was perhaps a dozen of them, too far away to make out any details, but he saw the mage clearly enough. His horned helmet was unmistakable, as was the purple-glowing whip that dangled from his hand.

As Fulgar crossed the field toward the water, he reached into his satchel for the comfort and strength of the novidian card. He had hoped to meet only the mage. It was no surprise that the mage hadn't come alone, but unfortunate nonetheless.

There was an uptick in the breeze as Fulgar neared, a penetrating chill that pushed away the warmth.

"Welcome, Fielder," said the mage. Even surrounded by open land, his thunderous voice had a menacing, echoing effect, as though one with the frigid wind.

"What is it you want?" asked Fulgar. He stopped about a spear's throw away. "Why did you summon me here?"

The mage returned a guttural chuckle. "Is it not obvious? Because of what you are. Your white energy blinds like fire to my eyes. It is an irresistible power."

"Then you want the power for your own purposes?" asked Fulgar. "I've spent months crawling out of the darkness. I am not about to plunge headfirst into Shadow."

The purple glow around the mage's whip pulsed in brightness. "With me, your power will become even greater."

"My power represents the Dynamism of the archastral Zophiel. I am a vessel of the Light. I will not be twisted and polluted by your Void sorcery."

The mage made a show of looking around. "Where is your archastral? Did the imparting of her so-called *power* not render her mortal? Did she not perish in her feeble attempt to stand against the might of Void, never again to return to this world? Zophiel is gone. It is the Shadow that is alive and well. It is the Shadow that shall dominate this land as in times of old!"

"That is but history twisted to suit your own desires. Lies and deception!"

"*Fool!*" hissed the mage. The word swirled in the air around Fulgar. "I offer you a renewed purpose. Are you too blinded by your precious Light to see it?"

Fulgar raised his sword. "I rather like my current purpose, actually."

The mage threw back his head in booming laughter. "Did you actually come here to *fight* me? Strong as you are, Fulgar Geth, you cannot hope to overpower me."

Fulgar's heart nearly stopped at the mention of his full name, but he tried to conceal his disquiet as he twirled his sword into a stance of readiness. "You will find I am quite relentless." He lowered his sword. "But I do not wish to fight you. I wish to understand. Were you once the man called Volk?"

"Volk is dead."

"You killed him? Or are you the one once called Volk?"

"I am more than Volk... more than you... more than any man."

"You are very arrogant," Fulgar replied. "Right now, it is only I who stands before you, but there are more—an entire Order, a brotherhood—united in principle under the Light of the ethereal. Against this, you will not prevail."

"Your *Order* is as nothing to the Following of *Khil-shi'dha* and the rise of Shadow. We will reap every ethereal." His voice was fraught with sinister glee. "We will have them *all*."

"You would have a world of misery and darkness, all for the sake of power for the forces you serve. And once you have it, what then? Will you have the gratitude of your *Following*? Will you find peace ruling a land fraught with suffering and destruction?"

"Here our banter ends. You have been given a choice—a choice to achieve what you once desired more than anything."

"You know nothing of my desires, but I do have one more question. There was another with Volk, a man named Binny. What became of him?"

"Ahh," the mage droned, a resonant sound such as would accompany a ground tremor. "Is this truly what motivated you to come? It is a souring meekness; yet, it is what your old friend suspected."

"Then . . . he lives?"

"Yes. I will take you to him. This, Fielder, is your last chance. You can join me in service to the Shadow willingly and partake of its might, or you can be taken by force."

"There is little will involved in coercion," Fulgar replied. "There is, of course, a third choice: you go away and leave me and Warvonia and its people in peace. You return Binny and any others you have taken. Keep the whims of your Following to yourselves."

The mage's ash-ringed eyes glared in darkness, followed by a deep, resonate growl that swirled around Fulgar as if he were standing with a bear in a cavern.

The mage turned to the gaggle of men and grimkins flanking his left and right. "Bind him."

Fulgar whipped the novidian card from his satchel in a flash of brightness. With a blast of white energy, he blew away two vermin

THE HEALER

coming from the left. To his right, he boomeranged the card through two more. They fell, screaming from fresh cuts as the card returned to Fulgar's hand.

Eight more—four men and four grimkins—charged toward him. He sent the card soaring in another blaze of light, but it was cut down by one of the grimkins.

Fulgar's palm tightened on the grip of his sword as he readied himself for a likely unwinnable duel against eight adversaries. And that was aside from the mage.

He lowered his sword.

"Wait!" he cried out. Everyone stopped. "If I agree to join you . . . will you leave Warvonia and my friends in peace?"

Silence reigned for long moments, such that even the rustle of wheatgrass in the breeze could be heard.

Finally, the mage spoke. "You have my word. I will no longer seek harvest within the streets of your town."

Of course, Fulgar knew better. He had no trust in the words of this mage, but he had hit an impasse. Coming here, he knew this outcome was possible, even likely. He still hated it. The mage had clearly set this trap, and Fulgar saw no way forward but to spring it.

If giving himself up was his one chance to get to Binny, then it had to be done. Once on the inside, perhaps he could find a way for them both to escape. He already suspected the mage underestimated the height of his power, if Fulgar could find the confidence to wield it. And if the mage continued to threaten Warvonia, then Zirion would have his chance to confront it without Fulgar, apparently just as he wanted.

Fulgar nodded to the mage. "Then I will go with you." He dropped his sword to the ground.

The eight minions strode forth and surrounded Fulgar. One burly grimkin with a hole in his beak pulled Fulgar's arms behind his back with the grip of an iron vice.

The mage cackled. "*I* will not seek harvest . . . but that will not stop others of our Following. Even you will join the cause of the Void, and when that time comes, you will do so quite willingly."

"You are an agent of deceit!" shouted Fulgar. "I might have known that your promises carried no worth."

"Come!" boomed the mage. "Let us show Fulgar the Fielder the true power yet present in this world."

"*Not so fast!*" shouted someone from behind. Fulgar closed his eyes in defeat. He knew that voice. It was Jinx, and by coming here she would be just as doomed as he was.

But she wasn't alone. As the eight around him scattered at the intrusion, he saw that Elcid and Silas had joined her. Silas wielded a staff of novidian, blazing white in the darkness, like an angelic boon pulled from the heavens.

Elcid, despite Zirion's warning of dangers Fulgar didn't quite understand, was armed with his golden sword of giamond. He'd come prepared for a challenge of ethereal significance.

The grimkin holding Fulgar's arms became distracted, and Fulgar pulled away, throwing himself to the ground and rolling toward his sword. He reclaimed it, sprang to his feet, and locked blades with the grimkin. His foe swung hard against him, but Fulgar's determination was renewed. He parried every blow through gritted teeth, overpowering the grimkin and backing him down. He swung low, opening a wide gash in the grimkin's thigh. With a squawk of pain and rage, the enemy dropped his cutlass and stumbled to the ground.

Jinx, Elcid, and Silas converged on Fulgar's position, staring down five remaining minions.

"Fulgar! Are you all right?" asked Jinx. She held the diamond sword before her, its surface gleaming like crystal glass under the white glow of the rings.

"I'm fine," he replied, "but you all are in grave danger."

"You seemed to be in far worse shape on your own," said Elcid. "You're a rather stubborn fool, Fulgar."

"If you were intent on doing something so rash as coming here," added Silas as they continued to stare down the remaining enemies, "did you seriously think we wouldn't join you?"

"But, Zirion—" started Fulgar.

"—is wise," Elcid cut in, "but he does not lord over our every decision."

"Perhaps this discussion is best saved for later," said Silas through his teeth.

"Just get me near that mage," said Jinx in a grim whisper. "I've got a special surprise for him."

Shouts and squawks filled the air as both small forces charged, and blades slammed together in combat.

Fulgar channeled his magnetism, skewing the swing of one man so he could punch him square in the face. Jinx dueled another with agility and the crystalline impacts of her diamond sword, cutting the foe down just as effectively as with any blade of steel.

One of the grimkins tossed Silas like a sack of onions. Elcid's opposition had a sword in each hand and swung with brute, fervid aggression, giving Elcid a clear struggle. Worse yet, a few of the fallen enemies had regained their footing and rejoined the battle despite their cuts and stumbles, adding to the chaos.

Fulgar noticed a faint glow of white in the grass near Jinx, where the novidian card had landed.

A loud crack rent the air with a flash of violet, rattling their senses like the crash of a thunderbolt. The mage stepped closer, looking especially tall and imposing, the whip held high like a viper ready to strike. As if without effort, purple plumes of darkfire ignited to the mage's left with a flick of his wrist.

"*Fulgar*," called Jinx in an urgent whisper. He turned to her and saw the novidian card in her hand. He began to reach for it, but she held up her other hand to stop him, shaking her head. He frowned in confusion. "Launch me," she said.

"What?" he whispered back.

Behind the Mask

"*Launch* me! You can do that, right?" In their time together, she had seen Fulgar magnetically propel objects in the same way she'd seen Dolion make his cards fly, but doing those things with a person attached was an entirely new spin on these moves.

"I . . . maybe. I don't know."

She held her diamond sword at the ready. "Go on!"

"You can't ask that of me, Jinx. I won't risk you like that."

"There's no time," she replied. "Just trust me, Fulgar. I can end this!"

Elcid and Silas were back to dueling foes. Elcid's sword blazed like a blade of pure sunlight burning in the night. When its yellow beam burned into his opponent's eyes, the man screamed and drew back, swinging his cutlass wildly and aimlessly in front of him. Elcid blocked a swing, landed a hard kick between the man's legs, smacked the cutlass from his grasp, and spun for a roundhouse kick to his face. Silas, with the novidian staff held horizontally before him, blocked every attack that came from two other adversaries.

The mage watched them all, likely seeking the best moment for a lethal display of power without damaging Fulgar, his prize; thus, Fulgar stayed close to the others.

Fulgar faced the mage and waved his sword in the air. "Mage of Shadow, you duplicitous wretch!" He stretched out his left arm and clasped Jinx's hand. The white around the novidian card in her other hand intensified. "*Here* is the power you seek!"

Channeled from the novidian held by Jinx all the way to the sword in Fulgar's grasp, a zap of white energy soared through the tip of Fulgar's blade. It missed the mage, exploding into the ground several feet to the side. Unexpected yet welcome to Fulgar, the blast extinguished the mage's darkfire. The mage recoiled from the impact.

"You missed," muttered Silas from behind.

Fulgar looked at Jinx. "No, I didn't."

He pushed his energy toward the novidian and stretched his

left wrist outward to evoke reverse magnetism. Jinx and the card launched forward. She landed beside the mage, twirled, and sliced into the mage's side with the diamond sword.

At first, the mage's cry was in the deep, powerful voice they had come to expect. After a moment, it reduced to the sound of a more ordinary man, groaning in rage and pain.

The mage thrust an arm toward the ground near Jinx. Black wind blew her back with an upheaval of dirt. She landed some twenty feet away, near Fulgar and the others. He ran to her and helped her up. She groaned with pain, one of her arms bleeding. The diamond sword was smeared with blood. Without any doubt, the strike had been true.

Fulgar yanked a paste consisting primarily of aloe and Cairn eucalyptus oil from his satchel, slathered it over Jinx's arm wound, and squeezed white energy into it.

"That's amazing," she said under her breath. "Thank you."

The mage's dark, lifeless eyes landed upon Fulgar. Fulgar looked back, anticipating any sign that the sword had lived up to its legendary expectations.

"You, Jinx, are more formidable than I ever gave you credit for," said the mage through a groan of pain, keeping a hand pressed firmly against his wound.

Jinx frowned. "How do you know my name? And your voice is familiar. *Why* is your voice familiar?"

Fulgar had recognized the same thing. But it couldn't be. It was impossible.

Still, the word escaped his mouth before he could even think. "Binny?"

All the fighting stopped, and any foes still conscious backed away, following their instincts to distance themselves as this situation unfolded.

The mage removed the horned helmet, and Fulgar finally saw the full face that existed behind the mask. Jinx stifled a gasp.

Behind the Mask

Although haggard and pallid, with ashen circles around his eyes, the mage's face was unmistakable.

"Binny," said Fulgar, his voice cracking. "How can it be?"

"I did it, old mate," Binny replied. "I got what you and I always wanted. Power. Raw, true power that no one can touch. The stories about the talisman were true. Now, I am like a god. Nothing can stop me. Nothing can stop the Shadow. *That* is the future, Fulgar. It is foretold. It is there, in the whispers of the mountain, a spiritual force that carries on through all who come into the Following. And the reward?" He laughed. "Everything! We shall have *everything*."

Fulgar felt like falling to the ground, drained of all strength. "Binny, *this* is not what we wanted. We wanted to live in peace, undisturbed and uncontrolled. This—what you've become—is something completely different."

Binny's blackened eyes flashed, his face twisted by horrible anger. "Do *not* deny the power we *both* sought!" He grunted a laugh, suddenly calmer. "I suppose I shouldn't expect you to understand. You always had power for yourself, even if below your true potential. It was there, Fulgar—the shrine, the origin of the talisman. That was where the transformation happened, where my devotion to the Void was sealed. That was where I slew Volk, who was worthy of nothing. I had used him, you see. After you and *minx* here got together, it was clear your focus had wavered."

"*Used* him?" asked Fulgar, his mind increasingly foggy. "You were captured and taken away on his ship . . ."

Binny grinned wickedly. "All part of the plan—the plan to get you both out of my quest for the shrine. That's what you wanted. Out. I knew it, even if you did not. And, at the time, it was for the best. You'd lost your desire, your dedication to our cause. So, what I did, Fulgar . . . I did it for you."

"I . . . I agonized over the loss of you for *months*, Binny! It tore me apart!" He glanced at Jinx. "Both of us!"

"And you think it was easy for *me*? We had a *vision*, Fulgar.

THE HEALER

A *future*! Day in and day out, we knew what we wanted. We were going to get there *together*! It was *you* who faltered, who started questioning everything we had worked for. So, I seized the chance. I learned that Volk knew where to find the shrine—the one in that old drawing we found—and I used him to get me there. He thought he might share in the power promised to me—the beholder of the talisman—but it was not for him. I gained favor with the spiritual forces there, and my strength only grows. Now, Fulgar, I offer the same to you, to increase the power you already have. We can finally both have what we set out for. Together, we will be at the height of leadership under the rising dominance of Shadow, under the inevitable kingdom to come."

Fulgar shook his head. "This is not you talking, Binny. Please . . ."

"Void accepts all. Bloodline does not matter—"

"You mean it *corrupts* all."

"You do not have to be *born* with special blood to embrace the powers of Void, but as a Fielder—yes, I've learned of etheretics—you can be that and *more*."

Amidst shallow breaths of distress, Fulgar could not believe what he was hearing, what his friend had been willing to become. "Binny . . . our goals were misguided. We could never have imagined the cost of achieving what we sought. I could scarcely even grasp the reality of it. Look at what has happened to you! This is not freedom! You are slave to the will of some insidious force that has succeeded in only one thing: *deceit,* for the prize of your allegiance. Binny, I beg you, come with us. You can yet be saved."

"No," Binny said, and there was a subtle flash in the purple glow of his whip. That flash pulsed, leaving the whip and coursing through its handle. It swam through Binny's arm, like fish through a stream, and gathered in his side, where the diamond sword had lashed him. It swirled over the spot, brightened as it whorled with blackness, and melted into the mage's body. When he spoke again, his voice had regained its thunderous resonance. "I *am* saved!"

Binny placed the horned helm back on his head. He raised the whip. "And, as ever, it is *you* standing in the way!" His devilish gaze was now aimed at Jinx.

"Fulgar!" called Silas. He tossed the novidian staff, and Fulgar caught it just as Binny cracked his whip.

A violet, fiery orb soared toward Jinx.

Fulgar lunged ahead of her, swung the staff in a radiant blur, and dissipated the orb midair. "Binny, no!" he yelled. "Please!"

The whip cracked again, and by the black magic Binny had succumbed to, its length extended, stretching the full distance to Fulgar. Its thong coiled around the novidian staff with a surge of violet tines of energy.

The novidian's glow disappeared, and Fulgar felt an intense vibration as he struggled to keep his hands on the staff. As the jolts intensified, the cold, dark energy crawled into his arms and bit in a hundred tiny places like frostbite delivered by fire ants.

Fulgar cried out in pain as a deathly chill pulsed through his veins. He heard the voices of his friends shouting all around, their calls as though from a great distance.

Jinx tried to cut the whip, but the energy pushed against her strikes and sent the diamond sword flying from her grasp.

As he held tight to the staff, Fulgar realized that he couldn't let go even if he wanted. The magnetism of his Fielder energy was engaged, although invoking it was not his doing. Something else was at work, and by the time realization dawned on Fulgar, it was too late. White Fielder energy flowed from Fulgar's body, through the staff and into the whip, where it intertwined with the violet Void energy and streamed into Binny.

Binny was stealing Fulgar's power.

Elcid severed the whip with his golden sword and cut off the energetic current. Fulgar barely had a chance to gasp before a blast of white-hot energy struck him like sideways lightning. His body convulsed and crumpled to the ground.

He raised his head enough to see his friends in action. Silas had claimed the novidian card from Jinx and used it to land a gash in Binny's shoulder. Elcid burned into the mage's chest with the golden light which beamed from his sword.

"No," Fulgar said weakly to the dirt. "Binny..."

Binny took a deep breath, seeming to draw in strength, and then blasted Elcid and Silas with swift, precise gusts of dark winds. Fulgar's comrades fell to the ground, their attacks neutralized.

"*Fulgar!*" boomed the mage. "Sooner or later, you *will* embrace the gift of the Void. I will not abandon you to the whims of others ... to the false power of the Light! I will not rest, mate, until you are once again at my side!"

Then he retreated across the fields to the northwest, minions scrambling and hobbling after him. Soon, they were gone, and all was still.

Fulgar pulled himself to his knees, his hands covering his face and his body wracked by wave upon wave of unbridled sobbing.

chapter 9
A WHISPER OF THE PAST
7/10/3178 P.A.

F ulgar opened his eyes the next morning to dusty, cobwebbed rafters of old, grayed wood. He lay atop a mattress, stripped of his black outer clothes in favor of his smallclothes—a thin white undershirt and drawers. Jinx was beside him, still wearing her white shirt and red skirt, her boots laid upon the floor. Two more beds, which had been used by Silas and Elcid, were vacant.

Jinx turned over and blinked awake. "Good morning," she said sweetly. "How are you feeling?"

"Chipper as a squirrel in a fox's mouth," he moaned. "Where are the others?"

"Down in the taproom," Jinx replied. "They left some time ago."

"Not you, though? Are you not hungry?"

She treated him to his favorite grin. "I'm fine. Quite comfortable, actually."

He took a long moment just to stare back at her. He squeezed her hand. "Thank you . . . for being here with me."

The night before, they had followed the edge of farmers' crofts in a generally northward direction until reaching the nearest merchant lane. That allowed them to find the quaint and rustic Prickly Trout Inn and Tavern, where they booked a large upper room.

"I have no money for this," Fulgar had muttered upon arriving to the inn.

"We've got it covered," Silas replied.

Fulgar remembered with glaring clarity the moment he learned that Binny was the Shadow Mage. Very little else had been discussed on the journey. Fulgar's mind was burdened by two overwhelming realities: Binny was the mage... and Jinx's diamond sword had indeed had no effect on the Void powers inflicting him. In his mind's eye, he saw Zirion glaring in reproof.

Fulgar knew he'd been a mess as they made their way to the inn, recalling childhood memories with Binny, denying what their eyes and ears had just witnessed, and venturing in and out of curse-filled tirades and fits of self-pity. Jinx had been there to comfort him every step, all the way to their room, until Fulgar calmed enough to find rest.

Now, as Fulgar emerged from sleep, his mental and emotional states had leveled enough for him to better manage the gravity of last night's revelations. As he looked at Jinx, her bare legs next to his, he found himself caught in a strange place between the trauma of his old friend succumbing to Shadow and the exhilaration of being with the woman he loved.

The door swung open, and Silas stepped halfway inside. "Elcid just hitched us a lift with a merchant back to Warvonia. He's loading up now." He left, pulling the door closed.

"Looks like we'd better get moving," said Jinx. She swung herself over the side of the bed and reached for her boots.

Fulgar sighed, lamenting the loss of more time alone with Jinx. "It appears that way."

Looking down at him, she smirked, making him certain she could read his thoughts. She bent down and kissed his forehead. "See you downstairs."

A Whisper of the Past

Fulgar quickly dressed and checked that Dolion's novidian card was still safely inside his satchel. Jinx had managed to hold on to it throughout last night's debacle and, once on their way, slipped it back to Fulgar. Satisfied he had everything, he left the room.

Clinking glasses and the scooting of chairs and barstools across a wooden floor greeted Fulgar as he descended the stairs. The smells of pan-fried meats and grilled vegetables wafted into his nostrils, and hunger rumbled in his belly.

Elcid tossed a small haversack at his chest. "You can eat on the way. We leave now." He made for the exit.

Fulgar looked down at the sack in his arms and opened the flap. Boiled potatoes, two small apples, warm millet bread, and a strip of salted jerky. He followed Elcid outside.

Jinx and Silas already sat in the open-air merchant wagon, accompanied by crates of cabbages, onions, carrots, and peppers and barrels of sugar, oats, barley, and grains. These articles had been shoved aside to create a thin sliver of space in the wagon's back and center. They would be riding all day on a hard, wooden, uncovered surface littered with wheat chaff and wilted greens.

"Welcome aboard!" greeted Jinx through a mouthful of bread from her own pack.

Fulgar pulled himself into the wagon, whilst Elcid stood to the side, conversing with the merchant. "I don't much fancy being in another wagon," Fulgar said, "but I'll admit I'm also far too drained to hike back."

Elcid joined them a few minutes later. "I feel I should tell you," said Fulgar, "that I don't have money for this."

"Yes, we know," Elcid replied as he hoisted himself. "We've got it covered."

The merchant, a gaunt man with a red face covered in graying stubble, checked over his cargo and hopped into the driver's seat without a word. A short time later, he reined his two horses into motion, and they were underway.

THE HEALER

The ride was quiet for a while. Everyone munched on their food from the inn to the calming vibrations of the wagon's movement and the clopping of horse hooves.

Silas, after a long draft of water from his canteen, was the first to break their silence. "You know, Fulgar, it was quite the irk and pain for three of us to track you for an entire day without being detected."

"That's how good we are!" added Jinx.

"Why didn't you reveal yourselves sooner?" asked Fulgar.

Elcid gulped down the last of his bread. "You seemed intent on facing the mage yourself, which was what he wanted anyway. We decided it best to let events play out and only interfere if we saw the need."

"Clearly we saw the need," said Silas.

Fulgar stared in thought at an old, wilted carrot green on the wagon bed. "How did you know to follow me? I was certain I had left the safehouse undetected."

"Oh please, Fulgar," Jinx replied, waving a pear as she spoke. "I knew even before I left that you were going to see that mage, even if it meant going alone. And *that* I simply couldn't allow." She nodded toward Elcid. "I convinced *him* of as much when he escorted me back to the market square, and I insisted I would be back to the safehouse later. That's just what I did."

"For my part," said Silas, "I volunteered to watch your chamber. I did not feel it right to cut you out, Fulgar, Zirion's talk of dangers be damned. Later, after I spoke with Elcid, we tried to ensure your expected exit would be unhindered."

Fulgar chuckled with a glance at Silas. "So, Jinx *did* find the safehouse."

"*And* got in," she added.

"Elcid *let* you in," replied Silas. "That's not the same as *getting* in."

Jinx smirked. "Just proves that all you need is someone on the inside."

"Still," said Fulgar, "as much as I appreciate the rescue, I fear things could now be worse. If you would've allowed Binny to take me, it might have satiated him. Now he will be all the more determined."

"And if he had taken you, he'd be all the more dangerous," said Elcid.

Fulgar shook his head, feeling frustrated in his ignorance. "But what does that even *mean*? Because he might use me? I want to *save* Binny from this darkness. I would never further encourage it ... never give in, as he did, to the desires of this Following he speaks of."

Elcid and Silas shared a look.

"Fulgar," said Silas, "if he and others of this Following are or become powerful enough in the Void, you might not have a choice. This alludes to the danger Zirion warned about. If one is powerful enough in the Void—a part of the darkest, most insidious devotions under Shadow—then you are likely to be sorely overpowered. There are accounts that lead us to believe it is possible for these Creepers—users of Void—to overtake and control people who have etheretic power."

"Can you begin to see the danger?" followed Elcid. Fulgar looked at him. "You, as a Fielder, could be consumed by Void and controlled by it, even against your will. Your powers would be joined to theirs, and you would effectively be their pawn."

"So, you see," said Silas, "the danger is not merely to yourself but to ... well, *everyone*."

Fulgar felt a shiver pulse through his veins. Zirion had been right in so many ways. Not only about the diamond sword's ineffectiveness but also in Fulgar's true misunderstanding of the stakes.

"What, then, can be done?" asked Fulgar.

"We need to speak with Zirion," Elcid replied, "and we must do so before your old friend comes to levy his full wrath upon Warvonia."

Fulgar sighed. "I was afraid you'd say that."

THE HEALER

Disinterested in deviating from his scheduled route, the merchant dropped them off in the Market Square district.

"We'll make do, if that's the best we can get," Elcid told the merchant, knowing full well they wouldn't have led the merchant to the vicinity of the safehouse anyway. Fulgar suspected this comment was to forestall the merchant's expectations for extra lyra.

While in the market area, they acquired a few morsels of food—Silas and Elcid covering the tab—and completed their journey to the Order's door in Old Bard. This time, no one bothered to blindfold Jinx.

They sat in the lounge, Zirion looming over them like an old giant roastwood tree whilst they described their encounter with Binny the Shadow Mage.

For long moments, Zirion stood still, scratching his beard and breathing loudly. His wordless standing transitioned to wordless pacing. Fulgar and the others awaited their leader's response in equal silence, hoping for words of wisdom above reprimand.

Zirion finally stopped pacing. "There are many things I would say, many things that I'm sure would go unheeded. Now we face a precarious time, a threat the likes of which have not been seen since before the founding of this kingdom. It is a fight we of the Order cannot ignore, although I fear we are woefully unprepared for it."

Jinx shook her head wearily. "I was so sure the Zoar legends were true and this sword would work."

"Within many legends are elements of truth," said Zirion, "but not every legend is true. Some have the evidence of continuity—accounts in alignment with historical events that we can track and find evidence for. Such is the case with ethereals. We of the Order, therefore, know there is at least one legend in which we can put our

A Whisper of the Past

trust: the legend of the Heroes of Time."

Elcid slapped his knee. "We *must* contact other conclaves of the Order. We need true ethereal weapons, such as those of legend, from our ancient armories."

"Time is too short," Zirion replied. "The nearest conclaves are in Stonehaven and Miskunn, if our old register is still accurate, and we do not know if they house any of the weapons of legend."

Fulgar groaned. "It seems the *entire* Order is woefully unprepared for such a conflict."

"You must remember, Fulgar, that the Order has not acted in a military capacity since the time of the Foundational War. Over the centuries since, we have acted more as stewards and protectors, our operations adapted to times of long-standing peace. We have warriors among us, but we are not an army."

Jinx snorted a laugh. "Probably the way the king wants it. Can't have competing armies now, can we?"

Silas cleared his throat. "It's a system in dire need of improvement. Getting multiple Order conclaves to coordinate is more like turning a three-masted ship than a rowboat. Inventories across the Order, as well as any roster of known persons with etheretics, are centralized near the Palace—none of us could access those any sooner than a month, at best."

The haze of desperation was beginning to give Fulgar a headache. "Then ... should we seek assistance from more local forces? Perhaps involve the Royal Guard?" Given his past with the authorities, the very suggestion made his stomach churn.

Zirion shook his head. "They are much less equipped for such a matter."

"Still," said Elcid, "there can be strength in numbers. I have friends in the Guard that I could engage."

"What have we got, then?" asked Silas, ticking his fingers. "A giamond sword with no Lumineer to wield it ... a diamond-and-gold sword of foreign legend which lacks ethereal might ... a scant amount of novidian ... and *us*, with ethereal affinities likely no match for that mage."

"And the Guard," said Elcid. "That could help disperse the mage's lackeys."

"Our ultimate problem is still the mage," said Zirion.

Fulgar raised a finger. "Binny is like me in one respect: He lacks experience. Surely there are bounds to what he can do."

"He is of a strength beyond his own," replied Zirion. "He should not be underestimated. We must remember that an ethereal problem requires an ethereal solution."

"And yet," replied Elcid, "what we have for ethereals is limited."

Fulgar looked around at everyone. Here they were, in a safehouse of the Order, and they had not even considered what might be right underneath them. "What *do* we have in our vaults? Could there be anything of use?"

Zirion pulled at his beard in thought. "Most of what we have here are unfinished novidian ore and records spanning histories from both Tuscawny and Korangar, along with various relics and the weapons you have already seen. I can't think of anything else that could help us now. There could be more that I'm unaware of."

"How could you not *know*?" asked Jinx.

"Over the centuries," replied Silas, "high-ranking Order and kingdom officials have been known to store valuable artifacts and materials in the vaults of different safehouses. Records of such items, as with those of the centralized inventories, can only be found near the Palace. They are kept even from conclave masters as a safeguard against temptation and unauthorized disclosure."

"This places much control in the hands of one branch—*overmuch* control, if you ask me," said Elcid, an acrid edge in his voice. "We could be sitting on the last of elder yew or celestialite and wouldn't even know it!"

"Careful of your tongue," Zirion warned. "Meetings do happen among conclave leaders, some even with our highest-ranking members in Sharm. While we might house a very few secret items right here in Warvonia, we are carefully aligned on other important truths about our kingdom and the world around us. When they tell me the First Ethereal is extinct, I must believe it, and I must take heart that the remaining ethereals have come in its wake."

Elcid's face reflected a hint of shame, an unusual look for him. "My apologies. I do not mean to question our Order's integrity. It is difficult to feel ill-prepared at a time such as this."

"And I share your discomfort," Zirion replied. "But we must remember that one purpose of our safeguards is to protect against the hasty usage and exposure of that which we protect. We may already have what we need . . . if we act with proper wisdom and skill."

"Are there more of these ethereals we could find somewhere besides your armories?" asked Jinx. "A hidden stash somewhere off-record? You guys protect this stuff for a living. Surely you have more than just bits of novidian and that sunlight sword."

Silas frowned. "Even *that* much, madam, is priceless."

"Of course, more ethereals exist," said Zirion. "Giamond, the Light Ethereal, is beyond our capacity to properly wield. Would that we could, as it might be our most potent weapon against a foe such as this. It is, in fact, an alloy of diamond, gold, and novidian."

Fulgar rubbed at his chin in deep concentration, recalling his studies of past conflicts involving ethereal energies. "The Strike of Faith," he said. "The strike of giamond at the heart, which in the past was recorded to have removed the Void's curses." He waved his arm toward Elcid. "We have a giamond weapon, do we not?"

"I do not believe it is pure," Zirion answered, "and the Strike of Faith required a true Lumineer to harness the full ethereal energy of the giamond. Otherwise, to attempt it might kill the wielder . . . or the one struck . . . or both."

Jinx shifted excitedly in her chair. "Ironic that my sword plus novidian equals . . . giamond, you call it?"

"Novidian," Zirion went on, "is still the Pure Ethereal, and I believe it can yet prevail . . . in the hands of a true Fielder."

Everyone looked at Fulgar.

Fulgar had trouble finding the same optimism. "I have already used novidian twice against the mage. It allowed me to escape, but it seemed to have little more than a glancing effect. It has done nothing to reduce his power."

"You still lack discipline," said Elcid. "You must learn to focus the energy within you, feed it through your confidence and benevolence."

Jinx arched an eyebrow. "Benevolence?"

"Emotional state is critical," Zirion replied. "Confidence—in yourself, in your actions, in your purpose—is where mastery begins."

"We mustn't kid ourselves," said Elcid. "Fulgar is the true weapon we need here. We must do everything to amplify his strength and give him the opportunity to strike true."

"Dolion!" Jinx perked. "He's another Fielder. That could help, right?"

"Fulgar's strength is easily double that of Dolion's," said Silas.

Fulgar shook his head. He barely understood the power within him and feared the others were starting to see him as a sort of panacea. That wasn't what Fulgar saw. "How can you possibly say that, Silas? I have done nothing to warrant that assessment."

Silas's brow lifted. "I have seen how naturally it comes to you. Significant strength, sometimes even by accident. As Elcid says, you simply need to learn how to control it."

"The most impressive thing I've done is trip some locks."

Silas sat up straight and slapped the arms of his chair. "Ah! But *that* alone shows just how well you *can* control it."

"Maybe Fulgar and Dolion can combine strengths," said Jinx, bouncy in her seat.

Elcid's intense stare landed on her. "That is yet another Fielder we must ensure the mage does not capture and use against us. I agree with you, Jinx, about Dolion's potential usefulness, but we must be cautious."

"He won't get Dolion," said Jinx. "We'll be sure of that."

Fulgar smiled at Jinx's words. If anyone had an abundance of confidence, it was her. *She should be the strongest etheretic among us,* thought Fulgar, *rather than me.*

"Will he join with us willingly?" asked Zirion.

Jinx nodded. "I'll talk to him. I'm sure he wouldn't miss this. Besides, I have something he wants, and he won't get it until I'm satisfied Tuscawny is freed of the mage." She shared a glance with Fulgar, who knew she referred to the sword of Kelau diamond.

"Good... good," replied Zirion, staring down in thought. "The source of the Shadow Mage's power still concerns me. This Following—that of *Khil-shi'dha*—is mysterious, yet the very name sends a ripple of fear throughout the pages of history."

"Korangar's history," Silas pointed out. "The weight of that depends on how much we can trust the accounts of the Sovereign Tracts of Kor—the sidelined 'Third Faction' of the Foundational War. Nothing about this Following is echoed in the accords of Tuscawny, not that I've ever seen."

"It's true," Zirion replied, "that even many of the Order disregard such accounts as vestiges of Korangar's foundation myths. But that is not the stance of Korangar's scholars. They regard the chronicles of Lord Zictavion with deep reverence—a warning for those who would pay attention. Usually these writings are dismissed by the Order, as if they exist only to place Tuscawny in a darker light, but I feel there is wisdom in heeding all points of view."

Jinx lifted her head, which had been resting on her fist. "I'm sorry, but are we still looking for solutions, or are we debating who's kept the best records?"

"Indeed," said Elcid. "Whatever the following behind this Creeper, we must gather all the strength we have to stand against it."

Silas gave Fulgar a solemn look and pointed at him. "Fulgar, allow me to be blunt. By all measures, *you* are the strongest among us in etheretics. Your abilities will be crucial to destroying this mage."

"We'll draw the enemy away from Warvonia," said Elcid. "Lower the danger to civilians. This will provide Fulgar the best opportunity to move against the mage and end it."

Zirion nodded. "It will take a well-coordinated offensive to catch the mage at his most vulnerable with the height of your powers."

Fulgar raised his hands for silence. "Wait, please! You all speak of destroying and killing the mage. That is not my intention. This mage is my childhood friend! I will use the height of my power, yes . . . but it will not be to destroy Binny. It will be to *heal* Binny—to save him from the darkness that has taken hold."

Silas frowned. "This is the same best friend that knocked you two off the deck of a ship so that he could work with a gangster in pursuit of an ultimate power, right?"

Jinx shrugged. "Well, anything sounds bad when you say it like *that*. And you might be right"—she hooked her arm in Fulgar's—"but I know where Fulgar's coming from on this one. We should save him, if we can."

"You both need to understand," said Elcid, "the very real possibility that your friend might be beyond saving. Many more lives than yours depend on your ability to recognize this." He gave Fulgar a hard, searching look. "When the time comes to do what must be done, will you be able to see it through?"

Fulgar returned the stare, his stomach feeling sour. "You mean . . . to kill Binny?"

"If that is what must be done."

Fulgar blinked wildly, staring at the floor. The weight of the situation was bearing down on him—a great, heavy burden that forced him to reflect on the possibility of killing the friend he'd

A Whisper of the Past

shared everything with since childhood. Even now, Binny was being an idealist. He didn't want to destroy Fulgar. He wanted Fulgar to join him—to share in what he now believed to be so important—much like he always had. Fulgar needed to break through that wall somehow.

He could now see what, in the past, they'd both been blinded to. In Binny's fervent quest to never be controlled by others, he had become slave to forces much more dangerous than those he had tried to avoid—first to the lure of the ancient talisman, then to the enticing idea that nothing was more important than the power the talisman could access, and finally to the forces behind the Shadow Following, all three of them shrouded in deception. He had become a puppet of Void mysticism, something so much worse than being controlled by guilders could ever have been.

Fulgar needed to show Binny there was a better way to live—that he could still be fulfilled and happy and at peace, without the powers he clung to. That he could still be redeemed by the Light.

But what if he refused? What if it truly was too late?

"I . . ." Fulgar struggled to find the words he knew Elcid wanted to hear. "I . . ." He shook his head. "Excuse me, please. I need some time to reflect."

As everyone watched in silence, Fulgar rose and left the lounge.

Fulgar knelt, eyes shut tight, before an altar of the Triad. Adorning the altar was a beautiful depiction of the world's three primary races—humans, grimkins, and anthropods—in harmony and grace. It was an Elohist portrayal of selflessness, a tribute to the bygone prophet Aholiah, recorded to have suffered three sinless lives, three deaths, and three resurrections, atoning for the inherent wickedness in all three races.

Fulgar was in the Cathedral of Saint Barnabas, located just

beyond the limits of Old Bard. The sanctuary was a haven of centuries-old statues, mosaics, and tapestries. Spicy incense hung in the air, and tall bronze candelabra lined the aisles of the sanctuary with small flickering candles kept lit and maintained by the acolyte on duty.

Fulgar raised his head and blinked away tears. He looked upon the kindly face of Aholiah in His human form, believed to be a surrogate of Eloh, one who walked the world among creation in love, grace, and compassion.

"Please," he said, barely a whisper. "Please, dear Eloh . . . I am too weak . . . too inadequate to bear the weight of this task."

He closed his eyes again. He desperately wanted to save Binny, but the logical side of his brain sensed that Elcid was right. There might be no choice but to destroy Binny, and it was a decision Fulgar would have to make in the heat of confrontation.

"Am I truly the one for this? Because I would sooner renounce the Order, everything I've learned, and leave this conflict for someone else to take this mantle from me. I beg you, please, give me a sign."

Subtle sounds—the slow drip of water, the electric hum of flocalcite light fixtures, even the whispering flutter of candleflames—resonated throughout the stillness of the sanctuary. All of it coalesced into a single, resounding truth.

Fulgar was completely and utterly alone.

Feeling defeated and empty, he lowered his head and stared at the tear-splashed stones beneath him. Alone. What he did next was his decision to make. No path would be forced upon him.

He could choose now to run away from everything and never look back. That felt the easiest path, probably one Fulgar would've taken at some point in his past. While it was a choice, Fulgar knew it was not an option, not now.

Fulgar had become Binny's next obsession, and Fulgar knew what lengths Binny would go through to get what he wanted. He

A Whisper of the Past

knew that now more than ever. No matter where Fulgar went, Binny would seek him.

Binny's corruption had been a slow one. Fulgar couldn't have seen it back then, back when he and Binny would've followed the talisman's call to the ends of the world. But it was there all along—that Void energy—polluting and deceiving Binny a little more every day, feeding from Binny's innermost desires, until Binny finally reached its shrine and the grip of Void squeezed ever tighter.

Now Binny was the feared Shadow Mage, committed to destruction of anything and anyplace, if that's what it took to get to Fulgar and his Fielder etheretics. And he wouldn't stop there. There would always be another pursuit—another person with power desired by Binny and the Void that enslaved him.

Fulgar, because of the very power Binny sought, was the only one who could stop him.

"I can't do it," he whispered. He looked up again at the altar. "Do you *hear* me? *I can't do it!*" The echo of his anguish carried throughout the emptiness and dissolved into oblivion.

His body shook, wracked by rage and desperation.

"Why should it be me? Why should such power fall upon my shoulders for it only to bring anguish and sorrow upon me?"

All he heard were the background drips, hums, and flickers of the cathedral.

"Please," he cried, weakened, shaking his head. "Please. You must answer me. Must this burden truly fall on me? Is there not yet hope?"

Complete silence surrounded him. It enveloped the drips, hums, and flickers of before, a stillness so absolute that even Fulgar's breaths were drawn into it.

A tiny whisper, the faintest brush of air, fluttered toward him.

Looking around, Fulgar found the source. His mouth fell open in wonderment. A butterfly of pure white beat its wings in gradual descent.

It landed in front of Fulgar.

He stared at it in sheer awe. Its perfect whiteness enamored him like the glow of novidian. Only twice before had he ever seen a butterfly such as this. First, in his childhood, the butterfly needed healing—a healing by faith. The second time, Fulgar's spirit needed healing—a rediscovery of faith. And now, just perhaps, by the exertion of faith, there was yet another to be healed.

Binny.

Healing could come to Binny by freeing him of the Void's grip. Even if that meant death to his corporeal body, it would be better than a life spiraling ever deeper into darkness. Fulgar would do all he could to save Binny's life, but his mortal life was not what mattered the most. It was his soul, and the lives and souls of those he endangered.

The butterfly flew away, its purpose achieved, and Fulgar stood.

Behind him, the heavy entrance door opened and closed with a deep echo. Fulgar turned to see Silas approaching. In his arms was a long, slender object in leather wrapping.

Wordless, Silas walked the length of the sanctuary, clomps echoing with each step. He came near to Fulgar and stopped.

"In devotion to protecting the ethereals and the sacred truths of our realm," said Silas, "it is not unusual for one to find purpose in one's efforts. Sometimes . . . you find those efforts are not for the purpose you originally thought."

He unwrapped the object. It was the novidian anelace, fully forged and refined, the most beautiful weapon Fulgar had ever seen. Its starlight pinpoints dazzled through a smooth, shiny sheen, the double-edged blade tapered with perfection to a point that seemed fit to pierce the night sky itself.

"As I finished this," Silas continued, "I came to realize that I was not making it for me or even for the Order." He extended it to Fulgar. "This weapon was always meant for you."

Fulgar took it by the grip, and it felt perfect in his hand. The

A Whisper of the Past

warm energy flowed within him, channeled and amplified by the anelace. A powerfully bright, white glow surrounded the weapon.

"I always felt my connection to this blade," said Fulgar. "When I lost it, for a time, it was as if I had lost a part of myself."

"Fulgar, one thing more. I know we in the Order can be set in our ways, and that can be difficult to trust. Eloh knows I have felt the same way myself before, but Elcid and Zirion are like the brothers I never had... and now you, Fulgar... you are among them. Whether or not you ever take your oath with the Order, you belong as one of us."

Fulgar lowered the weapon and looked at Silas. He was touched by Silas's words, nearly to the point of tears. Anything resembling a family connection was something he had lacked for so long that he had almost forgotten how it was supposed to feel. "That means more than you know, Silas. Thank you."

Silas returned a nod. "Now it's time to put that anelace to use."

"Know that I *will* try to save him, Silas," Fulgar replied, "but I will do what must be done."

"And know that we will be right there with you."

Together, they left the cathedral.

That same night, Fulgar came upon Zirion within the winding halls of the Order's safehouse. Zirion saw the anelace in Fulgar's grasp.

"Did Silas give it to you?" he asked.

"Yes," Fulgar replied.

"I believed he would, for it is connected to you. You are, for this point in the span of time, its rightful owner." He paused, looking over Fulgar, his eyes shining with something that could have been pride. "You are indeed of the Order, Fulgar, in the most honorable sense, for you are ordained as an ethereal protector. We all stand behind you."

THE HEALER

Fulgar swelled with a sureness unlike any he had experienced before. "To be of the Order is an honor above what my deeds in life deserve, and you have my thanks. Even more than that, Zirion, I am a *healer* . . . and, when it comes to Binny, healing is exactly what I intend to do."

chapter 10
LEGENDS COLLIDE
7/13/3178 P.A.

F ulgar paced about the taproom of the Prickly Trout Inn and Tavern, his anxiety rising by the minute.

Elcid had designated this and two other inns as lookout posts, all of them along the rural trade routes to Warvonia but well beyond the town itself. This gave them eyes across a broad expanse of land to watch for any movement from the mage and his followers.

Over the course of a few days, Elcid had managed to mobilize a company of the Royal Guard, the primary knights of the king's army, and station them throughout the inns. Some from among these soldiers further directed platoons of the town's localized Civic Force, who stood sentry at various posts throughout the streets of Warvonia, all of them on high alert for unusual activity of the sorcerous kind. Whether Royal or Civic, every one of them was eager for a plan of action against the mage and his troublesome forces.

Jinx had successfully recruited Dolion to their cause. Although Dolion proclaimed concern for Warvonia's well-being, Fulgar and Jinx knew he really wanted the gold-diamond sword of Zoar renown. Jinx had promised to give it up to reward his involvement, even if Fulgar thought the price rather high. Worthwhile or not, Dolion was now part of the plan, fully evidenced as he lingered about the taproom giving side-eyes to unfinished mugs.

The strategy was twofold: first to intercept Binny's forces, potentially from multiple fronts, and second to keep the fighting outside of Warvonia, so that risk to civilians and damage to the town would be minimized.

Despite their tightening strategy, Fulgar's nerves remained unsettled.

"I know Binny," he told Elcid and the others. "He will anticipate everything. And he won't be patient. When he wants something this badly, he'll move swiftly to get it."

"These soldiers are highly trained for a wide variety of scenarios," Elcid replied.

Silas raised a finger. "Not for *ethereal* scenarios."

Fulgar paced again, circling a small area of the floor. "I just have a bad feeling—that somehow he already knows what we're doing. This will be a game of who makes the first move."

"As with any military conflict, Fulgar," replied Elcid, "we have the benefit of an organized and disciplined force. The mage's is simply fanatical."

"Often the worst kind," Dolion interjected.

"We are widely deployed," Elcid continued, "and that should allow us to engage the enemy long enough for *you two*"—he pointed at Dolion and Fulgar—"to position yourselves against the mage."

"Major Cutler, a moment please!" called Elcid to Guardsman Girard Cutler, serving as Elcid's operational right hand and captain of the platoon at the Prickly Trout. They met over a square table, where Elcid had spread a map of Warvonia and the surrounding area.

Fulgar peered at the table from afar. Captain Tramon Bain held watch from Tree Blossom Inn on the western side of the forest, whilst Captain Neydalin, a rarity as a Guardswoman, sentried from

Belltower Alehouse on the eastern flank. Captain Clogg led patrol along the western fringe of town. They were "captains" more in the honorary sense for the purposes of this mission, not officially ranked as such within the Guard but handpicked by Elcid nonetheless. Elcid, in a similar fashion, had effectively become a general, owing to his relationship with those of the Royal Guard stationed locally. Higher-ranking officials over broader regions would likely have them all shackled if they knew of this unauthorized operation.

Coming a little closer, Fulgar squinted at the map. Almost without thinking, he dropped his finger on a specific spot along the woods outside of town. "There," he said. "Do we have anyone watching that area?"

Elcid raised an eyebrow. "Not specifically. Why do you ask?"

Jinx appeared beside Fulgar, leaning to see the map. "That's where we used to camp."

"Exactly," said Fulgar. "Binny will expect me to find him at a place of personal significance to both of us. I can think of none better."

Elcid nodded with a grunt. "Good insight. Girard, let's station some crossbow snipers around that location."

Fulgar took a broad step toward Elcid. "Remember, Elcid—I want Binny kept alive."

"Who's Binny?" asked Girard. "The *mage*?"

"Yes," Elcid replied to Girard, turning to face Fulgar. "But you must also remember that our primary objective is to end the threat of his sorcery—swiftly *and* completely."

Fulgar's hard stare did not waver from Elcid. "I know what must be done. Your prudence to ensure *nonlethal* attacks is much appreciated."

Dolion did a short, jittery hop. "Such precision does not come easily." He flashed a toothy grin. "Might cost you extra."

"Oh, shut it, Dolion," said Jinx. "I already explained this to you."

Dolion made a broad sweep with his arm. "But to hear it directly from Fulgar. Gives it such gravitas!"

"Our approach must be delicate," said Fulgar. "Binny should reasonably sense that I have approached him alone. I propose a signal. If I get a singular sense of where Binny might be, I will call out 'fan wide.' Circle broadly in my wake, and I must rely on each of you to ensure he doesn't see you. And please . . . do nothing unless I give the word, or unless I fall."

Jinx gave his arm a subtle squeeze. "We *won't* let you fall, Fulgar."

"I should hope *none* of us do," he replied, "including Binny."

Their first day and night at the Prickly Trout passed without incident, as did the second. No strange sightings were reported by any of the patrols.

On the third, a lanky, pale-faced member of the Civic Force barged into the taproom, his breaths heavy and labored.

Fulgar, Elcid, Silas, Girard, and Jinx sprang from their chairs in unison. Dolion, his usual placid self, remained comfortably seated. He was near the fireplace, where beside the hearth sat a small stack of anthracite logs chemically treated to emit red smoke as a means of signaling to other platoons.

"What is it?" Elcid demanded.

The man tried to speak through a dry throat, clearly struggling.

"Get him some water!" Silas ordered the nearest server.

A glass appeared from the kitchen within seconds, as though the need had already been anticipated. The man was mid-gulp when Elcid spoke again.

"You're one of Captain Clogg's men, aren't you?"

"Yes!" the man exhaled, nodding vigorously. "At least as for *this* mission, anyway. The name's Parry, sir."

"Well, Parry, you've had your quaff." He made circling gestures of impatience. "So go on, man! What's happened?"

"Disappeared, sir. At least five men, as of when I bolted. Simple as that. Can't explain it. I just knows what I saw. Lashed by that warlock's whip they were, and the next minute just *gone*, sure as the day is long."

"Surely not!" replied Elcid.

"There must be *some* explanation," said Silas.

Parry shook his head adamantly. "None we can figure, sir. They went somewheres . . . or nowheres . . . anywheres but where we was."

Silence followed, Silas and Elcid trading incredulous stares.

"I believe him," said Fulgar, stepping forward. "I've seen it happen before. It's something Bin—er, the mage—is able to do with his whip."

Silas pressed a hand to his forehead. "Sweet breath of Eloh. And with all our platoons watching, somehow they slipped through."

"Please," Parry continued, "what troops remain need reinforcements. Your Order leader has joined the fray, but our soldiers won't hold for long."

Silas's eyebrows lifted. "You mean *Zirion* has joined the fight? Things must indeed be dire."

"Right," Elcid replied. "Girard! Get our troops ready and mounted. They will ride with us. You ride to Captain Neydalin—it's only a minor detour to Belltower. Bring her force along with you . . . and pray we are not too late." He pointed toward the innkeeper standing by the kitchen. "Master Everhart, please send the red smoke from your chimney. Captain Bain is too far west for us to reach him directly, but hopefully one of his lookouts will see the signal and know that we have engaged. You have our thanks for your services." The innkeeper nodded dutifully.

Girard darted off. Elcid's intense gaze fell upon Fulgar. "It's time."

Fulgar's hand passed over the novidian anelace by his side. "I know."

"Oh, good!" chirped Dolion, appearing as though from nowhere and clapping a hand on Fulgar's shoulder. "I was beginning to think you might not go through with it."

"I'm much more concerned about *your* methods than mine," Fulgar replied. "I know what must be done. Let us be clear. When it comes to the mage, follow *my* lead. Do not attempt any surprises or unexpected heroics."

"Don't worry," said Jinx with a smirk. "He's not well-known for his heroics."

Fifteen men—eleven of the Civic Force and four of the Royal Guard—mounted horses alongside Fulgar, Elcid, Silas, Jinx, Dolion, and Parry. Horses were not kept by the Order, but they knew a livery in town suitable for when circumstances warranted renting beasts fit for speed and travel. Of course, such animals were readily available to the soldiers.

Elcid and Parry led the charge, urging their horses to a full gallop down the forest road. Ahead of Fulgar, hooves kicked up clumps of green moss and tufts of bluegrass, and occasionally he had to dodge sprays of dirt. It was an effort for him to keep up, his skill on horseback leveling about average.

At a fork in the road, they veered south, while Girard continued to the west. By the time they exited the forest for grassy hillsides, the sky was painted with the colors of dusk, the lowermost rings glowing in orange hues. This was a season of prolonged daylight, but, if they managed to head off the enemy, it would inevitably happen under nightglow. Fulgar's stomach did an unhappy little twist.

Warvonia greeted them in the distance with warmly lit windows and ships' lanterns glancing off the distant water of the harbor, all of them tiny flickers of life in the distance.

Flares of light rose along the city's edge, plumes of fire reaching twice the height of the buildings around them, like geysers of doom.

Legends Collide

Although still miles away, the sight was nearly blinding.

Fulgar felt a strange pang of relief that they were simply normal fires, rather than darkfire.

"*There!*" yelled the men ahead, urging their horses into maximum speed. A short time later, they reached the first buildings along the town's westernmost housing district.

The bright orange of the flares was almost hypnotic. Fulgar figured it was similar to seeing a lighthouse from a ship, otherwise surrounded by fog and dark ocean. Such a light becomes the cynosure, the thing to which all eyes are drawn, like mosquitoes to a campfire.

A reality that Binny would know all too well.

"Wait!" called Fulgar. "That's where they *want* us to go!"

He'd barely gotten the words out when a mass of grimkins rushed them from the left. Horses were tackled, men dragged to the ground with yelps of surprise. Birdlike screeches rent the air, joined seconds later by the clanging of swords and the screams of men stabbed before they could defend themselves.

Fulgar leapt from his horse before any grimkins could drag him down, ripping the anelace from his belt midair. All the anxiety and nervous anticipation he had previously harbored vanished, chased away by something he couldn't quite admit was courage, but it was close. The anelace channeled his Fielder energy and burned white in his grasp, invigorating him with warm power.

Crying out, he swung against foes, barely aware of his own actions through the fog of adrenaline. They toppled before him as he severed their steel blades like toothpicks and cut them to the ground with squawks of anguish.

Frantically, he gave healing power to as many of his wounded comrades as he could. Such quick work was only suitable for simple cuts and scrapes. He felt sick over the few men he could not help, the ones stabbed and bleeding too badly.

"Jinx!" he called.

"I'm here, Fulgar!" she answered, providing him an instant wave of relief. She was only about ten feet away, teamed up against the assailants with Elcid and Silas. She used her standard blade of steel, undoubtedly not willing to risk damage to the gold-diamond sword still by her side.

As Fulgar's senses realigned with his body, he saw Dolion scattering enemies with his novidian cards, which blazed in the dark like white-hot boomerangs. A short distance away, Parry fought along with two knights of the Guard. Many others, mostly of the Civic Force, had been slain by the grimkins.

"Elcid! Fulgar! Silas!" shouted a booming voice from some other direction.

It took Fulgar a few moments to realize who it was coming from. "Zirion!" The large man ran toward them with big, clomping steps, like a battle-ax-wielding bear on the charge.

"You came right toward the fire spouts! That's exactly where they *wanted* you to go!"

Elcid pointed toward Parry. "We followed the one from *this* platoon who retrieved us!"

"There's not much left of this platoon, I'm afraid," said Zirion. "We've barely held them off."

"I ordered signals for Captain Bain's platoon," said Elcid. "Watch for them, and they can help you secure the town."

Zirion nodded understanding. "Aye, will do. Your prowess as a military leader never ceases to amaze me, Elcid."

"Have you seen Binny?" asked Jinx.

"The mage took maybe five soldiers with that whip of his. As the fighting picked up, we lost sight of him."

The wild, animalistic scream startled them all, and Silas leapt away just before a purple-enflamed horse crashed to the ground. Fulgar dowsed the darkfire with a white beam from his anelace as the creature writhed weakly, cold steam rising from its body. Whether it would live Fulgar could not say, but he soon saw the

Legends Collide

perpetrators—three grimkins conjuring the violet fireballs.

He bolted toward them, even as one of the pulsing orbs shot toward him. Jinx's shout was muffled and distant against his focus on the foes ahead. With his anelace, he cut through the orb as if through like a flickering snowball, and the grimkin glared at him with a mix of shock and hatred. In unison, they drew steel.

Fulgar smirked.

His sights set on the one that had already tried to kill him, he achieved a magnetic lock on two of the grimkins' swords and forced them to stab each other. With a mighty leap, he landed before the remaining foe, slashed through the opposing sword with a streak of light, twirled, and severed the head from its body, which crumpled in a grisly, feathery heap at his feet.

He turned back to his comrades, his determination never so strong. Binny had been here, had fought this platoon, and Fulgar hadn't been among them. He knew where Binny would go—knew it down to his very core—the one place Binny would expect Fulgar to find him. "*Fan wide!* I'm going after Binny!"

He sprinted off toward the forest in the west, ignoring every voice that called his name from behind.

Seeing their old campsite was a haunting experience for Fulgar. Though obscured by a thin veil of weedy overgrowth, everything was as they'd left it. The stones surrounding the firepit, the logs they'd rested upon—everything was there. He realized it might be a construct of his mind, but he believed he could still see the worn spots on the ground where Binny, Jinx, and he used to sleep. He stared at the spot where he and Jinx had lain side by side, his mind flooding with memories across the emotional spectrum.

"It really takes you back, doesn't it—being here again?" said Binny's voice from the darkness.

Fulgar did not move his eyes from the ground. "It does."

"I knew you would come here, eventually."

"As did I expect of you." Fulgar looked up and saw Binny, perhaps thirty feet away, standing just outside the edge of the forest. It was the appearance of what he had become, the Shadow Mage, but that was not what Fulgar saw. He saw beyond the helmet of tusks, the heavy garments of black, and the ashen skin surrounding the mage's eyes. To him, it was just Binny, his old friend.

"Then you have finally decided to join me?" asked Binny.

Fulgar crossed his arms. "Of course not. What you propose leads not only to my own death but that of this land and countless others."

"That is absurd. You really think I fight for a purpose of *death*? This is life—this is *salvation*! I've seen the inevitability of the Shadow's rise and the Light's demise. The Shadow's roots permeate this land, as veins pulsing and branching, ever spreading in influence until the time is right. We must learn to *embrace* it so that we might truly thrive in the times ahead."

"To embrace the Shadow is still a form of death—a *spiritual* death, the worst kind. I also have learned much, my old friend. And so it is *you* whom I hope to save."

Binny paced a small area, pounding a fist against the black padded jacket covering his torso. It was thick and heavy, a defensive gambeson such as traveling knights often wore. "This conflict ends only one way: you coming with me. Otherwise, you will have to best me, and *that* is not going to happen. For one, because you won't, and we both know it. For another, because you *can't*. You've done well stepping into your power, but you are still inexperienced."

"The Light has always been with me, Binny, longer than you've been polluted by the Void. Although, I daresay that started the moment you embraced the talisman."

"*Polluted?*" said Binny. "You didn't always see it that way, if you can bring yourself to remember." Fulgar opened his mouth to respond, but Binny cut him off. "I know what you're going to say: we were *misguided*. I don't see it that way. You got distracted and followed a different way, the way that felt most natural to you. This *power* you have—it's much different than mine. My strength in the Void is not some tired, dwindling inheritance from a long-dead presence. Your power is slow, like some old man trying to remember what he used to be good for. My power is fresh . . . more accessible . . . more eager to surge toward its full might."

"You're partly right, Binny. The Void is eager to corrupt anyone who will have it without prejudice. But the Light—even though a part of me, it must be accepted. It is not like an old man that forgets but rather like a close friend who meets you where you are, walks with you, aids when you need it, and helps you become more than you can be on your own." He held out his hands, a gesture of invitation. "Binny, it is not too late for you. I can help you remove this darkness from within you. What you are doing—what you have become—this is not the path to true life."

"How blinded by your Light and your precious *Order* you have become." Binny's voice had a growling undertone, a bit of the mage showing through. "Surely, by now, it's clear that you must join me. That is the only way all of this ends." His voice softened again, back to Binny. "That is the only way we can move on with our purpose and be friends—be brothers again. You and me, together, on new quests, with new power and purpose, until we reap our inevitable rewards. It is what we both *deserve*"—the word came out like a hiss—"after all we've been through."

"Inevitable? Binny, you are deceived! Tricked . . . *enslaved* by the following of this ancient Umbramancer. There is no reward in this but death, darkness, and damnation!"

Binny laughed—a pitiless, demeaning laugh. "As one of the Following, I shall be above death, riding upon it like a timeless wave and never slipping into its waters. Only the weak do that."

"You are wrong, Binny. Only the spiritually weak fear death

such that they will do anything, no matter how wicked, to avoid it."

Binny sighed. "Eventually, you will understand. You will understand, and you will realize how *foolish* you were for resisting me now. But tonight is not that night." He took the whip from his side, and it hung loose from his hand, like a serpentine pet waiting to do its master's bidding.

Fulgar, sensing trouble, drew the anelace as Binny continued.

"Tonight, I do what must be done," said Binny. "I do it for you . . . for *us* and our dreams of old. I do it, whether you submit willingly . . . or *not!*"

The whip cracked. Fulgar assumed himself ready for any attack, but the blaze of purple light that beamed at his eyes was completely unexpected. It blinded him like a blow to the face, the entire world washed in purple and white flashes with each blink of his eyes. He raised his anelace by instinct and, by some miracle, blocked something else that he surmised was a gout of darkfire.

Sight returned just enough for him to see Binny charging, something indiscernible held overhead. Another blink clarified that it wasn't invisible but rather a broadsword blacker than night.

Their weapons clashed with an unworldly, vibrational thrum. White and purple jolts intertwined as though engaging a battle of their own. Fulgar parried Binny's thrusts, holding back the sword of black doom with his anelace, nothing like the blade of steel that had melted in Fulgar's hands before. He found strength with every counterstrike. If Binny was a mage of Shadow, then Fulgar had become a mage of Light.

He and Binny now inches apart, Fulgar dared glance at Binny's eyes. Fulgar was devastated by the surrounding ashen skin which revealed the extent of his friend's corruption, as well as the determined hatred that dimmed the once natural brightness of his eyes.

Their blades locked, each man matching the strength of the other, prongs of light dancing between them. Careful to hold his position, Fulgar listened to the magnetic impulses in his body,

Legends Collide

finding metal within Binny's garb, perhaps plate armor within the gambeson.

He spun out of the hold and reached out to engage his magnetism. With an effort, he locked on and thrust sideways, flinging a surprised Binny some twenty feet away.

Growling, Binny stood. "You will *not* want to try that again!"

He charged, and again they dueled. Fulgar leapt a low swipe to his legs. Upon landing, he thrust his arm forward with a blast of white Fielder power.

Binny caught the energy, such that it gathered into a white ball between his hands, and flung it back at Fulgar.

Fulgar couldn't stop it. The energy itself didn't hurt, but it blew him back and seized his muscles momentarily. The anelace landed a few feet away from him.

"*Bind him now!*" roared the mage.

Black-garbed men and grimkins emerged from the surrounding trees and ran toward Fulgar. He tried to force his sluggish body into motion, reaching with all his strength for the anelace.

He heard movement from behind, more bodies approaching, and the inevitability of defeat nearly overwhelmed him. He was helpless, surrounded, and barely able to move.

Then white lights like glowing bats zipped past and dive-bombed two of the mage's men, electrocuting them unconscious. Relief bounded into Fulgar like a running embrace. *Dolion's cards!* he thought, recognizing with great fondness his fellow Fielder's unique way of making an entrance.

Silas and Elcid appeared from the trees behind, taking the mage's men by surprise. They unleashed their own shining weapons of white and gold—Silas a novidian staff and Elcid his short giamond sword—and tore into the foes with brilliant flashes of light.

Parry and their accompaniment of soldiers from the Prickly Trout charged ahead, joined by Girard and the additional platoon under Captain Neydalin, perhaps thirty soldiers in all. They spread around the old campsite and engaged the remainder of the mage's attackers. A few enemies fell to quarrels from high in the trees, a reminder to Fulgar that Elcid had ordered crossbow snipers throughout this area. Binny took a step back toward the woods, seeming to let his minions take the brunt of the charge.

Jinx knelt beside Fulgar, retrieved his anelace, and handed it to him. "You know, you don't have a history of faring well going it alone like this."

Fulgar felt an instant resurgence of strength and stood. "You make a fair point, but meeting Binny alone was the only way I could even hope to engage him on a personal level."

"Yeah? And how'd that go?"

"I fear for him, Jinx. He is deeply deceived. And, to him, *I'm* the one deceived."

She gave his arm a squeeze. "Keep trying. If anyone can get through to him, it's you."

Fulgar glanced about their forces. "Where's Zirion?"

"He stayed back to secure the town with what was left of Captain Clogg's platoon."

Fulgar's gaze caught Binny, who stood in place, also watching the events around him. He struck with his sword only when anyone dared come against him, and the soldiers were clearly no match.

With a flash of violet, the mage lashed out with his whip, catching one of Parry's legs and yanking him to the ground. Dark-purple-and-black energy pulsed from the whip to Parry, surrounding his body as the soldier winced and cried out.

Fulgar bolted ahead, stopping about a spear's throw from the mage. "*Binny!* Stop this! It is not your way to harm innocent people!"

"*None* of you are innocent!" Binny roared back. "Not so long as you stand against me! More will share his fate, Fulgar, if you continue refusing me."

"There was a time when you only wanted power to protect

yourself, not to dominate others!"

Binny tugged, and the whip released Parry's leg with one final jolt of energy. Steam rose from his body as he writhed weakly upon the ground, the glow of Void still around him.

Captain Neydalin ran to his side, knelt, and gently raised Parry's head. Staring into her battle-hardened yet caring eyes, Parry struggled to speak. "I go now . . . to join my brothers."

"You honor them," Neydalin replied, "as we shall honor you."

Even under the soft glow of night, they could see the color leaving his skin, as though frostbite crawled over it. With a shudder, Parry froze like a statue. The glow surrounding him pushed into his body, and he vanished.

Elcid appeared at Fulgar's right, Silas at his left, both facing the mage. Dolion and Jinx flanked Fulgar from just behind.

"You are going to regret that!" shouted Elcid.

"Where has he gone?" demanded Silas.

The mage grinned, a sinister twist of Binny's face so disturbing that Fulgar had to look away. "Where none can follow."

Elcid raised his giamond blade, its radiance like a rod of golden sunlight. "I will send you where none can return!"

He charged, quite against their plan of Fulgar and Dolion stopping the mage with combined Fielder attacks.

"*Elcid!*" Silas called too late. Elcid was already halfway to the mage.

Binny, with an unsettling calm, widened his stance and faced Elcid. He held his black broadsword longways, the tip of its blade resting in his left palm. A thin nimbus of purple light surrounded it.

Elcid aimed his giamond sword at the mage and unleashed two small, yellow orbs of Aether energy.

Binny, still holding his black sword of byrne longways, thrust his arms forward, and from the weapon a frigid gale of wind blew into Elcid. Fulgar and the others felt its wintery chill gust throughout the area.

The orbs of light from Elcid's sword vanished, and even the light within the blade itself guttered out like a spent candle. Flailing, Elcid crashed into the forest.

With seemingly little effort, Binny had overpowered the Light Ethereal. With Elcid, it was not in the hands of one with true etheretics. Even so, Fulgar recalled the historical accounts of such sorcery during the Foundational War, and it chilled his blood.

It was a stark reminder that history could always repeat itself.

"Dolion," said Fulgar quietly. "Please be ready at my mark. But remember, if at all possible, I do not want him mortally wounded."

"Just say the word, mate," Dolion replied.

An eerie quietude swept the area, like the eye of a hurricane. Fulgar kept his focus on Binny. Through a wicked half-smirk, Binny met the stare.

Then he darted off into the woods.

"*Shoot him!*" screamed Elcid from the middle of a brambly bush. "Shoot him down!"

Fulgar took off after Binny, sprinting as fast as he could, flashing a glare at Elcid as he passed.

"*Fulgar!*" Silas and Jinx called in unison.

He saw Binny just up ahead. Crossbow bolts zipped through the air, sticking into the trees and ground as if into loamy pincushions.

Fulgar engaged his magnetism, trying his best to throw the bolts off course to prevent them striking either him or Binny. He felt like sending one back to Elcid as a statement. No one else, likely aside from Jinx, truly cared if Binny lived or died, least of all Elcid. Fulgar couldn't entirely blame him, but it made him no less agitated.

Binny emerged from the thick growth and darkness of the forest into an expansive glade. He finally stopped upon reaching the center, turning to face Fulgar.

"Has it come to this, then?" asked Binny.

"Only if you will it so!" Fulgar replied, his anelace luminous and ready.

Legends Collide

One by one, his friends and comrades appeared behind him. Whiteness shone from Silas's staff to his right and Dolion's cards to his left. Jinx stood between him and Dolion. Elcid was there too, somewhat farther removed, his giamond again shining gold, although not as brightly as before. Major Girard, Captain Neydalin, and a couple dozen soldiers joined them.

No one stood ahead of Fulgar. Everyone remained behind him, waiting to follow his lead. The mage gazed upon them all . . .

. . . and threw back his head in boisterous laughter.

"We of the Following are more numerous than you realize," said Binny. He raised his arms, and another swarm of men and grimkins stepped out from around the glade, rallying behind their leader. He pulled on a chain around his neck and freed it from beneath his gambeson.

Fulgar immediately recognized the swirling, fiery design of the object in Binny's hand. It was the talisman.

"Don't you see?" Binny continued. "They are ever in waiting. Waiting for a torchbearer—the strongest, most capable, most willing to serve as a vessel of the cause. It's not so unlike your ancient Order, I suppose, except that we are ever *growing*, ever gaining strength, rather than slowly fading into the pages of history and, ultimately, into extinction."

"It's not like the Order at all, Binny," said Fulgar. "You've been poisoned by outer influences, that you might dominate others by force. The Order looks at what is already inside—the goodness and purity in the soul of each person—and helps build that to its greatest potential and purpose."

"We shall see," replied the mage. Binny dropped his arms, and the horde behind him sprang into action, charging along the edges of the glade like roaches skirting walls.

"We'll take 'em this side!" shouted Girard.

"And we'll take the other!" followed Neydalin.

Both platoons took off, and Fulgar said a silent prayer for their survival. He remained in the glade's center, along with Jinx, Dolion, Silas, and Elcid, soon to be encircled by troops in battle. It was the sort of dramatic flair only Binny would orchestrate.

Binny widened his stance, facing them down, filled with the unnatural power of the Shadow Mage as he held the byrne broadsword in one hand and the whip in the other. He must have attained some heightened level of strength to wield such a large sword with so little effort.

"Spread out and cover me," said Fulgar, setting his feet. "I'm going at him directly."

He dashed forward, wary of the whip, and slammed the anelace against Binny's broadsword. They tore into fervent duel—high, low, side to side, Fulgar looking for any opening to land a strike and dispel the Void energy flowing through his old friend.

Binny swiped wide, and Fulgar attempted to lock on with his magnetism.

Fulgar felt a curious buzz pushing back through his arm. His eyes widened in a moment of realization. Binny was reversing the magnetism back toward Fulgar.

"I *said* you'd regret trying that again," growled the mage.

The magnetism slammed Fulgar hard into the ground, rolling him back.

His friends charged in. Dolion's cards zapped and cut into Binny, until he swatted them away like horseflies and blasted Dolion with a dark-purple orb. He caught Elcid's sword with his whip and flung it away, turning to hammer his broadsword into Silas's staff. Silas got in a few good hits before Binny slammed the pommel of his sword into Silas's shoulder and kicked him away.

Jinx remained near but didn't engage directly. It seemed she was waiting for a better opportunity. The gold-diamond sword was now in her grasp. Fulgar wondered if she still clung to the legends of Zoar and thus remained determined to again strike Binny with that weapon.

Legends Collide

Fulgar recovered himself and lunged at Binny, slashing with his anelace.

Binny caught the blade in the same hand holding the whip—not a move Fulgar expected, considering the novidian could slice through steel like warm butter. Through beaded sweat and gritted teeth, Fulgar pushed with all his might, but Binny matched his strength.

"I can best your every move," hissed the mage.

Binny's other fist, broadsword hilt in hand, slammed into Fulgar's jaw. Then one of Binny's knees shoved into Fulgar's abdomen, stealing the wind from his lungs. Fulgar doubled over. Binny followed with an uppercut, this time with the whip-bearing fist, that sent Fulgar reeling backward and flat on his back at least ten feet away.

Fulgar groaned and arched his back in pain. His face throbbed, and it felt like the joints of his jaw were filled with sand, their movements gritty and coarse. Warm wetness on his cheek confirmed he was bleeding.

Turning on the ground, he saw that his friends were still near, ready to rejoin the battle. He scanned the glade's perimeter and glimpsed occasional bursts of purple. Some of Binny's minions were using byrne to attack, something the soldiers were not equipped to handle.

"Go help the others!" he ordered while forcing himself to stand. "Let no one else fall to this Void devilry!"

Elcid, giamond sword back in hand, nodded and ran off to the right. Silas hesitated but soon took off to the left. Jinx and Dolion lingered behind.

"Can't let you keep all the glory to yourself, mate!" Dolion replied.

"Jinx, go!" Fulgar waved her off. "It will take Fielder strength to end this!"

She remained rigid. "I'm still waiting to see that work!"

THE HEALER

"Right," said Dolion. "Then let's have us another try!"

He ran a wide, circular path around Binny, flinging three cards into the air. Dolion directed the cards to soar high overhead and into the mage on their return, like a massive juggling act. With some struggle, Binny warded them off with his helmet and sword.

Fulgar followed Dolion's lead and began running the same circle across from Dolion. He summoned what strength of magnetism and white blasts he could, anything to throw Binny off.

Worry tapped at Fulgar. It was no surprise that Binny had refused Fulgar's pleas to follow him. Thus, Fulgar's primary hope was that enough carefully placed strikes of Fielder energy would dispel the Void possessing Binny without killing him. But, so far, that hadn't been enough, as the mage absorbed hit after hit and the Shadow remained.

Binny swatted away one of the cards, pointed his sword, and blasted Dolion mid-run with a fiery purple orb. The remaining cards dimmed like cooled embers and dropped to the ground.

When Binny snapped his attention back to Fulgar, it seemed his eyes glowed with the cold burning light of darkfire. Fulgar lost himself for a moment and slowed his circling.

Swift and terrifying was the whip's pounce. Before Fulgar fully realized what had happened, it was coiled around the blade of his anelace. A distorted, sizzling tangle of white and purple discharges emanated from the weapons. Coldness pulsed into his arm, interfering with the warm buzz of the Fielder energy channeled by the anelace.

Even if he'd wanted, he couldn't let go. His fingers would not move. Then his arm. Then his legs.

Until he took a step toward Binny, a step that he had not commanded his leg to take. Fulgar reached a chilling realization. The Shadow Mage was taking control of his body.

A thin dark haze started to cloud his vision just at the moment Jinx slashed at the whip with her diamond sword. Once before, that hadn't worked; this time, perhaps because of the energies surging through the whip, her strike was just enough. The whip released Fulgar's blade, and the haze immediately receded. Slowly, feeling began to return to extremities that had gone cold as death.

The mage looked upon Jinx with pure rage. "*You!*" he growled. Then he charged, and Fulgar could not move fast enough to intervene.

Jinx and her weapon withstood a barrage of strikes from the black broadsword, but the mage's strength forced her to step backward. With a broad swipe from the mage, the diamond sword was wrenched from her grasp with a crystalline scream. She stumbled and fell upon her rump, scrambling to back herself away as the mage raised his sword for a kill strike.

Fulgar was there in a trice, his anelace blazing and ready to meet the mage's weapon of darkness. He parried Binny with hard, fervent swings that erupted with white sparks and zaps, this time forcing the mage back. He landed a kick into Binny's torso that sent him to the ground.

Silas had returned from fighting around the glade's perimeter and now stood near Dolion. "Give me that!" said Dolion, snatching the novidian rod from Silas's hands. With it, he aimed and shot a thin beam of white Fielder energy, but it wasn't at the mage.

It was at Fulgar.

The beam surrounded the anelace and Fulgar with an even brighter luminescence. Dolion was using his strength to enhance Fulgar's. Pointing the anelace, Fulgar directed a wider, stronger beam at Binny, using it to hold him to the ground. Binny struggled against it, pushing hard to stand back up, and Fulgar found it increasingly difficult to hold him down.

"Channel your power through my sword!" shouted Jinx from behind.

Fulgar opened his mouth to protest but stopped himself. Thoughts of the histories he'd read and conversations with Zirion flashed through his mind, and suddenly pieces of a centuries-old puzzle seemed to fit together. Heroes during the Foundational War had used the Strike of Faith—a giamond blade to the heart—to free comrades possessed by Void's Shadow. Elcid's giamond wasn't pure; even if it was, they had no Lumineer to properly harness its energy. Jinx's sword wasn't giamond, but its gold-diamond alloy combined with the energy of novidian might be close enough.

As much as Fulgar hated the risk, Jinx might be right. This might be their best hope.

He looked into Jinx's determined, eager eyes. "For the heart, Jinx. Be careful!"

She launched forward, brandishing the sword of Zoar legend.

Fulgar would have to aim his outlay of Fielder energy away from Binny and to Jinx's sword, a move requiring utmost careful timing. At the moment he determined best—when he was sure Jinx could strike before Binny could react—he released Binny and directed the white beam at Jinx's sword as she charged.

But his best was not good enough.

Jinx already had the sword poised to strike when the whip lashed out and coiled around one of Jinx's legs, pulsing in cold, purple energy. Fulgar would not have believed it possible—he had seen the whip severed by Jinx—but the mage must have made the whip longer with his Void sorcery. The mage tugged on the whip, and Jinx toppled with a scream, her body glowing and writhing as steam rose from her skin.

"*Jinx! No!*" bellowed Fulgar. "Binny, what have you done?!"

Binny got up on his knees. "I've removed that which came between us."

"You . . . selfish, murdering spawn of Gheol!" He looked at Dolion, who was sweating from the exertion of his own Fielder beam. "Keep your energy on me, no matter what!"

"Doing . . . my best!" Dolion replied through gritted teeth.

"It's over, mage!" shouted Elcid, the giamond shining its

golden light.

Fulgar crept closer to the diamond sword.

From the mage's other side, Silas stood with Dolion's cards in hand. "There will be no return to your master this time."

Binny looked all around, as Girard and Neydalin and a full complement of soldiers formed a ring around them.

"Your followers are no more!" shouted Girard.

Fulgar took the sword of Zoar from the ground.

"Our followers," the mage boomed, his attention on those around him, "ever lurk right under your noses. Our *master* reigns unseen with the wisdom of millennia, and *nothing* can—*UGH!*"

Diamond sword in hand, Fulgar struck true, straight through Binny's heart.

Binny's eyes widened and locked on Fulgar's. In them, Fulgar saw flashes of anger, betrayal, fear, and shock before they clouded with unnatural blackness. Dark energy surged all around Binny's body, even as a ball of whiteness spread from the impact of the sword. Elcid yanked away the mage's whip, and Silas took the byrne broadsword. Fulgar withdrew the diamond blade, and Binny crumpled to the ground, shuddering.

Fulgar tossed the bloodstained diamond sword aside and ran to Jinx. She was nearly frozen and fading fast. He knelt and took her in his arms. She was almost unbearably cold.

"Always wanted to go d-down in a blaze of glory," she said.

"Why? *Why* did you have to do that?" he asked, tears forming. "It should have been me."

Jinx shook her head weakly through constant shivers. "Th-there you g-go, trying to steal all the fun. We all . . . h-have our role to p-play."

"I'll fix this. I'll heal this. There must be a way."

Her icy hand brushed his cheek. "N-not everything has a f-fix. Some things simply have a p-purpose."

"But . . . I need you . . ."

THE HEALER

"And the world needs you." She blinked several times, almost as if seeing something far away. "Th-this... isn't goodbye... F-Fulgar, my love..."

She froze solid, the purple glow around her drew within, and she disappeared.

Fulgar stayed on his knees for uncounted long moments, staring at the ground in incomprehensible grief. He was numb, and the world spun around him in profound darkness.

From behind, he heard moaning.

"Fulgar," Silas said softly, "it appears Binny has survived... and it seems the Void has left him."

"Yes," said Fulgar, not turning around. "He must be taken to safety. I beg pardon to ask this boon: Can the rest of you please secure and take him? I... cannot look at him now."

"Of course," replied Elcid. "Fulgar, you have done the Order—and all of us—a great service."

Fulgar stood, picked up the diamond sword, and turned to face the others, taking not even a glance at Binny. "Thank you, my friends. I will see you soon."

With that, he left them for the quiet of the forest.

chapter 11
SHADOW AND LIGHT
7/20/3178 P.A.

A full week had passed when Fulgar returned to the Order safehouse. Rain pattered on the dreary streets of the Old Bard district, giving them a much needed wash. Under the cover of a rain cloak, the anelace by his side, he cut quite the untouchable figure. Not a single unsavory soul crossed his path, and Fulgar's steady gait did not falter as his boots clomped heavily upon the cobbles and splashed undaunted through grimy puddles.

Zirion opened the disguised alleyway door. "Ah, Fulgar! My heart is glad to see your return."

Fulgar shook the rain from his cloak and lowered its cowl. Zirion cocked his head ever so slightly at the sight. Fulgar had decidedly changed his look while away. His head was now clean-shaven, the three colors of his natural hair no longer visible.

"A bold move," Zirion assessed, but he followed that with a short nod, laying a big hand fondly upon Fulgar's shoulder. "Sometimes, just as in nature, a new season in life brings changes that are visible. This suits you."

"My thoughts exactly," Fulgar replied with a thin smile.

THE HEALER

"Come. The others will be overjoyed to see you."

He led Fulgar to the Keepers Lounge and left him there alone. In the quiet of the spacious parlor, Fulgar glanced around in fondness and reflection. His time in this space had previously been characterized by intimidation and conflict. Upon first arriving here, he was truly a broken man.

So many walls had come down since then, so many demons faced. From lost to found, from thief to protector, from dejected to loved, from misguided to redeemed, from darkness to light—the man he had been was now but a memory.

Silas was the first to enter. "Fulgar! You old, cheeky, bloody-minded git!" He pulled Fulgar into a brief, friendly embrace. "I was beginning to wonder if you'd return."

"My home is here, Silas. That is as clear to me as ever."

Elcid followed soon after, giving the golden dagger by the doorway a firm tug. He grunted loudly when it remained as stuck as ever. "After that whole altercation with the mage's forces, you'd think I might finally be worthy." He looked at Fulgar. "You've proven yourself quite the warrior. Why don't *you* give it a try?"

"Oh, don't be ridiculous," said Silas. "It won't work for him, either."

Fulgar gave the dagger a glare of challenge. "Sure, why not?" He grabbed the dagger's grip and pulled with all his might. It gave him not the slightest budge. "*Phew!*" he said, giving up. "Are you sure the dagger isn't *part* of the rock?"

Elcid looked well-pleased. "Ha! Here we have one with ether-etics, and even *he* isn't worthy to free it."

Silas sighed through an eyeroll. "It's not about being *worthy*. It's just not meant for you—*either* of you."

He approached Fulgar and extended his hand for a firm shake. "Even so, I'm pleased to see that you're well and back among us."

Fulgar glared at the golden dagger, wondering how he had not considered it more before now. "Is that . . . giamond, then?"

SHADOW AND LIGHT

"Supposed to be," replied Elcid with a derisive snort. "Blasted thing won't even glow for me. I suspect it's some form of trickery that Silas has heaped upon us."

"I assure you, it's quite real and quite pure," said Silas.

Zirion finally joined them. In the kitchenette, he steeped a delightful rosehip and honey tea, at which point they all sat in pleasant conversation as friends and brothers.

"Where *have* you been this past week?" Elcid finally asked.

"I sought closure," Fulgar answered.

"And did you find it?" asked Zirion.

"If I'm being honest . . . no, not entirely. I reflected on my time and experiences by going to various places—the harbor, our old campsite, the forest glade, and various shops and establishments throughout town. I got to a point where I could appreciate my memories with Binny . . . and with Jinx . . . but I could not remove my grief. The loss of Jinx . . . is especially difficult." Eyes closed, he paused for a deep breath before continuing. "I finally decided that it was acceptable to feel grief. It was not a thing that had to be removed completely. I willed myself to abide it, and I decided that I would best honor those I'd loved and lost by living my most purposeful life."

Silas raised his teacup. "Few wiser words have been spoken. Good on you, Fulgar."

"On the matter of Binny, I understand he is safe . . . ?"

"And secure," replied Elcid. "Girard and his men have agreed to keep watch over him in the northern coastal cliffs, but not so closely that he is restricted from coming and going as he pleases. So far, he has been exceedingly quiet."

"And the talisman?"

"It is now out of the enemy's reach, stored within our vaults."

Fulgar stood. "Zirion, I am quite ready to take my oath."

Zirion adopted a somber expression and stood to face Fulgar. "Place both hands over your chest, starting with the left, for it is closest to the heart." Fulgar did as instructed, and Zirion did the same. "Fulgar Geth, kin under the Light and fellow kingsman of Tuscawny, you come of your own conscious volition to give of your greatest self, talents, body, and soul to the brotherhood that is the Order of Aether Diamond. Is this your will?"

"It is."

"Repeat now the words of our oath: Protection of that which protects us. Perseverance over falsehood. Purity over pride, that the Light should stay the Darkness."

Fulgar repeated the words sentence by sentence.

"Do you covenant to hold these words in your heart in service to the Light?"

"I do."

"Then, Fulgar Geth, with brothers Elcid Ursid and Silas Schmeid having borne witness, I, Zirion Tevet, Lord over the Warvonia Conclave, hereby declare you an official member, protector, and brother in the Order of Aether Diamond." At this, his solemn demeanor broke with hearty laughter, and he pulled Fulgar into a bone-crushing embrace. Silas and Elcid followed with claps on the back and congratulatory utterances.

Although Fulgar had already been a part of the Order for months, this moment was monumental for him. It was a path forward that he had chosen to walk, a commitment to and beyond himself, and he did so without an inkling of doubt or hesitation. This was the first time he had ever truly felt so certain.

He might have presumed sureness back when he and Binny walked in lockstep, back when they'd placed their hope in the talisman and the power it represented. Ultimately, that had been Binny's passion, which had influenced Fulgar like a contagion. They had both been deceived by the talisman and its promises of legend. They made many of the same mistakes, shared many of the same beliefs. Fortunately for Fulgar, his life veered down a different path.

He really *did* have Binny to thank for kicking him and Jinx off

Volk's ship that fateful day. It was the move that had forced Fulgar into a period of reorientation, winding and treacherous though that time was.

But this milestone of Fulgar's life was also bittersweet, for now he carried on without Binny and, most painful of all, without Jinx. Fulgar could think of no greater purpose than opposing the forces that had ruined those closest to him.

"Fulgar," said Zirion, "I both laud and regret that the taking of your oath has come at perhaps a very critical time in the ongoing struggle between Shadow and Light. I cannot help but feel that there is a deeper stirring of dark forces as yet undetected."

Silas spoke while walking his emptied teacup to the kitchenette. "I agree. More than a mere shrine and talisman transformed Binny into the Shadow Mage. Binny himself told us his Following was more prominent than we know. I think it'd be wise to take him at his word."

"We tried questioning your friend," said Elcid, "to no avail. Even now he is cognitively . . . vacant."

Fulgar stared at the floor, emotionally unsure how to react. "I admit . . . the charge we face is a daunting one. As I am a true etheretic, the responsibility weighs heavily on my shoulders. I was drawn to the Shadow Mage, I think, because even before I realized it was Binny, I knew it was somehow connected to me and my past. Going forward . . . I feel quite blind."

"As an etheretic," said Zirion, "you have been given much—gifts and talents, yes, but also the heavy burden that you so wisely recognize. The world will expect much of you, often without even realizing it. Others will not understand what you have and what you are. There will be those who seek to take it from you. Countless beings will owe you their lives, but you will be thankless. Your road is marked with betrayal and opposition. You straddle the border between balance and chaos . . . but take heart, Fulgar. You are not alone in this conflict.

THE HEALER

"We are soldiers in a war not merely with mortals but with forces that will do anything to overpower all that we are and all that keeps us together. We are a vapor in the ongoing legend of the Heroes of Time, and within us dwell the spirits of all heroes before us."

He placed both hands upon Fulgar's shoulders and looked him square in the eyes. "You—*we*—are the Order of Aether Diamond."

Seabirds lurked about the harbor, circling, waiting for fish to swim near the ocean's surface. They hovered in air thermals, screeching as though for dominance over each other. Around the pier where Fulgar sat, water rippled with the breeze and curled into impromptu waves as the late Jovidor sun's warmth heralded the start of the fall subseason.

This was one of Fulgar's favorite places for reflection, although today's visit held another purpose. Seated with his legs swinging off the edge of the pier, he rested a hand upon the elongated package beside him—the gold-diamond sword of Zoar concealed within leather wrappings.

The clomping of boots against wooden planks grew louder from behind.

"You're late," said Fulgar, rising with the wrapped sword in hand.

"Important business," replied Dolion. "Plus, I hated to interrupt what appeared to be some very deep thought."

Casting it a final glance, Fulgar held out the leather-bound weapon. "I believe this now belongs to you."

"You're a man of your word." Dolion reached out and took the sword, briefly peeling back the wrapping to confirm its contents. "Don't see many like that anymore."

"Well," said Fulgar, "perhaps you should keep some better

company."

"Ah, but *that* wouldn't be very profitable."

"Remember the terms of our agreement—that sword is to find its way back to Zoar, and *not* into dangerous hands. I trust you'll be able to discern as much."

Dolion arched an eyebrow. "Terms I did not negotiate with *you*."

"I am Jinx's surrogate in this matter, as you can imagine."

Dolion gave a lopsided smirk. "Of course. Well then... you have my thanks, and my condolences. Muriel's feelings were always for you."

Fulgar extended a hand, and Dolion shook it. "I would welcome you as a colleague in the Order as a fellow Fielder. Our strengths combined could prove invaluable against the ever-gathering darkness."

"We shall see. I rather enjoy Zirion's attempts to woo me."

"See you soon, then."

With a wave, Dolion neatly spun around and clomped off, Fulgar watching him walk down the pier.

Two days later, Fulgar found the seaside chalet in which the Order had situated Binny.

Located a short distance north of Warvonia, the small wooden dwelling was nestled within cliffs offering a picturesque view of the idyllic scene below, where ocean waves battered rocky shores with foamy aggression. As Fulgar neared, he noticed the deep reddish color of roastwood in the chalet's walls and overhanging eaves, a very stout wood that would stand well against the environmental elements.

Getting there wasn't terribly difficult once he found the right path—a narrow passage winding around columns of rocky crags.

It was very easily missed and no barriers protected travelers from multiple steep drop-offs.

Once the dwelling came into view, Fulgar stopped, gathering his breath and his thoughts. He wasn't sure which made him more nervous, seeing Binny as the mage or seeing Binny after the power he had long sought had been wrested from him.

Fueled by sheer bravado, Fulgar willed his steps the rest of the way to the front of the house, then to the front porch, and finally to the door. He paused at the door and nearly turned back, but his hand had a mind of its own and knocked without his permission.

Silence.

He craned his neck to peer through the front window, seeing no lights or movement.

He knocked again. A faint stir from inside told him someone was there.

"Binny," he said. "It's Fulgar. I would very much like to speak with you."

Again, nothing.

Fulgar looked behind him, to where the crashing waves engaged their battle against the sea stacks and rocks. *Like Shadow and Light*, thought Fulgar, *a never-ending conflict. One of them attacking, one of them ultimately standing against the whims of the other. So then, which is which? Of the Shadow and the Light . . . which one is the rock?*

Of course, he believed it to be the Light, but there were certainly those who would disagree.

He turned back toward the house and tested the door handle. It wasn't locked, so he pushed the door open.

Inside, a small entrance hall branched left, right, and straight. The air was mildly rancid with dusty undertones. The place was mostly empty, with a few simple tables and chairs. Of course, Binny had only been here a little over a week, and the dwelling itself had been an old seaward lookout post from days before their modern, robust harbor. Fulgar had heard that a lighthouse used to be nearby, but it had ultimately crumbled due to disrepair and unstable ground. Zirion had arranged this location via his connections with Mayor Suvok of Warvonia and Dugard Pratt of the seafaring mercantile guild, which apparently still held some dominion over the property.

Fulgar found Binny in the sitting room to the right, where he silently stared back at Fulgar from a tall armchair.

Binny wore a simple gray shirt and taupe trousers, the might of the Shadow Mage clearly removed from him. Now he looked frail and gaunt. His face was stubbly and his hair an unkempt, oily mop, indicating he had bathed very little, if at all, since coming here. Around his eyes, the skin was still blackened like the surface of a burnt log left over from an old campfire.

Slowly, Fulgar stepped fully into the room. Bookshelves lined the walls with more titles than Fulgar would've expected, random figures and figurines occupied various surfaces, and an assortment of mismatched furniture circled the interior. Almost everything in here had been furnished by the Order, who might also have allowed Binny to bring some items of his own choosing, provided they posed no danger to others.

"Hello, Binny."

Binny turned his gaze toward a window.

Fulgar stepped around the back of a couch patterned with fronds and leaves in evidently every shade of color possible. It might've been someone's attempt to cheer Binny up, but Fulgar found it almost painful to the eyes. Once away from that, he found a small wooden chair and sat, facing his old friend.

"I had hoped to come sooner," Fulgar started timidly. "I . . . needed some time. I thought that, perhaps, you might also. Are you doing okay here? Your view is absolutely marvelous, a completely wild and untamed coastline that many only dream of seeing."

Binny's gaze was unmoved.

"Look, I know I'm probably the last person you want to see. I also know that others of the Order of Aether Diamond have come to see you, as well. We hope . . . if there are others out there who have fallen into the same deception you did, we might be able to help them as well."

Fulgar's chair creaked as he shifted in the quiet room, waiting for some response from Binny, receiving none.

"If I'm being honest, my interest at this time is more focused. I need to know about Jinx, Binny. The way her body completely vanished, frozen like an ice sculpture. I need to know . . . is she truly gone? Is there a way to bring her back?"

Fulgar stared at Binny another silent minute. He stood abruptly with a scoot of his chair, restraining himself with much effort from leaping at Binny's throat. His calmer senses prevailed, knowing a violent outburst would not be productive, nor was it really how Fulgar wanted to react.

That restraint, however, did not stop Fulgar from raising his voice a level as he paced about the room. "Did your tongue somehow leave your body with that mage? Have you lost the ability to remember? What *exactly* did that whip do to people?"

No response.

By this point, Fulgar began to wonder if Binny's silence was more than simple resentment or stubbornness. Perhaps the Void had taken more from his body and mind than Fulgar had anticipated.

Fulgar pushed aside his line of thinking and sat back down with a long sigh. He joined Binny in staring out the window as he spoke. "You and I always felt the attraction of different forces, and they affected us in different ways. The Void of the talisman had its effects on you; my ethereal genetics—etheretics—had its effects on me. We were so young. How could either of us have known the gravity of our choices, what these powers really demanded of us?

"I'm reminded of that old clergyman, back in the cathedral where we found the scroll of the talisman's shrine. He said some-

Shadow and Light

thing that I never forgot, even though I went most of my life not understanding it: 'In life we have ourselves, we have those close to us, and at the core of it all we have the guidance of Eloh.'

"I know belief can take so many forms and meanings. Belief in *what* exactly? Even that which I know as Eloh may take on different names to other people and yet be the same thing. I do not have all the answers, but what I have come to believe is this: The presence of Eloh has been to me like a guiding spirit that dwells within. That guidance, I think, is how one can come to know the nature of Shadow and Light, Void and Aether. Once I became open to that guidance beyond the self and the fallible, I could begin to see the opposing effects of these forces."

Fulgar faltered when he realized that Binny was now staring at him. He recovered himself well enough to complete his thought.

"I think it boils down to this: The Shadow seeks and devours, whereas the Light beckons to be sought. The Shadow moves to empower itself, whereas the Light moves to reveal power that already exists. The Shadow, by deceit, proclaims itself the truth and the future, whereas the Light, for those who will listen, shows itself to be the truth that always was and will always be."

Binny looked down at Fulgar's anelace. "You got the blarkle after all, didn't you?"

Slightly taken aback, it took Fulgar a few moments to answer. "Yeah, Binny . . . I got the blarkle. Novidian. Maybe one day I can teach you more about it."

Binny slowly ran his thumbs up and down his stubbly jawlines, his stare on Fulgar unwavering. After what felt like long minutes, he turned and took a book from a nearby shelf. Fulgar squinted to see it and soon realized it was an old children's tale, a set of adventures featuring Grimy the Grimkin. Binny opened the book, slowly thumbing through its pages.

He stopped on an illustration of a hovering figure, cloaked in black, surrounded by grimkins in various acts of dancing, kneeling, and chanting. He turned the book around to Fulgar, placing a finger on the cloaked figure.

"It's real."

Fulgar blinked. "Umbramancers, as from children's stories?"

"*The* Umbramancer. The Following. They are real."

Something about Binny's tone sent a chill up Fulgar's spine. He slowly nodded. "Yes. I've read and heard about such from the Order—the old Following of *Khil-shi'dha*."

Binny shook his head. "It's not just old. It exists even now... and it is *coming*." He rocked nervously in his seat and clutched himself as though suddenly cold.

"Coming when?"

"I don't know."

"Coming how?"

"However it can. Worthy vessels... as I was. Ancient powers such as we have only begun to witness. Even artifacts hidden over the ages. There is one—the shard of *Ni'shan-qa Til'la-ni'tha*, what laypeople call the Grimstone—that is something the Umbramancer sorely desires. Your *ethereals*—he will have them all. And those outside his grace... are doomed." His voice dropped to an airy hiss. "*Now even me.*"

"Seek Eloh's grace, not his," replied Fulgar.

"It's a matter of time," said Binny, "and then we'll see what truly comes to pass."

"Binny," said Fulgar, feeling the unbridled tug of such a sudden, ominous revelation, "what about Jinx? What happened to her?"

"The whip—it was an endowment of his power." His eyes shifted sideways, as though lost in remembrance. "All along... it was you." He looked up at Fulgar again, his words venomous. "It was *you* that took it all from me. *Everything* I had strived for."

"I hope you can come to understand why that had to be. You *killed* people, Binny. You're fortunate to have as much freedom as you do."

Shadow and Light

Binny stared back at him, his expression empty, almost droopy. "I never killed anyone, not really."

"What do you mean? What really happened to them—to Jinx? Is she *gone*, Binny?"

Binny stared at him for long, unsettling moments. "She is gone, but not in the way that you think."

"Gone to *where*? Where can I find her?"

Binny seemed to struggle, pressing a palm against his temple. "I might eventually have been worthy enough to know, but I do not."

Fulgar wanted to press further, but he knew it would gain him nothing. Already, he had heard enough to give him a flicker of hope, and that alone was priceless.

Another long silence followed, not quite as uncomfortable as before. "I feel . . . empty," Binny finally said.

"I would expect so," Fulgar replied. "You had that talisman almost as long as I've known you. All that time, it poured darkness into you. That is what . . . filled you up, you could say, and that left no room for *you* to be your own person; at least, not completely. With that darkness removed, I believe the emptiness you feel is just space left for you to grow into."

"Hmm," Binny murmured, seeming to take Fulgar's point.

Fulgar locked eyes with his old friend, that ashen skin a persistent reminder of how much he'd changed, and Fulgar tried to remind himself that no one was too far gone for redemption.

"You had become something that wasn't really you, even if, at some point, you had followed it willingly. We both did, and we both underestimated the weight of our choices. Even with all that has happened, Binny—my brother—know that you have my love . . . and my forgiveness."

Standing, Fulgar made his way toward the doorway, Binny's gaze following him. "I did not ask for your forgiveness."

Fulgar stopped behind the couch. "You didn't have to." He

continued out of the room.

As he placed his hand upon the door handle to exit, he heard Binny speak once more.

"You'll come back, won't you?"

Fulgar smiled, a flicker of genuine gladness he had not felt for a long time. "Of course, I will." He opened the door. "May the Light become you, my friend."

TIME AND SEASONS OF ELIORIN

Dates and times are referenced many times throughout this book. Eliorin has both longer days and longer years compared to Earth, taking 28 hours per day, and 425 of these 28-hour days to make a year. (Seconds, minutes, and hours are the same length as on Earth.) A leap-year occurs every five years, adding one day to the month of Sivarch.

A typical clock on Eliorin might look like this, with a single hand pointing to the hour:

THE HEALER

The calendar used throughout Grandtrilia, and almost universally throughout the Great Crescent, is divided into twelve months with three seasons, four months each in length, as well as six two-month sub-seasons:

Month	Number of Days	Season	Sub-Season
Janiose	34	Sprout	Spring
Febtose	34	Sprout	Spring
Sivarch	35 (Leap-Year: 36)	Sprout	Sprung
Avreal	36	Sprout	Sprung
Mav	37	Harvest	Summer
Jervens	37	Harvest	Summer
Jovidor	38	Harvest	Fall
Agust	38	Harvest	Fall
Sleptindor	35	Lull	Fallen
Octcolore	35	Lull	Fallen
Novashtay	33	Lull	Winter
Freezindor	33	Lull	Winter

Time and Seasons of Elioron

Year 3177 PA
May

Soulsday	Lunsday	Tunesday	Whitesday	Thorsday	Flamsday	Sitsday
	1 ○	2 ○	3 ○	4 ◐	5 ◐	6 ◐
7 ◐	8 ●	9 ●	10 ●	11 ●	12 ●	13 ●
14 ●	15 ●	16 ◐	17 ◐	18 ◐	19 ◐	20 ◐
21 ◐	22 ○	23 ○	24 ○	25 ○	26 ○	27 ○
28 ◐	29 ◐	30 ◐	31 ◐	32 ●	33 ●	34 ●
35 ●	36 ●	37 ●				

THE HEALER

Year 3178 PA
Jovidor

Soulsday	Lunsday	Tunesday	Whitesday	Thorsday	Flamsday	Sitsday
			1 ◐	2 ○	3 ○	4 ○
5 ○	6 ○	7 ○	8 ○	9 ○	10 ◐	11 ◐
12 ◐	13 ◐	14 ◐	15 ●	16 ●	17 ●	18 ●
19 ●	20 ●	21 ◐	22 ◐	23 ◐	24 ◐	25 ◐
26 ◐	27 ○	28 ○	29 ○	30 ○	31 ○	32 ○
33 ○	34 ○	35 ◐	36 ◐	37 ◐	38 ◐	

Time and Seasons of Elioron

Year 3178 PA

Soulsday	Lunsday	Tunesday	Whitesday	Thorsday	Flamsday	Sitsday
	1 ☽	2 ☽	3 ●	4 ●	5 ●	6 ●
7 ●	8 ●	9 ●	10 ☽	11 ☽	12 ☽	13 ☽
14 ☽	15 ☽	16 ○	17 ○	18 ○	19 ○	20 ○
21 ○	22 ○	23 ☾	24 ☾	25 ☾	26 ☾	27 ☾
28 ●	29 ●	30 ●	31 ●	32 ●	33 ☽	34 ☽
35 ☽	36 ☽	37 ☽				

ABOUT THE AUTHOR

Wayne Kramer lives in the Southern Indiana countryside. He loves the open spaces and fresh air. His family keeps a small greenhouse, usually a little garden, chickens, and an overweight cat. He has been married to his wife and best friend, Kaly, since 2004. They have five daughters with the nature-themed names of Dawn, Brooke, Holly, Ivy, and Jade.

Wayne wanted to be a published author for nearly 25 years before finally publishing *Heroes of Time Legends: Murdoch's Choice*. Life finally afforded enough flexibility that he is able to focus a lot more time developing the "Heroes of Time" series that he is very passionate about. Another major novel in the series has already been written.

From early on writing was one of Wayne's favorite pastimes. He wrote short stories throughout middle school and high school for Young Authors contests and group projects. Before "Heroes of Time" dominated his mind, he worked extensively on creating an epic-fantasy novelization of a popular role-playing video game. Over the years Wayne received frequent feedback on many revisions of this novelization, making it one of the primary vessels through which he fine-tuned his writing.

He graduated from the University of Louisville in 2005 with a Bachelor of Business Science degree. He worked for his parents' company in the field of medical imaging equipment and parts for a total of fifteen years. Wayne also pursued business opportunities in licensed products, which included helping to run a traveling retail presence, ecommerce, and product design.

Wayne currently owns and runs his own business, W7 Global, which sells parts for medical imaging equipment all around the world. Throughout his professional and personal endeavors, Wayne has visited nearly 40 countries and about 25 states in the US. He especially loved visiting Hobbiton in New Zealand.

Wayne feels truly blessed by God to pursue his dream of writing and publishing stories. The world of Eliorin was inspired by Wayne's love of stories of classic fantasy and time travel, and he is incredibly excited to share this rich world with you.

FOLLOW THE LEGEND OF THE HEROES OF TIME

Thank you for reading
Heroes of Time Legends: The Healer

Watch for more to come in the
Heroes of Time series!

www.heroesoftime.com

Please leave this novel a review at Amazon, Goodreads, or wherever you bought this book.

Follow Wayne Kramer and Heroes of Time at…	
Facebook:	http://facebook.com/heroesoftimeseries
Instagram:	http://instagram.com/heroesoftimeseries
Discord:	http://heroesoftime.com/discord
YouTube:	http://heroesoftime.com/youtube
Goodreads:	http://goodreads.com/waynekramer
Amazon:	http://heroesoftime.com/amazon

Follow https://heroesoftime.com/thehealer/amazon to go directly to the Amazon review page.

May the winds fare you well!

FULGAR GETH RETURNS IN

HEROES OF TIME LEGENDS: MURDOCH'S CHOICE

Captain Murdoch has the chance of a lifetime in his grasp ... or is it just a fool's errand?

Zale "the Gale" Murdoch, one of the greatest seafaring merchants in the kingdom of Tuscawny, is at the top of his game. No one has reached the guild's grandmaster status in generations, and he's but one job away, with his biggest rival right on his heels. When a mysterious stranger approaches him with information that will seemingly ensure his success, Zale is tempted. The mission: to retrieve the Grimstone, a mythical artifact obscured by the shadows of history and religious folklore ... an object of immeasurable value ... if it's real. The journey to find out could cost him more than his reputation and a leisurely retirement. He'll have to battle dark magic on a perilous voyage to the hostile land where the Grimstone is reportedly hidden ... a land very few sailors return from alive.

Starlina Murdoch, Zale's estranged daughter, wants nothing to do with the sea. But Jensen, the boy she loves, is a member of her father's crew and determined to make a career as a sailor. As she becomes unexpectedly entangled with her father's voyage, she must find her bearings amongst the crew and decide for herself where her dreams truly lead.

Join Zale, Starlina, Fulgar, and the rest of the crew on an epic adventure of daring, danger, and magic! This is just the first installment of the "Heroes of Time" series, and you won't want to miss the rest!

Visit **shop.heroesoftime.com** to get it now!
Use Promo Code BLARKLE to get 10% off your order!